The *Miracle* *of* FORGETNESS

ROBERT F. SMITH

ASPEN
BOOKS

The Miracle of Forgetness
© 1997 by Robert F. Smith
All rights reserved

Library of Congress Cataloging-in-Publication Data

Smith, Robert F., 1970–
The miracle of forgetness : a novel / Robert F. Smith
p.   cm.
ISBN 1-56236-235-6 (pbk.)
I. Title.
PS3569.M53792M57   1997
813' .54–dc21   97-41895
CIP

Design by Robert Davis
Printed in the United States of America

Also from Robert Smith:

BAPTISTS AT OUR BARBECUE

To the girl with the skylike eyes and sealike soul.
Stormy, clear, wild, calm.
Krista

Acknowledgments

A gigantic thank you to everyone who has supported me thus far. I would list you all by name, but I would undoubtedly forget someone and end up feeling awful. I'd eat to hide the pain, gain ten pounds, and then have to spend a miserable afternoon at the mall shopping for new clothes. So as to avoid the horror I decided on this. Thanks to, "ABCDEFGHIJKLMNOPQRSTUVWXYZ6." I figure everyone I know, aside form a few foreign friends who use those confusing alphabets, can find thier personalized thank you within these letters (foreign friends, please squint and pretend). Thank you, thank you, thank you!

Two clear exceptions: To Richard H. Cracroft, who has gone far beyond the extra mile for me. His kindness has been the catalyst for so much of this. And to Paul Rawlins, a friend whose patience and know-how have made this trip fun.

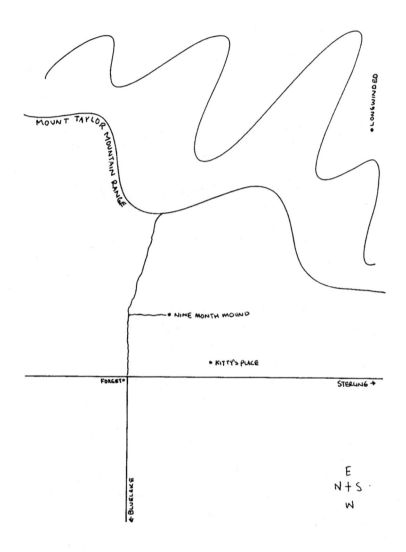

MOUNT TAYLOR MOUNTAIN RANGE

• LONGWINDED

• NINE MONTH MOUND

• KITTY'S PLACE

FORGET•   STERLING →

← BLUELAKE

E
N + S
W

Some Bit from Later on in the Book

 Like a giant hand it swooped from the sky, plucking my body off the earth and then hurling me towards the ground with such force I could feel my bones popping. What once was wind now was water.

It was thick and surrounded me like needy children on a giving Santa. I pushed desperately at the water with no effect. I could feel the cold liquid slowly filling up my lungs.

It was no use. I was a dead man.

I put my hands to my side and let my body sink deeper. My eardrums pounded and swelled as the pressure became too great for them to bear. I quickly considered my relatively short life and the tragic end it was about to meet.

This was it.

My mind became flooded with thoughts of my old neighbor Ernie who had died a horrible death years earlier. He had been swimming in a large lake, near his vacation home, when a huge aircraft skimmed the surface, scooping up several hundred gallons of H2O to put out a fire miles away. Poor Ernie was plucked up in the giant bucket and then dropped into a burning forest. He was found many days later dressed in his scuba garb, his spirit long since departed.

It was an awful story.

But now here I was, pleading with God to send me a miracle. Pull me out of this big blue abyss and deposit me onto greener pastures. Drier pastures.

My hands went numb, and an odd sensation shot up my left arm. Then, like a warm pickle spear being violently shaken, my body started to convulse.

Death appeared on the horizon. He stuck his large, hairy arm out as if to shake my hand and welcome me into the next world.

I put forth my trembling mitt and then politely declined.

Chapter One

Hot and Bothered

Phoenix sucked the life right out of you. It was too big, too much, and far too crowded. And then, as if those three attributes weren't unappealing enough, Phoenix was hotter than the fabled afterlife of Mormon Heck. Yes, this was the place people in Purgatory feared. I felt confident the superintendents of the burning underworld used Phoenix as a threat.

"You shovel that coal or it's down to Phoenix with you and your miserable soul."

I strongly disliked it.

I had been forced to grow up here, and for some demented reason I had returned from my mission back here to the city of the sweltering sun. And it was here in the two years since my mission that I had grown stubbornly inactive. I blamed a large part of my inactivity on my warm surroundings. What had I been thinking to return here? I should have gotten out before the heat had melted my brain and damaged my spirits.

I had no real reason to be here anymore. My parents, Tim and Harriet Stevens, had passed away the day after I sent my mission papers in. And my older sister, Maria, had since fled Phoenix, vowing never to return.

Maria hated the heat, and she had a particularly hard time living where my parents had raised us—too many reminders I

1

guess. My parents' death had not been easy on the two of us. Four years later we were both still trying to deal with it. Mom and Dad had died in a automobile accident. They had been on their way to Mesa to visit my dying grandmother when an inebriated motorist decided to drive in the wrong direction. I never did see the wreck, but it left Maria and me destroyed and had changed our lives forever.

I was a nineteen-year-old high school senior at the time of their death. We only had seven days of school left, and I had just sent in my mission papers, with the hope of leaving shortly after I graduated. I could still vividly remember when and how I got the tragic information.

I was pulled out of my high school shop class and given the news by my shop teacher. It was a very surreal experience. There is nothing like having someone yell at you for poor buffing one moment and then having him turn around two seconds later and inform you that your parents are gone. Crazy Milton, my shop teacher, tried hard to give me some sort of analogy dealing with wood and welding to soften the news.

"The wood may be gone, Gray, but the sawdust remains," he had said. "Sweep up the shavings boy. Sweep up the shavings, add a little glue, and mold yourself a key chain out of all of this."

I just stood there and stared at him until he became self-conscious and returned to his other students. The school superintendent drove me home, said he'd be there for me, and then sped off. I cried for three days straight.

When my mission call came two weeks later I decided that the best thing for me to do was go. I knew that's what my parents would want. Besides, I didn't want to be in Phoenix then, like I didn't want to be in Phoenix now.

My sister, Maria, got married to a nice guy while I was serving in Austria. She and her husband had chosen to settle down in Oregon. Me, I had little desire to get married, but I craved some sort of reprieve from the heat and huge city I was now stuck in.

It was my backsliding that eventually afforded me a way out.

The Miracle of Forgetness

I had been a pretty good child up until the end of my mission. My parents' death had been a huge trial, but I had remained strong through all of that. It was the weaker sex that did me in. After I had been home almost a year, my girlfriend, Mindy (whom I had dated for years and written to my whole mission), told me that the Spirit had informed her I was not the right one for her. Mindy and I had been toying with the idea of getting engaged, but I just couldn't step up to it. And now because of my procrastination the Spirit was going around behind my back whispering to her that I was unfit to marry. The nerve.

I went off the deep end. Well, I didn't really go off the deep end, but I waded around in the shallow end of the pool of wrong choices for a good long while. I had no parents, I was femalely disenchanted, and I had a lot of free time. I started going to church less often, and I read my scriptures so sporadically you could clock the seasons by it. My mind soon decided to stop retaining information. Everything became so clouded and confusing.

With a decline in scripture reading came poorly constructed personal prayers. I went from half hour prayers on my knees to ten second sound bites mumbled into my pillow as I dozed off sleeping.

I was slipping.

I dropped out of college and spent a while trying to decided what to do with myself. It was during this period of inactivity and laziness that I developed a major addiction to Pepsi. It started innocently enough, one can on a hot day when there were no other choices. But three weeks later I was so hooked I had a hard time functioning without a can of the dark demon constantly in my hand. Sure, many would say it was no big deal. There were plenty of stalwart Mormons who saw no harm in consuming caffeine in its fizzy form. But I had been raised in a household where cola was a sin akin to actually boozing it up in a bad part of town on a Sunday. We were a zero-tolerance home. My sister Maria had once been grounded for a week after my

3

mom caught her with a half-empty can of Dr. Pepper. Now here I was openly rebelling against my upbringing by making Pepsi a staple in my diet.

Ironically, it was this vice which provided me with a way out.

It was a hot last day of March. I had been home from my mission for about two years now. I had just gotten off work at Sears where I currently was the assistant manager over lawn mowers and hand tools. I went to the corner store and purchased two king-size Snickers bars, a *TV Guide,* and a big bottle of Pepsi. I then stopped at one of the city parks and read my magazine with the car air conditioning on high. Sadly, this was how I was spending far too many of my afternoons. My life lacked direction, substance, and purpose. Mindy, my ex-girlfriend, was married, with a kid on the way. She had a career and she had a husband whom apparently the heavens approved of. And here I was nursing a Pepsi and circling shows I didn't want to miss in the *TV Guide.*

Tragic.

I wanted more. But deep in my lazy heart I knew I would never find within myself what it took to get out of here and on with my life. My sister was gone, and my parents obviously had more important things to do in the next life than whisper hints and helps down to their struggling son here on earth. Life seemed so stale.

Pathetic.

I took another drink of my soda. I noticed the label on the front of the container advertising "The Great under the Cap Giveaway." I flipped over my cap fully expecting it to say "Sorry pal, you're no winner." Instead it said "$500,000."

Five hundred thousand dollars?

I read it again.

"$500,000."

If this wasn't my parents whispering to me from beyond, then what was it? I didn't know what to do. I read the container twenty times, making sure there wasn't some already expired date involved in this. There wasn't—the contest didn't end for a month. I read the bottle twenty more times to see if it said something like "Collect five '$500,000' game pieces to win a free Pepsi." It didn't.

I had won five hundred thousand dollars.

Suddenly I was everyone's best friend. My sister called me. Relatives I never knew called and wrote incessantly. Charities called. Shelters called. And a couple of high school buddies I had not seen for years started hanging around my place. Everyone wanted a part of my new wealth. In fact, the only place that didn't want my money was the Church.

I had figured the heavens and I were on good terms now. I mean there had to be more to my new fortune than luck. Then when I decided to get my life in order and pay my tithing the Church said no, informing me they did not accept tithes on games of chance. Oddly, I was bummed.

So, I politely told everyone who needed my money "No." I then socked all of it away. I didn't want to use any of it until I found the right thing to spend it on. I then patiently waited around for something to happen.

Two months later something happened.

The thick stream of letters from relatives and needy people had tapered off. I had kept my job at Sears, thinking that was the sensible thing to do. I mean the money wouldn't last forever. I figured I needed something to fall back on, and unfortunately this was all I had at the moment. I returned home from work one afternoon to find a letter from someone claiming to be my uncle. He called himself Uncle Stick, a nickname, he explained, he had received because of his height and weight. He had heard from my Aunt Janis that I had come into some easy money, and he was now offering me an investment opportunity of a lifetime. It seemed that Uncle Stick owned a trading post in a small town called Forget. Apparently the store was located at the crossroads of two major highways and did pretty good business. His offer was that I could buy him out for a fairly large sum, and then he would run the place for a small salary. The store came with a house, thirty acres of land, and a car. Yes, for about half my winnings I could have myself a home, a business, and thirty acres of Forget's finest soil. He enclosed a picture of some fuzzy mountains that I could not clearly make out.

I set the letter down and laughed. It was an interesting offer, but that was it. I mean I had never heard of an Uncle Stick. And living in a town called Forget didn't really sound too exciting. I wanted out of Phoenix, but I didn't really want into Forget. Did I?

I was about to throw the letter away when there was a knock at the door. I answered it to find Mindy standing there. She looked pregnant and uncomfortable, which made me pleasantly happy.

"Mindy," I said, surprised, jabbing my hands through my black hair in attempt to make myself appear more together than I actually was.

"Gray," she said, her eyes puffy as if from crying.

I smiled. This was it. Someone or something had finally whispered to her that she had messed up. Now here she was, coming back to me. Sweet justice. Mindy was the only girl I had ever loved. She was beautiful, funny, and at one past point in time she had been mine. She had comforted me when my parents had died and had dated me during my feathered hair and braces stage. She wrote to me faithfully my whole mission and had the courtesy to dump me gently when she actually did. Now here she was coming home to me, pregnant and confused. I vowed to be the father that child almost never had.

"Mindy, you've come back," I smiled, pulling her into my apartment.

"Back?" she questioned.

"To me," I clarified.

"What are you talking about?" she said, sitting down on my small couch.

I held my tongue. It was obvious she had an agenda.

"Gray, I have told myself a million times that this was none of my business." Mindy motioned for me to sit down in a chair next to her and dabbed at her eyes with a well-used tissue.

I quickly obeyed.

Mindy continued. "It's none of my business, but my religion teacher keeps talking about how we are all responsible for each other. He's the smartest man in the world," Mindy gushed. "Except for my husband of course," she quickly added.

I rolled my eyes. It was becoming apparent that Mindy had not come back to me.

"Gray, I'm concerned about you," Mindy said.

"Concerned," I laughed. "About what?"

"I know you're not going to church regularly."

"Nice of you to keep tabs on me," I smiled.

"My brother said you're still working at Sears."

"I am," I confirmed.

"Sears," Mindy laughed. "That's pathetic."

Mindy was losing some of her shine.

"Hey, it's a job."

"With no future," she added.

"I don't think you need to be worrying about me," I said. "Your concern for me should have ended the moment you dumped me."

"Well, I can't just turn my heart on and off," she cried.

I stood up to get myself a drink. "Why did you come here?" I asked casually, feeling like one of the soap stars I had been watching too much of lately.

"I'm concerned about your future."

Mindy was actually starting to bug me.

I pulled out what I considered to be my only ace.

"I'm rich you know."

"Oh Gray." She dabbed. "In my opinion all you own is a big pile of dirty money that will disappear as quickly as it came."

I had not remembered Mindy being so self-righteous.

"You have nothing," she whispered. "No future."

Perhaps it was my parents pushing me from behind the veil that caused me to say what I next said. Or perhaps it was the simple fact that at that moment I would have said whatever it took to make my life look and feel different than it now was. That, and at this exact second I wanted nothing more than to make Mindy as jealous and as remorseful over her decision to dump me as I possibly could.

"I'm moving," I said proudly.

"You're what?" she asked.

"I'm moving. I've bought myself a business and a home on thirty acres of the most beautiful land you could ever imagine. Mountains, rivers, ponds, lakes, streams, springs (Mindy had mentioned to me once how much she wanted to live by water).

Mindy looked uncertain. "What business?"

"It's a thriving grocery store and gas station in a nice little town called Forget."

"Are you making this up?" she asked.

Suddenly I wanted all of this to come to pass. What the heck? Forget might just be as nice as I was making it out. And if it wasn't, well, it didn't matter, because I would be out, gone, and I would never have to see Mindy again.

I spent the next hour painting a picture of my new mansion and business. I really painted; the medium of dishonesty seemed to suit me. The picture I created made Forget look so great, so friendly, so family and gospel oriented, that no righteous Saint could not desire to live there. And when Mindy finally left she was having a hard time concealing her burning envy.

Mission accomplished.

Chapter Two

Flying Blind

My sister thought I was crazy. She could think of lists of things my money could be better spent on. She had heard of Uncle Stick, but she couldn't remember if she had heard good or bad things about him. Maria extended an invitation for me to come and spend a month at her place, to think this thing through.

I refused.

I didn't want to be talked out of my decision. I couldn't bare the possibility of running into Mindy later in life and having to tell her that the entire Forget thing was just a big joke.

I sold my car and the few pieces of furniture I had. I then settled my affairs, which was an embarrassingly uncomplicated thing for me to do, packed up, and flew out of Arizona forever.

I traveled to the city of Sterling in a nice big jet. I was very excited. I didn't particularly like to fly, but I was making an exception in this case. I had bought myself a future, and in a matter of minutes I would be looking at my investment. I just wanted to get there fast.

The Sterling City International Airport was huge, and nobody was there waiting for me when I got off. Like a disoriented two-year-old, I wandered around until I found the luggage area. Once I had recovered my bags I looked for my Uncle Stick. He was supposed to be waiting for me. I had talked to him on the phone a few times, but I didn't really have a good idea what he looked like. Tall, skinny, and my Aunt Janis had described him as having either a dirty mustache or a filthy mind—I couldn't quite remember. People cleared out, and eventually I was standing there next to the revolving luggage port all alone, feeling like the unwanted runt of the litter of life.

I was digging through my bags, looking for Uncle Stick's phone number, when a thick, short man with gigantic hands and sunken eyes tapped me on the shoulder.

"You Gray?"

"Are you Uncle Stick?" I asked, knowing from his build he was not.

"Nope, Stick's busy. Follow me."

He was direct. I followed this man out of the airport and over to a small plane with rust spots all over it. The plane looked like something you would see littering a battlefield. Its wings sagged, and its nose was pealing like Mindy after her trip to Mexico last year.

"We're flying in this?" I asked, afraid to hear the answer.

"She may not be pretty, but she'll get us there," he said haltingly.

I stuck out my hand. "The name's Gray Stevens."

"I know," he said, looking at me as if I were some sort of idiot. "Let's go. I've got things to do."

I put my luggage aboard and then climbed in myself. Mr. Friendly started the engine and then with reckless abandon he took off down the runway. The plane made all sorts of troubling noises as it struggled to get up to speed. Eventually the sagging wings lifted us off the ground and into the clear blue sky. The noise of the engine made it impossible for my mind to conjure up anything except visions of this gruff stranger and me hurling toward the earth in this rusted little plane.

My pilot looked over at my white knuckles and smiled.

"You lack faith," he observed.

"In what?" I yelled, feeling that he was being entirely too vague.

The Miracle of Forgetness

"In the laws of aerodynamics. If you follow the rules nothing can go wrong."

Great, I thought. I was trapped in a small plane with one of those people who had to turn everything in life into a lesson.

He started to use his hands to explain lift. I begged him to put both his hands back on the controls. He did so reluctantly, grumbling something about my acting like his wife.

We flew in relative silence for a while. It gave me a little time to wonder about what I was getting myself into. I watched the sky grow bigger and bigger as we pushed through the open air and away from civilization. The plane followed the tiny, string-like highway down below. There were no clouds around, but occasionally I would see a small bird soaking itself in the blue sky and wondering where we found the nerve to interrupt its peace and quiet.

After about twenty minutes my pilot pointed towards what looked to be a couple of small buildings sitting at the crossroads of two highways. I couldn't make them out too well because of our height and my view, but it looked pretty desolate. Certainly this was not my investment.

"What's that?" I yelled.

He mumbled something back that I could barely hear over the engine. It sounded like he said, "Forget," or, "I Forget."

I prayed that he had forgotten. What we had just flown over was no more than a blip on a flat brown screen. Where were the mountains? Where were the rivers, lakes, and streams I had lied about? There was a big mountain range off to the right aways, but it was at least thirty or forty miles away from what my pilot had just pointed at. A few minutes later our plane began descending.

A medium-sized town pushed up all around us. Moments later we were safely on the ground and I was staring at the small terminal of the Bluelake Airport. The pilot killed the engine. Silence ensued.

"Nice flight," I commented.

The pilot turned to me and finally gave me his name. "I'm

11

Todd," he said in a rather unfriendly voice. "Your Uncle Stick sent me to get you."

The information was flowing now.

"Do we drive from here to Forget?" I asked.

"You do. I've got church work to attend to."

"Are you a Mormon?" I asked.

"Yeah," Todd said, looking at me once again as if I were stupid. "I'm in your bishopric."

Mixed reactions.

I was excited by the fact that he was Mormon. I really did want to get my spirituality back in shape and consequently I was happy to meet a fellow Mormon. But I wasn't thrilled by the fact that he was in my bishopric. From what I had seen so far he didn't appear to be someone I could feel completely comfortable around. He was like thick wool on a hot day.

"Does Forget have its own ward?"

"Forget has nothing but Stick's place. Bluelake is the ward you will be attending. Largest ward in existence."

"In existence?" I guffawed.

"In existence," he snapped back.

"You're kidding?"

Todd gave me another one of his looks. Apparently he didn't kid.

"Is my Uncle Stick a Mormon?" I asked. I had forgotten to find out for myself earlier—I had just assumed he was. I came from a long line of Mormons. My great-great-great-grandfather was one of the men who helped settle the lesser-known pioneer incident, "The Morter Creek Slapping."

"Stick's Mormon on the records," Todd said. "But that's about it."

Todd climbed out of the plane. I did the same. I followed Todd into the terminal. He turned around, annoyed by the fact that I seemed to be tailing him.

"Your car's over there," he said, pointing out the window at a tiny orange car. "Keys are in the ignition."

"How do I get to Forget."

The Miracle of Forgetness

"We do have road signs," he said bitterly.

I took my cue and stopped asking him questions. I hoped long and hard that the other people in this area were just a tad bit nicer than Todd. No offense to him personally, but he had the personality of a gamy badger. God had probably put him in my bishopric to make my return to full activity as hard as possible. I constantly felt fatherly pressure from above concerning my coming back into full activity. It was as if God wanted to make sure I was fully committed before he believed me. He knew me far too well.

I drove around Bluelake looking for signs that would point me to Forget. I couldn't seem to find any. Bluelake was completely flat. No hills, mounds, or bumps. Only its abundance of buildings broke up the flat line. But despite its lack of lumps Bluelake was a neat city. It wasn't huge, but there seemed to be lots going on. I passed a community college where coeds were lounging on the lawn sunning themselves. A couple of them looked worth enrolling for.

I drove under a huge banner that was joyfully announcing the upcoming Bluelake Parade. I passed well-maintained banks and hotels and what seemed like fifty restaurants. There were people all over, going about their business here as if they were following a pattern. I passed a small cemetery that was now home to those town folks who had finished their earthly projects.

In the center of town sat a Mormon chapel. It was large, brick and unusually shaped for an LDS building. A huge American flag hung limp at the top of a silver flagpole out front, and a completely bald man in overalls was driving circles around the chapel on a riding lawn mower. I thought about stopping and talking to him, but I still had signs to find.

At the edge of Bluelake was its namesake. A gigantic blue lake that seemed to stretch on for miles, white sands surrounding its flat shores. At the moment the lake lay limp and lazy looking, its water creeping up against the shore, searching for more area to stretch itself out on.

There were a couple lakeshore businesses, and there was an area designated for vendors. Velvet blankets covered with sparkling turquoise jewelry and trinkets seemed to stretch on for miles, making sort of a patchwork quilt along a good section of the shore. I could see people intently haggling and exchanging money for wares and food.

I pulled up next to a mobile pretzel stand and parked. I bought myself a cheese-filled pretzel and directions to Forget. Surprisingly both made my stomach uneasy. The pretzel vendor was curious why someone would want to go to Forget.

"There's nothing there," he informed me.

"There had better be something," I returned.

"Well, there's a gas station or something,"

"That's it?" I asked.

"I think there's a tree," he replied.

"A tree? A single tree?"

"Listen, I don't know what's there, and to be quite honest with you kid, I don't care. I just happen to know that if you follow Witch Road you'll run right into it. It's ten miles out of Bluelake. Which makes it about ten miles closer to Sterling than we are. And whatever is out there sits smack dab at the intersection of Highway 62 and the old Witch Road." This informative gentleman then turned his back on me to help a couple of new customers.

I headed out for Forget.

I had to go back through Bluelake to get to there. I kept wishing my new home was located in this nice city. This was the kind of place I had always wanted to live. Kids played in the streets, people waved at each other, yet there were still places for a person to get Chinese takeout.

Bluelake ran out after a few minutes, and past its borders was nothing. It was as if God had run out of decorating ideas. Off in the distant distance I could make out the mountain range I had flown over, but besides that there was only flat, brown, and unattractive. I half wished for a tornado of mercy to simply touch down and carry me off to someplace more appealing. No luck. The skies were clear.

About a mile out of Bluelake I passed a large sign announcing that I was now entering Katford County. Five miles later I passed a weathered old billboard that was doing its best to spread the word about a little piece of heaven just up the way.

Forget.

A short while later Forget came into view. It had looked a thousand times better from way up in the sky. From down here below it was nothing but two buildings and a thick, uneven fence that seemed to box off a couple of the acres I had foolishly bought. In front of the store Witch Road crossed the highway. The crossing was pinned down by two stop signs and a couple of well-weathered, wood streetlights. A red bench sat next to one of the stop signs, empty and welcoming society to sit and watch the world pass them by. There was a giant tree which stood in the middle of the fenced area behind the house. It looked so out of place and lonely I wanted to cry. The house was old, and its roof was covered with clay tiles that looked as if they were just waiting to slide off. The two buildings and one tree were huddled together, shunning the rest of the barren world.

What had I done?

I pulled up to the front of the so-called thriving store. There were four gas pumps with a concrete shelter covering them. Above the door to the store was a sloppily hand-painted banner that read "U-Swap-Em-Trading Post and Gas Station." There was obviously nobody swapping anything at the moment; the place looked deserted.

I parked and stepped out. A small sliding window about three feet from the front door slid open.

"Are you Gray?"

"I am."

The window slid shut. I stood there expecting someone to come out and greet me. No one ever did. Eventually I walked inside.

The shop was a disaster. Trinkets and faded cardboard signs adorned every inch of space. There were some glass refrigerators with sandwiches and drinks in them and a rack of magazines—

every one of them with word *Field* in the title: *Field and Stream. Field and Guns. Field and Fire.* The checkout counter was unfinished plywood, the front of it filled with pinned up notes that were announcing all the locals' needs and wants.

"Bed for sale."

"Need help with math?"

"12-gauge must sell."

On top of the counter was a cash register and a glass case filled with pink frosted donuts and a couple of loose pieces of really tough looking beef jerky.

"Suck it all in," the man behind the counter said. "Let the eyes get a real good gander at all the fine merchandise we have."

I was sucking.

"Uncle Stick?" I asked, sticking out my hand.

"Just Stick."

That he was. He was at least two inches taller than my six-foot-four frame. And from the looks of his physique it didn't seem like he was carrying around anything other than skin, a few important innards, and a large pile of bones. He was a stick. He wore a tattered old cowboy hat and a faded T-shirt that said "Just do it" on the front. His ears were as big as his tiny hands, and a large, gray-at-the-bottom-brown-on-the-top mustache hung under his long skinny nose. I liked him right off.

"Nice to meet you, Stick."

"Listen, I don't want to appear unkind, but any moment a customer could pull up, and I will need to take care of his needs and his needs alone. I can't be talking to no relative while people need help selecting a soda. So let me say what needs to be said before we are interrupted." Stick drew in breath. "I'm your Uncle Stick, yeah, yeah, yeah. Your father was my stepbrother, but I never knew him. We never lived together, we didn't keep in touch, and I can almost bet he would not have approved of us doing what we're doing, but he's dead, rest his soul, and you and I, well, we're living."

That was stretching it.

"Your father was a good man," he continued. "I don't know

that personally, but my sister Janis says that's the straight truth. And except for that story about the plumber Janis has never lied to me."

I nodded, showing Stick I was still with him.

"I saw a picture of your father once. He looked a lot like you, only prettier. That's a good thing. I don't want no girl-looking nephew of mine to be my business partner. This is the wild west, and pretty boys get picked on like sugared gizzards."

I mentally added another item to my list of things to never eat.

"Listen," Stick went on, "I'm only going to say this once so listen up. I'm real grateful for what you done. This business needs some capital and, well, you supplied it. We were able to pay some bills and get a lot of fine new merchandise. But I must tell you, I answer to no man. I'll do my job, you do yours, and things will go just fine. What I'm trying to say is that don't go trying to bring in all kinds of fancy changes. I don't want to wake up tomorrow to find I'm peddling gift baskets and crouton rolls."

I think he meant "croissant," but I let it slide.

"I'm a simple man with a bad back and a weakness for cards. Please don't try and make me something I'm not. People are going to tell you things about me, but just don't believe them. Deep down I'm fairly ordinary. Just 'cause I don't ever like to leave the store doesn't mean anything. I'm committed to this business. I think you'll find that to be a positive thing about me."

"Commitment is good," I added.

"What do you know about commitment?" he suddenly snapped. "You ever been scorned, I mean really scorned?"

I wasn't sure what he was talking about, but I felt confident I would have remembered being really scorned. I mean the Mindy thing had hurt, but I never felt scorned.

"Listen, Gray, I didn't mean to jump all over you," Stick apologized, "and Jenny is none of your affair. So let me just finish what I started saying, okay?"

I had no idea who Jenny was, and the only thing in my entire life that I had wanted from my Uncle Stick was for him to finish this stupid conversation so I could check out the rest of my investment.

"I've got a cot and a shower in this back room. And if I choose never to leave, then so be it."

"You never leave this store?" I asked.

"What, is that weird?" Stick responded.

I shrugged my shoulders, not really caring one way or the other.

"Why do they call you Gray?" Stick asked. "I mean your eyes are green. Do you got some sort of wishy-washy, gray type personality or something?"

"Nope, that's just my name."

"Well, I suppose that's all right. At least you're not some lukewarm fence sitter."

Actually those were the perfect words to describe me at the moment. I wanted to ask Stick what his real name was, but I decided to wait until later. He gave me the keys to the house, explained some of the things I needed to know immediately, and then started straightening the candy aisle. I still liked Stick.

The house was locked up securely. It was obvious Stick had never used it. It wasn't too ugly inside. In fact, if you could look past the thick shag carpet and the curling linoleum, the place almost had a sort of rustic charm. I felt comfortable in it despite its age. I pulled down the thick blankets that had been pinned up in the windows. Sunlight spilled into the house, attempting to scrub out the dark and dreary. The darkness was a stubborn stain that required the strength of every uncovered window to lift it.

The pretzel man really had been right, out back there was just one tree. No bushes, no flowers, just a whole lot of dirt and one tall, tall tree. It stood towering and thick, rubbing up against the blue sky with its green, leafy, and untamed hair. Stick had called this tree the miracle tree. You see, something Stick had failed to mention in his letters and phone calls was the fact that Forget had no water.

The Miracle of Forgetness

No water.

It was more than just Stick's unusual personality that prevented others from building neighboring houses and businesses. It was the fact that if you chose to live here you had to bring in water. Stick informed me that water day was Tuesday. There was a large holding tank, and once a week a truck from Bluelake came and filled it up. It was expensive and inconvenient but there was no other way. I got thirsty looking at the dry scenery. I went back inside my new house to find the bottle of water Stick had given me at the store.

I drank as if it were my last drink. Who knows, out here it possibly could be. I then started to clean and organize my abode. The house was furnished, but it was so dusty inside that as soon as I began to move things around I couldn't breathe. I opened all the naked windows and started airing the place out. I then turned the electricity on and opened the water valve connecting my place to the store and tank. Most everything seemed in order.

I was unpacking my stuff when I noticed a letter lying behind one of the bedroom chairs. It was in a faded blue envelope with only one word on the front, *Francis*. I dusted it off and opened it. I figured since it was my house I was entitled to read it.

I should never have touched it.

Chapter Three

The Bitter Pill
of Paper and Pen

Dearest Francis,

I know I am only going to make things harder by leaving this note, but I feel that you deserve some explanation. The thought of you reading this breaks my heart, but it is what must be. Like my Aunt Reema used to say, "A loose string is an embarrassing blemish."

You were right about Paul and me. If I were to stay with you, my life would be a lie. I know you Francis, and I know deep down you would not want me to live my life that way. I know you would want me to be with Paul, happy like that colt you freed from that wire gate.

Paul and I have decided to run away. There is no future for the two of us here, so we must leave. I couldn't bare to bump into you while shopping for groceries, or catching a picture show. I must go.

I will never forget you or the kindness you showed to me, but in the end it is just not enough to make things right. Please forgive me for doing this to you.

Try and remember the good times, like that night at the state fair. Who knew one person could eat nineteen corn dogs. You devil, I was never prouder.

Don't dwell on the bad times. Like that night at the state fair when you became ill and ruined Melissa's good shoes. Life's too short for petty grievances. You will always be a positive in my life, albeit distant.

This is goodbye, Francis. It is not meant to be.

Yours in the past, Paul's in the future,

Jenny

Stick's Jenny? I didn't know if Stick had ever seen this letter, and I was a little bit leery of showing it to him. Was this what he meant when he said scorned. I mean this letter had scorned written all over it. Stick's Jenny was either incredibly dumb or socially and pathologically cruel. She reminded me a little of Mindy.

I sighed.

The letter didn't look like it had been read before. And it was so old that it was browning at the folds. I put it back in the envelop and contemplated just what to do with it. If Stick had read it before, then showing it to him again would be like pouring salt into a Sticky wound. But if by some chance Stick had never seen it, then it might be best if he did.

Too many decisions.

I didn't even know my uncle that well. What if I showed it to him and he became so outraged that he did away with me? It could happen. I mean I had a tendency to be annoying at times, and then to produce a raging Dear John letter and give it to a convenience store hermit. Well, all those things combined might just be the death of me. I needed to sleep on this.

By the time I drifted off I had successfully talked myself into showing Stick the letter. It would be wrong of me to keep it from him.

I prayed I would be doing the right thing.

Chapter Four

The Rug Girl

The next morning I helped Stick open up the store. I then spent some time memorizing the merchandise. The capital I had just injected into the store had resulted in our shelves appearing stocked and full. Bright labels from new products winked and snapped all over the store. The store was set up just like every other convenience store I had ever seen. There were rows of candy, food, and supplies, and by the counter there was a soda island topped with pop dispensers and condiments for the hot dogs near by. I took a moment to straighten the little packets of ketchup.

I wanted desperately to show Stick the letter I had found yesterday, but sleep had made me a coward. The fire I felt last night at eleven when I finally fell asleep was now just a tiny spark that was about to be smothered under the weight of my second thoughts.

I needed to get to know Stick better. I wasn't anxious about springing something like this on him if he was not up to it. Besides, he seemed so happy that I was there to talk to. I would hate to burst his bubble.

I was busy alphabetizing the breath mints Stick had briefed me on, when a small white truck with a banged up tin camper shell pulled up to pump four. A tall girl with dark skin and a loose dress got out of the truck and began pumping gas.

Through the front window I could see her run her hand through her long dark hair. It suddenly occurred to me that she was unusually good looking. She couldn't get the gas to start up so she put the pump back in its cradle, looking confused. I was going to go out and help her but Stick took care of it. He simply slid open his little behind-the-counter window and yelled at her.

"Flip the switch."

"Which switch?" she yelled back.

"Gray, would you go show her what to do?" Stick asked.

"I don't know what to do," I replied.

"You just flip the stupid switch," Stick cursed. It was becoming clear just how much he treasured his blessed customers.

I stepped outside, fairly sure I could find this evasive switch. I walked to the pump trying to appear confident. This dark-haired girl was about a foot shorter than I was, and I rather enjoyed looking down at the top of her head as I stood there trying to find the switch. Her hair was so black and so shiny. My glance slid down her like water off a soaped up oil drum.

I couldn't find the switch.

Stick slid open the window again and in a bothered tone gave instructions.

I found the switch. Apparently the pumps were turned off nightly for security reasons. It struck me, however, that with the switch to turn them on and off being located right next to the pumps things were not really that secure.

I flipped the switch.

"Thank you," she smiled, putting on display one incredibly white set of teeth.

"Are you from Bluelake?" I asked.

"No, Sterling," she replied.

I commented on Sterling, the whole while wondering if my breath was good enough to face her directly and talk. I had brushed good and long just a couple of hours ago, but morning breath was a tricky thing—Crest wasn't always enough. I wished I had helped myself to some of the breath mints I had previously been organizing. I wanted desperately to make a worthwhile impression on this girl. Her naked fingers made it obvious she wasn't married or seriously committed to someone else. This was a good thing. I couldn't remember ever meeting a more beautiful woman.

Mindy who?

And call me dizzy, but she seemed to be, yes, I think she was flirting with me.

"Sterling's nice," she observed. "I was born and raised there."

Could it be any more obvious?

I set the pump to run itself and then started in on this woman's windshield. She leaned against the hood of her truck and watched me. I tried hard to make washing a windshield look important—more like an art than a chore. The last thing I wanted was for her to think of me as a common gas station attendant. I had to make myself look like more than I appeared to be. I wanted badly to blurt out that I owned this place, but I just couldn't think of a good way to introduce the fact. Sentences with no real beginning and weak endings danced around in my stimulated brain. This girl instilled an instant attraction. Like a blockbuster movie where no one cared about the plot, she drew me in. I needed to impress her.

"Are you just traveling through?" I asked.

"Yes," she answered.

The gas pump clicked, signaling her tank was full. I put the nozzle back and she followed me inside. Stick was nice enough to let me ring her up. She used her credit card to pay and I took notice of her name.

Angela Cortez.

I ran her card and then reluctantly handed it back to her.

"Nice meeting you," I said casually. "I hope you travel safely."

"I hope so too."

"Have a nice life," I added, still not sure what I wanted to say to these customers as they came and went. She turned towards me.

"I'll tell you what," she smiled. "You can keep tabs on that for me. I'll be back through in a week. I sell rugs."

She sold rugs.

She would be back.

I watched her get into her truck and drive away. Two seconds later Stick came and stood besides me.

"I've seen prettier," he said.

"Out here?"

"Looks aren't everything." Stick picked up a comb from out of the store comb bin. He ran it through his mustache and then returned it to the bin.

"No one wants a used comb," I complained.

"My point exactly," Stick replied, obviously thinking I was referring to Angela.

I was a little bothered by Stick's attitude towards Angela.

"Do you know her?" I asked.

"Not real well," he answered. "She tried to swap me some rugs for a tank a gas a while back."

"Did you do it?" I asked.

"You kidding? What in the heck am I going to do with a bunch of Hispanish rugs?"

"Hispanic," I corrected.

"Really?" Stick asked.

I nodded.

Stick wrote something down on a small piece of paper. "Well, what am I going to do with a bunch of rugs?"

"Sell them," I offered.

"Listen, Gray, don't go trying to guess the buying patterns of my customers. I've tracked their spending habits for years now. Jenny always said I had a mind for merchandise."

I think she meant science.

"I can tell you what the next customer is going to buy before he even comes through the door."

"You're on," I said, willing to wager for fun.

I used to be far more reluctant to even place a friendly bet, but ever since my Pepsi payoff I felt I had fate on my side. It was something I needed to correct. I made a mental note to talk to my new bishop about it. Lately I had been making up a nice long list in my head of all the things I wanted, and needed, to repent of. I really wanted to be a better person—a new ward seemed like the perfect place to turn over a new leaf.

"I'll bet you my monthly salary I can tell you what the next customer will buy just from looking at him, or her," Stick challenged.

We shook hands.

Two minutes later a big green Buick pulled up to the pumps. A man with a huge, spherelike beer belly got out from behind the wheel and started to put gas into his car. He scratched himself on the arm a few times and then stretched, his shirt ascending to show the perfect whiteness of his tummy.

"This is too easy," Stick said. "The man will buy a pack of chewing gum, one prepackaged deli sandwich, a book on tape, a fountain drink, and one of these pink frosted donuts."

I sat back and watched.

The man finished pumping gas. He then came in, asked for a pack of free matches, paid for his gas and left.

I held out my hand as if to collect my winnings.

"You don't honestly expect me to pay up?" Stick asked.

I smiled, turning to head back to my house.

"Besides," Stick said, "a young kid like you wouldn't know what to do with a lump sum of money."

"I bought this place," I replied.

"You invested in this place," Stick corrected.

"I think you're wrong there," I retorted. "The papers now say that this place belongs to me," I said, trying to remain friendly.

"You wouldn't last an afternoon here alone," Stick huffed. "The papers may have your name on it, but this place is mine. Don't start thinking I work for you."

"You do," I argued.

"There ain't no piece of paper in the world that can make me a slave."

I should have let it go. I knew Stick was just trying to hold on to a small slice of his diminishing pride. But I had my ego to worry about as well. It wasn't like I had a mountain of positives working for me at the moment. Sure I had a few dollars, but I also owned a pathetic pit stop in the middle of nowhere and a life with no direction. Regardless, I still should have behaved myself.

"What about this piece of paper?" I asked, pulling out Jenny's letter from my back pocket and dangling it in front of Stick.

"What's that?" he complained.

"I found it in the house."

Stick took a look at the handwriting and stepped back. "Is this a joke?" he asked.

"No joke. When was the last time you were in that house?" I asked.

"I haven't been in there since Jenny left."

"How long ago was that?"

"Twenty some years ago."

That explained the dust.

"Who's Francis?" I questioned.

"That's my real name," Stick said. "But no one ever calls me that. No one. Understand?"

I understood.

"Have you ever seen this?" I asked, waving the letter.

Stick shook his head no.

"Jenny must have left it for you the day she went away."

"She said she would come back," he whispered.

Stick kept staring at the envelope like it was alive. I suddenly had the urge to put it back in my pocket and act as if I had never pulled it out. Stick looked wounded from the neck up and lifeless from the neck down. He sensed my possible withdrawal and sprang to life, grabbing the letter from my hand.

I stood there staring at the Hostess fruit pies as he read Jenny's declaration of indifference. When he finished he set it on the counter, smoothed it out with his left hand, and rubbed his forehead with his right. His eyes were wet and yellow, pain leaking from them like tears.

"I'm sorry, Stick," I offered.

Stick took off his hat, revealing a mess of tangled, wild hair. He tugged on his ears, set his hat on the counter, licked his palms, patted his cheeks, and stepped out from behind the counter. He then pushed me aside and walked out of the store.

"Stick," I yelled.

It was too late, he was out the door. He walked to the highway, crossed the road, and just kept walking in the direction of the distant mountains. I contemplated going after him, but I didn't want to leave the store alone. I didn't even have keys to lock it up.

I had really done it.

Three hours later Stick was still gone. I had tried my best to help customers, but I really had no idea what I was doing—and everyone kept asking where Stick was.

"Stick hasn't left this place in years," they would say.

"Well, he's gone now," I kept having to say back.

I didn't have any idea what to do. I felt like I should tell someone about Stick, but I didn't know anyone around here yet. It was early afternoon when I noticed a number written on a sticker that was attached to the base of the phone. The name above the number said "Todd."

I dialed the number, hoping it was the Todd from my bishopric.

After ten rings somebody picked up.

"Hello," I said.

"Hello," a female voice sobbed back.

"Is Todd home?"

"Who is this?" the voice asked.

"My name's Gray. Todd flew me here yesterday."

"Todd flies everyone everywhere," she cried.

This woman was obviously distressed. She sounded like my sister, Maria, after two days of no sleep. Stressed, cranky, and ready to scrap with anyone who didn't see things exactly like she did. I approached cautiously.

"Are you all right?" I asked.

"Oh, I'm all right, all right. I've no money, my hair's falling out due to stress, my husband has just left me, I've been fired because I snapped back at the bank president, I don't have this month's mortgage payment, everyone thinks I drove Todd away, and he had the nerve to take most of my furniture and my mother's heirloom refrigerator. What kind of man takes a woman's heirloom? Tell me that, will you?"

"I barely know Todd," I whispered.

"Well then maybe there's hope for you." Todd's ex-wife ended the conversation with a click.

This was just great. What had I been thinking? I wanted to live in a small town. I now owned the smallest town in this state. I wanted to improve my future. My future now consisted of trying to master the Slurpee machine before the next customer pulled up. I wanted to make Mindy jealous, and here I was in a location so remote that jealousy would be hard pressed to find it with a map.

Shoot.

Just when I was about to write myself off a cop car pulled up to the store.

I was never so happy to see the law.

Chapter Five

Bob and Weave

I use the word "law" loosely. This officer got out of his car holding a McDonald's bag in one hand and a carton of fries in the other. He lifted the fry carton up to his mouth, pouring the last of the fries in. He then opened the sack, looking for any strays that may have escaped to the bottom of the bag. Success. He pulled out a rather long fry and smiled as if he had just found a cure for cancer. He headed towards the door but stopped and sniffed the air. He then picked up his feet checking the bottom of each of his boots. Something on the bottom of the right one made him laugh. He sat down on the hood of his car and pulled off his right boot. He then waddled inside.

As soon as he was in the store he sensed there was something awry.

"Where's Stick?" he asked.

"He's gone," I answered.

"Gone where?" he prodded.

"I don't know, he just took off walking in that direction."

This cop didn't like my answer. He dropped the boot he was holding and pulled out his gun. "Stick hasn't left this place in years," he accused. "Now what did you do with him?"

Two seconds ago he was a bumbling, fry-eating idiot. Suddenly this cop was a heavy, angry man pointing a gun at me.

"Really, Stick left."

The cop waved me out from behind the counter. He then checked back in Stick's room; finding nothing he returned to me.

"What's going on here?" he asked. I pointed towards the letter from Jenny. The very letter that had driven Stick away.

"What's this?" he asked, picking it up.

"It's from Jenny," I answered.

"She's come back?" he asked.

"Nope, I found that in my house. Apparently Jenny's never coming back."

The cop tisked.

"I knew it," he then said. "I didn't wish it, but I knew it. Stick never had a chance with Jenny. Long curly hair, nice figure, and boy could that girl whistle. Can you whistle?" the cop asked me.

"Well...sure."

"Let me hear you."

"Now?"

"Come on, let me hear you," he smiled. "Do you know 'Red River Valley?'"

I shook my head, indicating I didn't really know anything at the moment.

"'Star Spangled Banner?' Everyone knows 'Star Spangled Banner.'"

"Well, I..."

"Come on, let's hear it."

I puckered my lips and blew. It wasn't the greatest noise in the world, but modesty aside I wasn't hurting for whistling skills.

"That's nothing. If Jenny were here she could whistle rings around you."

"Jenny's not here."

"That's true. Still I'd hate to be beat by a girl at anything. Having a nice, calm, self-assured feeling when I look at myself in the mirror is priceless."

He must have had mirrors of mercy.

The cop started whistling the "Star Spangled Banner." He walked out from behind the counter and leaned the bulk of his weight against the magazine rack, whistling the whole while. After a few moments he motioned for me to join in. I looked around, embarrassed about the whole ordeal. Luckily we had no other customers at the moment.

I joined in, though visions of the rug girl catching me in such a state and deciding to buy her gas elsewhere made me jumpy.

A small station wagon pulled up to the store, and what looked to be seventeen kids tumbled out and began pouring into the store. I momentarily paused.

The cop walked up to the counter and slapped his palm down, motioning for me to continue. I started whistling again.

What was happening?

Two of the kids stopped and stared at us. Finally the older of the two said, "Mom's got to see this."

I could have stopped. It's not as if I would have been breaking the law if I ceased to pucker. But two things kept me going. One was the fact that this cop had sort of an endearing personality. For some weird reason I felt compelled to make him comfortable. The second reason was that if I actually stopped I would have had to explain what was going on to these customers who had just come in. I was hoping they would simply think we were weird and then just go away.

No such luck.

The mother and the father made their way over to us. By this time the cop was not only whistling but he was directing. And of course the only person he had to direct was me. I could feel my face burning. I was just about to die from embarrassment when one of the younger kids, recognizing the familiar "Star Spangled Banner," began to whistle with us. It wasn't long before all of his brothers and sisters had joined in. Two seconds later the mother of this brood broke out singing along in a voice so falsetto I felt the cop should have arrested her right then and there for impersonating a human.

Where was I? Images of me working at Sears and Mindy

dumping me kept popping up in my mind and reminding me of the wonderful things I had left behind. This had to end.

I began coughing.

The music played on.

I began coughing, holding my stomach, and signaling for them to stop. Finally the father asked, "Are you all right?"

"I could use some water," I said.

The cop, put out by my interruption, got me a cup of Sprite from the soda machine. He then helped the family find diapers and Ding-Dongs, cashed them out, and sent them on their way.

"I know you were faking," the cop said once we were alone again. "But I can't say as I blame you. That middle kid was whistling the wrong song."

I stopped coughing and smiled. "I'm Gray, Stick's nephew."

"I'm Bob," the cop said. "Nice to meet you, Gray."

He stuck out his hand as if to shake mine, but in actuality he was reaching for one of the pink donuts on the counter.

"So do you live in Bluelake?" I asked.

"Me? No. I can't stomach those big cities. I'm from Longwinded."

"Where's that?" I asked.

"You see those mountains over there," he said, pointing toward the direction Stick had gone.

I nodded, "Yes."

"Well, if you take Witch Road far enough, eventually it leads over that mountain and into the greenest piece of earth God's ever scribbled on."

"Longwinded?"

"Yep."

"Quite a name," I commented.

"Actually it's a nickname but we like it."

"So how long does it take you to get here?" I asked.

"Well, you can't actually take Witch Road. Sure it's a straight shot, but it's a real dinger. Leopold Smilton got stranded on that road just last spring. Mud so deep he almost lost his boy, Pat." Bob stopped, adjusted his belt one notch looser, and then continued. "No, the way to get here from there it to go through Sterling. You come down from Longwinded to Sterling," Bob was moving his finger through the air as if that helped make his directions clearer. "Then Forget's a straight shot from Sterling," he varoomed.

Bob then was silent for a bit while he finished his donut. Well, it wasn't actually silent. Bob was a rather celebrated eater.

"So how long does it take you to get here," I asked.

"With my sirens on I can get here in two and a half hours flat."

"And why do you come here?"

"Oh, Stick and I go way back. He grew up in Longwinded. But like so many, the big mountain walls of Longwinded were a bit too smothering for him. He wanted action. He came to Forget about thirty years ago. Bought this place from an Irish man named Noble. Met Noble?' Bob asked.

"No," I answered.

"Well, too late now then, he's dead. Anyhow," he segued, "Stick met Jenny at a Mormon dance in Bluelake. He was as crazy over her as a pig in a sty of butter-whipped pudding." Bob stopped, suddenly remembering the boot he had brought in. He walked over and picked it up from where he had dropped it. He grabbed a wet nap and began to clean the bottom of it while continuing with his story. "Jenny never really liked Stick like a boyfriend. No, Jenny liked short boys. But Stick kept pestering her to marry him. Finally one afternoon the two of them had it out. It wasn't pretty."

I felt confident it hadn't been.

"Jenny's all weepy, Stick's all weepy, and people are picking sides like this is some sort of game. Lot's of folks thought Jenny was too good for Stick, and a good number of people felt Stick was getting the short end of the stick." Bob laughed at his little surprise joke. "I didn't even know that one was coming," he commended himself. "Anyhow, within a couple of days rumors of a guy named Paul start to surface. Stick took no stock in it, but it appears that he should have. The Mormon bishop was the one who convinced Jenny to choose Paul. Stick can't stand Bishop Withers because of it.

"The last time Stick saw Jenny was when she said she was going to go make up her mind. She told him she would come back to him and let him know, but she never did. She didn't have the guts to tell him to his face."

"So Stick's been waiting for her?"

"He has. There have been only a few times that he has actually left the store. The time Wendell got his head stuck in a tree down at the Bluelake chapel. I mean that's something you just got to see. I wasn't fortunate enough, however. I heard about it after the fact."

"I'm sorry," I said.

"These things happen," Bob said sagely. "And of course Stick left his post for a couple of hours many years back when he heard that John Wayne was eating at the Bluelake Steak House. It turned out to just be Otis Jennings with freshly dyed hair on a particularly heavy water retention day. But Stick still had his picture taken with Otis," Bob pointed to a picture hanging behind the counter. "Stick figured he could fool some people with it."

"So my uncle has really not left this store for years?"

"Straight shooting truth. Stick was scared to death Jenny would come back while he was away."

"Odd."

Bob looked at me as if I had just introduced a new word to his vocabulary.

"Well," he said, "I should probably go find Stick. Will you be all right here?" he asked.

"I don't have a store key," I said.

Bob took a key off his key ring and gave it to me. "Stick made one up for me," Bob explained. "You've got to jiggle it when you turn it. It works on both the front and back door. Now, which way did Stick go?"

"Straight that way," I pointed.

Bob stuck his boot back on, grabbed another donut, and

headed out. I couldn't decide if I was worried that Bob might not find Stick, or if I was worried he just might. Those two together seemed a rather lethal combination.

The next customer to come in bought a pack of gum, a prepared deli sandwich, a book on tape, a soda, and a pink frosted donut. If only this customer would have had the courtesy to come earlier. Then maybe my uncle wouldn't be wandering around in the sand, headed nowhere in particular, and positioned to be picked up by an incompetent whistling cop. Actually I couldn't help thinking that a couple hours of staring straight into the sun wouldn't hurt either of them.

I waited patiently for word.

Chapter Six

Love Is a River

The sun was growing lazy in the sky, its posture sorely lacking. It looked as if it had removed its girdle and was now letting it all hang out. I read the hours on the door to find out just what time we closed up shop.

Nine. One hour to go.

There was still no sign of Stick or Bob. I would have been really worried about the two of them, but I was more worried for myself. I had managed to serve customers all day, but this was not something I wanted to do again tomorrow. Stick had said he would man the store and I would be free to pursue other avenues of interest. But I had blown it. I had produced Stick's letter of resignation. I had the ideal situation and I had ruined it. Who could ask for more than an employee who never left the job? Oh well, it was water under a very stressed bridge. I could only hope that Stick would return to his perch and I would be free once again to start thinking only of myself.

I was awful.

I really did need to talk to my bishop about getting my life together. I picked up the phone and dialed information.

"What city?"

"Bluelake."

"What listing?"

"The Church of Jesus Christ of Latter-day Saints."

"Oooh, are you sure you want them?" the operator asked.

"Sure, why not?" I answered, surprised to get more than just a number.

"They've got a lot of wives."

"Not anymore," I returned.

"Well, I've got a sister in-law that read a book about them."

"And?" I prodded.

"It's not good."

"Really?"

"My brother was in Scouts with one of them, and he said they always talk about God."

"Is that bad?"

"Well I'm sure the way they talk about Him is."

"Interesting," I commented.

"Do you still want the number?" she asked.

"Why not?"

"It's your soul."

She gave me the number and a quote from some guy named Johnny concerning true Christians. I thanked her for both.

I rang the number. A friendly, animated voice answered the other end.

"Bishop Withers."

I explained who I was and how I was hoping to be a positive part of my new ward. The bishop seemed so excited about this I thought any moment I was going to hear a big bursting noise. We talked for quite a while. He even held on while I helped a couple of customers. Eventually we had said enough for one phone call.

"We need you Gray," he said.

"I heard it's a pretty big ward."

"Not big enough."

"Well, I'll be there Sunday. Oh," I added. "I don't know if you know yet, but apparently your counselor Todd left his wife. I didn't know if there was something we could do for her."

"One step ahead of you Gray. I've got the lovely Cloris Plot in my office right now."

"She just came in?" I asked.

"No, she's been here the whole time."

I was suddenly embarrassed.

"Sorry," I said, "I didn't mean to interrupt."

"No interruption. We are all one big concerned family. Sister Plot doesn't mind.

"Do you mind?" I heard the bishop ask.

"I don't mind," she answered back.

I sort of minded. "Am I on speaker phone?" I asked.

"You are," the bishop answered.

My sudden embarrassment turned to total humiliation.

Here was this poor sister whose whole world had just come apart being put on hold and listening in while I prattled on about my desire for caffeine and my hit-and-miss activity.

"I thought we were talking privately," I complained.

"We're building Zion here," the bishop said excitedly. "One heart, one mind, one ward."

One word. Weird.

"Thanks, bishop," I said halfheartedly.

"Nice talking to you, Gray," he returned.

"Sorry for snapping at you earlier," Sister Plot chimed in. "I hope you'll forgive me. I just haven't been myself lately."

"I hope you'll forgive her," the bishop instructed.

"Of course," I stuttered.

"Good then. We'll see you Sunday."

I hung up a little leery of the whole deal. He seemed like a nice bishop, but his tactics seemed a bit unorthodox. Regardless, I was going to do what ever it took to be the best Mormon I could be. I couldn't let anything stand in the way of my becoming the person I knew I needed to become.

I was just about to turn off the store's open sign when a car pulled up to the front. A man in a suit came strolling in with a fistful of papers in one hand.

"Do you have a rest room I could use?" he asked.

I pointed ours out.

He started walking towards it but stopped. He turned and looked at me closely.

"Do you belong to a church?" he asked.

"I do."

"What faith?"

"Mormon," I answered.

"I thought you looked like a Saint. I have an uncanny ability to pick out Mormons. It's a gift I guess. My wife says I am one in a million."

She was dead right.

"Here, read this," the man said. "I think you'll get a kick out of it." He put a folded piece of paper on the counter and walked off. I thought for sure it was going to be a flyer for Nu-Skin or Amway, or maybe some anti-Mormon literature, but I was wrong. It was a church bulletin cover with the meeting schedule of the Fremont Seventh Ward in Sacramento, California. I had no idea why this guy had given this to me. California was a long way away.

I took a good look at the bulletin. The front of it had a picture of pioneers crossing a stream, and the inside was filled with the standard stuff. I read through it. Conducting, speaking, praying, announcements. I still had no idea why this man had given me this. I flipped to the back to finish reading the announcements.

> Thelma Hopskins has an excess of wheat. If anyone is wheat deficient in their food storage please contact Sister Hopskins.

There was nothing worse than an excess of wheat. I felt for Sister Hopskins and her grainular dilemma. The announcement beneath it read...

> There will be no APYW this Tue. The YW will be preparing for their heritage buffet, Thur. at 7:00 p.m. The AP will be required to prepare the spiritual moment for the BYC which will be held next Sun. immediately following PEC at 6:00 p.m.

It took me a couple of minutes just to figure out that APYW stood for Aaronic Priesthood, Young Women. I was worried for a second that during my inactivity something important had been added to the Church without my knowing.

I read the next and last announcement.

> Rivers Jordan is looking for someone to write to. If interested please contact Sister Jordan at 2152 East Golf Avenue. Sacramento, California.
>
> Rivers is at present waiting for Elder Darrell Higgins to return from his mission in Florida. She feels correspondence with someone other than Elder Higgins would be healthy. Applicants will be screened.

I read the announcement a couple of times, unsure of just how to take it. For a moment I thought it was cute. Then I found it disturbing. I then concluded that it must be some kind of joke. Certainly no one would really put this kind of thing in the ward announcements. Excess wheat, sure, but openly promoting correspondence between a waiting woman and just anyone certainly was not Church condoned. Someone had slipped something past the program lady, and if my suspicions were confirmed, heads had already rolled over it. This had to be someone's idea of a joke.

Rivers Jordan? Obviously made up.

If not, Elder Higgins needed to be contacted immediately and notified as to just what kind of girl he had waiting for him. I mean the ward bulletin, come on.

Now, inspiration and I have sort of an uneasy relationship. I had the hardest time deciphering what was inspiration and what was just dumb junk my mind was producing. I had read a book once detailing just how inspired thoughts made it from the presence of God to us feeble-minded people here on earth. It was an inspiring book, but I had since forgotten exactly how it said this happened. Was warm and tingly rock solid proof that the universe was trying to signal me? Because for some reason this dumb little announcement made me lightheaded.

I set it down. I picked it back up.

There it was again.

I set it down for good. The man who had given it to me emerged from the bathroom. He walked up and down the chip aisle, finally settling on a bag of cheese strings.

"What a hoot," he said as he came to the counter.

"I assume you mean this announcement for a pen pal,"

"I do."

"Is it a joke?" I asked.

"I think it's serious."

"Is this girl normal?"

This gentleman laughed and opened up his bag of cheese strings even before paying for them. He stuffed a handful into his mouth and began speaking. I wish he would have done things in reverse order.

"Yeah, she's normal all right. In fact," he chewed, "she's an impressive young lady." This man then set down his handful of papers. "Could you throw these away for me?" He asked. "I just brought them in to read in the bathroom. I'm heading back East for a conference. Just needed to make a pit stop."

I took the papers and the program and threw them in the trash can behind the counter. I charged this Californian for his few items and then sent him on his way.

I turned off the open sign and the store lights. I then went out front and stared off towards the mountains. I felt as if I should feel lonely, but I didn't. I kept thinking I was out of place and out of sorts, but I wasn't. Forget was nothing but a barren piece of land, but something about it made it seem like so much more than that.

Strange place.

I went back in and managed to wiggle the key enough to adequately lock the door.

Rivers Jordan? Ha.

I was closed.

Chapter Seven

We Are Not Alone

Forget was kind of eerie without the knowledge that Stick was at the store. My home was big, lonely, and moaned like my sister, Maria, enjoying an oily bowl of pasta. The windows rattled with the wind, and they looked out upon yet another reason why Forget had me spooked: it was so much darker here at night than any place I had ever lived before. Black like an unrepentant soul surfaced from the dirt. It didn't matter that a half-moon was out or that the skies were freckled with stars like acne.

It was dark.

The two streetlights at the crossing stood there like dull-eyed sentinels guarding the road to nowhere, but that was it. Their weak light meekly illuminated the lonely red bench which sat there sunburned from the long day. Otherwise, I had never seen such darkness. Like thick tar, the sky rested upon everything. Only occasionally did the black muck get smeared around by the headlights of a passing motorist.

My father had liked the dark. He thought everything and anything looked much more appealing veiled in night. I remember when he took me to my first fathers and sons' outing. An older boy with a severe weight problem caught on fire while aggressively roasting marshmallows. Luckily he had been working on his fire safety merit badge that day, and the instructions to stop, drop, and roll were fresh in his mind. This kid did okay at stopping, and he was above average at dropping, but the rolling was where he excelled. His shape and the steep slope of the campsite sent him hurtling down the mountain. He fell off a ledge and traveled a good long way down into the forest before he got caught up in some thick ivy bushes. It took us all a while to even find him. I remember thinking how much easier he would have been to locate had he still been aflame. After we found him we all took off in different directions, each thinking we personally knew the best way back to camp. My father and I got terribly lost. No moon, no stars, and no idea where we were. Dad finally made us a little shelter and we spent the night under a huge pine tree covered in darkness.

Dad loved it.

Every once in a while—because I couldn't really see him—he would remind me that he was there and that there was no need to worry. How I wished I could hear his voice now.

I missed Dad.

Heck, at this moment I missed Stick. I had only known him for twenty-four hours but I felt like we had been friends for at least three days. And oddly enough I missed Angela the rug girl. I kept seeing her in everything. The outdated, incredibly busy kitchen wallpaper reeked of her, and in its pattern she was multiplied a thousand times. The long, dark shag carpet reminded me of her hair and made my fingers so nervous that only a clenched fist could calm them. I diverted my mind from Angela by thinking of the bulletin girl. Now there was a thought worth pursuing. I had always wanted a girlfriend whom I met in an unusual fashion. And a personal ad in the church bulletin was all that and more. Very intriguing. Sure, she was waiting for a missionary, but that only increased my chances. There is nothing like a girl on ice.

Rivers.

Angela.

I was dreaming in both cases.

I thought back to the time I had first met Mindy. It was at Pinny's Bowling Alley in downtown Phoenix. She, in her flared corduroy pants, wearing a short sweater and sporting some of those ugly bowling shoes. Me, playing the pinball machine, trying to work up the courage to simply say "Hi" to her. In the end it was she who came up to me.

Ours was a less than spectacular beginning. Mindy shyly wandered up to the pinball machine, and after watching me for a few minutes, nervously began to tell me about a lizard she had seen the other day in her front yard. I then said something like, "That's neat," and she then said something like, "Yeah, I thought you'd like to hear about it."

That was it.

She walked back to her friends. I made my way back to mine, and it was over. I had never been happy about our beginning. Of course, I was even less ecstatic about our ending. But none of that mattered now. Mindy was gone for good.

The wind outside began to get restless, reminding me that there was still no one out here but me.

I was it.

How utterly discomforting. To think that I might need to rely on myself was a disconcerting thought. What if I slipped and knocked my head? I could lie here for days before someone found me. Or what if I choked on a big piece of food? It was a proven fact that the self-Heimlich was not very effective. I made a late dinner and cut my food into tiny pieces—better safe than sorry.

I wasn't sure how to feel about things. I was slightly homesick for what used to be, but the deepest regions of my fickley soul were surprisingly undisappointed by what I had ended up with. I only hoped I could make something of it.

This, after all, was my one shot.

After dinner I cleaned out the refrigerator and fixed a couple of the kitchen cabinets. Then I started in on the main bathroom. While I was scrubbing the bathtub it occurred to me that I was mad at myself for letting Bob go to look for Stick alone. I could have closed up the store and joined him. The thought of hanging out with those two seemed better than the social evening I was now enjoying. I had no one to call and nowhere to go. I didn't even have a TV to watch. I considered driving into Bluelake, but it was already eleven o'clock; besides, I didn't want to miss Stick when he returned. It occurred to me that he was now my Jenny.

Forget was way too isolated.

I went outside and got into my orange car. I reclined the seat a bit and then messed around with the radio for a few minutes, trying to find something decent to listen to. Every station except one was playing country music. The other was a Christian rock format. If I was going to stay in Forget I needed to get myself a cowboy hat or find God. I turned off the radio and sat there in silence. I counted passing cars for a while—each vehicle sliding across my vision like beads on a abacus.

I finally got out of the car and closed the door, then looked up at the black sky in awe. Forget was so small and yet it seemed to be the point were the sky and the vast stretches of land plugged themselves into the earth. I watched a star streak across the black, painting a thin scratch of light that the night healed quickly. I walked back into my home letting the strong wind push me forward.

Once inside I double checked all of my doors to make sure they were locked and then got ready for bed. I must have been asleep for a while before I was awakened by a heavy pounding on the front door. The noise ran through my house like startled rabbits. I fell quickly out of bed.

I fumbled around for a big stick or something I could use as a weapon in case the knocker was someone with malicious intent, but I couldn't find anything other than one of my shoes. Intruder beware. I held the shoe in front of me and approached the door—it sounded as though somebody out there was in trouble.

"Who is it?" I yelled.

"It's Bob," Bob screamed back. "For the sake of all that is shiny let us in."

I'm always supportive of a good cause. I quickly unlocked the door and Bob and Stick came tumbling inside. Bob pushed the door shut again and made sure it was locked.

"Turn off the light," he ordered.

I was quick to obey.

With the lights off I could barely see either Stick or Bob. They were easy to locate, however, due to their heavy breathing. It sounded as though they had both just finished a twenty-mile marathon in ten minutes, their sour breath mixing with the night air.

"What do we do?" Stick finally whined, sounding like a completely different person than the uncle I knew just hours ago.

"I don't know," Bob said. "I just don't know."

"What happened?" I asked.

Bob "shhhhed" me.

The wind was really going wild outside now, and you could hear sand violently blowing against the windows. Stick started to moan, and Bob began mumbling things about God and the particularly poor state of mankind. I was beginning to get a tad bit spooked.

"You guys are creeping me out," I said, half joking.

"What we just saw ain't pretty," Bob warned.

I suddenly missed the big city and the comforting sound of ambulances racing to the scene of a crime or accident. I missed dead-bolt doors and the knowledge that a 911 call might actually be responded to in less than an hour's time. I missed well-lit parking lots, community watches, and the soothing sound of my upstairs neighbors fighting over whose night it was to do the dishes.

"What happened?" I asked.

Bob's breathing slowed, followed by a couple dry gulps. It was beginning to smell like sweat in the room. I wanted desperately to open a window and let some of that wild wind in.

"Should we tell him?" Bob asked Stick.

"He'll find out soon enough anyway," Stick cried.

"Tell me," I begged.

I could hear both Bob and Stick settle themselves on the floor.

Bob finally began to paint the picture. "I went out after

Stick," he began. "I couldn't find him anywhere. I drove around for an hour just honking and yelling his name. I got a little tired, so I stopped and took a short nap."

I could see how an hour of honking and yelling could wear even the best man down.

"I woke up just as the sun was going down," Bob continued. "Well, the setting sun made Nine Month Mound stand out like Billy Johnson's bald head. It seemed to just rise up in the distance."

"Nine Month Mound?" I asked.

"It's a small hill about halfway between here and the mountains," Stick explained.

I motioned for Bob to continue, although it was doubtful he could see me do it. He started back up nonetheless.

"Well, I suddenly remembered how Stick used to take Jenny out to Nine Month Mound. Remember that Stick?" Bob asked.

"Of course," Stick remembered.

"Anyhow, when I got to Nine Month Mound there was Stick sitting alone and rocking back and forth like he was one of them crazy, stressed-out city people. He wouldn't talk to me, he wouldn't look at me, he just sat there swaying. I finally had to get some water from my car and throw it at him."

"That wasn't water," Stick argued.

"It was getting dark," Bob explained. "So it was windshield fluid. Honest mistake. Stick started talking after that." Bob stood up and looked out the window.

"Anything out there?" Stick asked.

"Nothing."

"Is that the story?" I queried.

"That ain't the half of it," Bob said, once again sitting down on the floor. "Well, that's probably about half of it, but it's not the weird half. You see, once Stick started talking, things got better. That's sort of what I'm about," Bob bragged. "I bring people out of their skin and up to my level. Most people see people. Me, I see colors."

"Is that true?" Stick asked skeptically.

"It is."

"Well, what color am I?" Stick wondered.

"You're somewhere between amber and..."

"Finish the story," I pleaded, still sleepy and not yet confident I had been awakened for a good cause.

Bob was sober once more. "I was helping Stick to the car. It was pitch black out now, but I had my headlights on. Suddenly there was this incredible rushing sound, like a huge vacuum," Bob made a sucking vacuum noise. Small bits of spit came out of the dark and hit me. "Like the sky had been ripped open," Bob continued, "and everything was being sucked out of the hole. Stick really started to come undone, and it was all I could do just to remain composed."

Bob was talking slowly now. Each word he said was whispered and unsettling. I didn't know whether I should get goose bumps or start to laugh.

"Two seconds later," he went on, "we saw this, this thing fly over our heads and slam into the ground at the exact spot where Stick had been sitting when I got there. The exact spot!" Bob overemphasized. "Years back I'm pretty certain that I had once sat on that spot as well." Bob thought about this for a moment. "What are the odds," he finally said.

I don't know about the "what," but I think Bob made the "who" perfectly apparent.

"This flying...thing banged into the ground and exploded. Fire squirted everywhere. I think it singed some of my forearm hair," Bob complained.

"It was the most frightening thing I've ever seen," Stick whispered.

I would have put more stock in Stick's words if it weren't for the fact that he had not left Forget in years.

"What do you think it was?" I asked.

"It was shaped like a dish," Stick offered.

"No, no," Bob said, "it was shaped bigger than a dish, it was more like a platter. Sort of like that nice relish platter your mother used to have," Bob said to Stick.

Stick was about to comment on this but I stopped him.

"It was no bigger than a platter?"

"We're talking shape, not size," Bob scolded.

"Besides," Stick jumped in, "everyone knows that aliens are tiny."

I shook my head.

"Actually," Bob said, ringing in the voice of reason, "it was shaped like a gigantic brick. I got a real good look at it as it hovered over my head. I figure the occupants were no taller than Enis McCaffy."

Stick nodded his head in agreement. I had no idea who Enis McCaffy was, but I deduced that she was no giant.

"Come on," I laughed. "Hovered? I thought you said it whizzed past you and slammed into the earth."

"I did," Bob said. "But this thing had the potential to hover."

With my eyes now well adjusted to the dark I could see Bob look over at Stick and shrug his shoulders.

"The hover potential was there," Stick confirmed.

"See," Bob taunted.

"So just what was this gigantic, platter-shaped brick with hover potential?" I asked.

"It was nothing from this planet. I can swear to you that," Bob said. "I've seen man-made, and this was anything but. We ran over to the site to see if there was anyone alive, but there is no way anyone could have lived through that. We shined my searchlight, looking for anything moving but there was nothing. Just pieces of material and what looked to be tiny innards or something."

I was going to be sick for more reasons than one.

"They were almost cute," Bob added.

I wanted to yell. Instead I calmly said, "Shouldn't we call somebody or something? Someone should go out there and see what we can do."

"There ain't nothing we can do," Stick cried. "We've been invaded."

"Invaded?" I scoffed. "There's been a terrible accident and we need to do something about it." I stood and flipped on the light switch. Light flooded the room, revealing two middle-aged, ashen men and one twenty-four-year-old with a head full of second thoughts concerning buying into Forget. This was ridiculous. The charm and foibles of the locals had been almost pleasant when I arrived, but this was a life or death situation. There was no room for folklore or superstition now; lives might be on the line.

"What can we do?" Stick moaned.

"I don't know," I said, flustered. "But we have to do something."

"Now wait a second," Bob interjected. "I don't know how you handle things like this in the big city, but out here we do things differently."

"Do, or don't do?" I asked.

"Come on now," Bob chastened, "there's no need to get vulgar."

I unlocked the door and walked out of my house and into the night.

"Where are you going," Stick asked.

"To call for help."

The phone was not yet hooked up at my house, so I had to use the store phone. I unlocked the back door and went in. The store was eerie at this time of night. Empty and cold. I dialed 911.

Bob and Stick came in through the back door. Bob had his gun drawn and Stick was carrying a frying pan lid in front of him like a shield. Obviously they were protecting themselves from other life forms. I know if I had been an alien and I had stumbled upon them, I would have fled and never returned.

Bob put his fingers down on the phone, disconnecting my call. "They'll think you're crazy," he said. "You'd better let me call."

I waved Bob away. I dialed again. The phone picked up on the third ring.

"There's been an accident," I said calmly.

"Hold on," the voice said, "let me find some paper. All right, what happened?"

"There's been a plane crash."

"It was no plane," Stick shivered.

I shushed him.

"There's been a plane crash, and I think some people may have been seriously hurt or possibly even killed."

This person got some information about me and then started asking about the accident. I was having a hard time describing the location of the incident, so I put Bob on the phone.

"Is that you, Dot?" he asked. "It's Bob from Longwinded."

Bob talked to this Dot woman for almost ten minutes, and only twice did I hear any reference to the accident. He finally hung up and smiled

"Boy, that Dot is the friendliest person I know. Hard to imagine a woman with so much warmth could have gone through what she did last year. I've always said that doctors can make mistakes."

"And the accident?" I asked impatiently.

"She's sending someone out there."

"What should we do?" I questioned.

"Well, I don't know about you, but I'm spending the night here," Bob informed us. "There's no way I'm going to drive home when there's space people flying around."

I put my head in my hands.

"Well, you're welcome to sleep in my house," I surrendered. "I've got an extra bed in the guest room."

"I'm not going to sleep in the store alone," Stick complained. He had gone from a self-confident, devil-may-care cowboy to a scared and desperate man.

"You can take the couch," I said, inviting Stick.

Bob looked at us and in hushed tones began to speak. It felt like he was going to make us all take a blood oath concerning what had gone on tonight. Instead he said, "Just so you both know I have a little snoring problem."

"I've heard," Stick said.

"I can't help it if my body produced big adenoids," Bob defended.

I didn't know much about adenoids—annoyeds seemed more applicable.

"Are you sure there isn't something else we can do about the wreck?" I said as we locked the back door and headed to the house.

"The Bluelake police will take care of everything," Bob said. "Dot knows we're here if they need us."

How comforted she must be, I thought.

Chapter Eight

Pricked

Bob didn't snore, he honked and thrashed as if he were having some kind of terrible circus war flashbacks. He woke me out of a dead sleep with his "little snoring problem." At first I was concerned for him, but when I turned on the light I could clearly see that he was smiling the whole while.

I closed the door to Bob's room. It was still so loud I couldn't sleep. I buried myself in blankets. It was no use. Bob's snoring cut through everything.

After enduring his throat theatrics for almost an hour I finally became so frustrated that I went into his room and tried to shake him awake. Eventually he rolled over, and while still asleep he licked his lips and with a big friendly smile said...

"Chester was a good horse."

"Bob," I yelled out of frustration.

He turned over and then went right back to producing sounds that not even congested whales could imitate.

I wanted to wake Stick up and get him to help me move Bob to the store, but I was scared that if I did Stick wouldn't be able to fall back asleep either. Besides, I wasn't sure the store was really far enough away to drown out the sound of Bob. I decided to go and find out for myself.

I gathered a few blankets and pillows and headed out.

The Miracle of Forgetness

The store was an awful place to sleep. There was no way I was going to slumber on Stick's cot in the back room. I just wouldn't feel comfortable. So I laid down a few blankets and tried to make myself a bed on the store floor.

No matter what I did I still couldn't knock off. Not only was the floor too hard, but things were bouncing around inside my head like rubber balls in an electric dryer. It was as if I had a five-hundred-piece puzzle in my head which my mind kept throwing together unsuccessfully—the pieces just wouldn't fall into place correctly.

The hard floor started to make my back sore. This whole thing was dumb. I shouldn't be where I was at the moment—and I didn't just mean camped out on a hard tile floor. I shouldn't be setting myself up for failure like I was. I shouldn't be letting Pepsi caps and my feelings for an old flame set life's course for me. I shouldn't be postponing marriage. What had I been thinking? Who was I to ignore the blueprints? All my spiritual struggles would be so different if I had just followed the rules. I thought of Todd Plot, my pilot and local wife deserter. His words concerning flying and how nothing could go wrong if you just followed the rules rang clear now. I didn't want to end up like Stick.

Lonely.

I couldn't count on lotteries and chance meetings with the rug girls of life to keep me happy forever. I needed to actively work on myself and stop just hanging around life waiting for someone worthwhile to pull up and want more than self-service. Geographically, I was stranded for awhile, but spiritually I should be moving on. I couldn't believe I had laughed at that Rivers girl for putting an add in the church bulletin. At least she was doing something. At least...

My thoughts had been moving along so rapidly I had hardly noticed the completed puzzle in my mind. Each piece fit, and like a thick coat of clear shellac, thoughts of Rivers were now covering the puzzle, preserving it and making it fit for framing.

What was this all about?

My mind was calm, my spirit pricked. I got up and went over to the trash can, where I dug the bulletin out and placed it on the counter.

What the heck.

I found a piece of clean paper and there under the light of the glowing glass refrigerators, using a box of cold cereal as a clipboard, I composed a letter to this Rivers girl.

What did I have to loose? Words seemed to come incredibly easy. What a sign. Apparently I had gotten myself onto a worthwhile track. I finished the letter, folded it up, and put it in the same envelope Jenny's letter had been in. I crossed out the name Francis and scribbled Rivers' name and address on the front underneath it. When I was finished the letter looked old, tacky, and uninspired. I figured if Rivers could look past that we might just have a future.

I had considered the fact that this entire Rivers thing could be just a big joke. But if that was the case I figured it would be something funny to talk about years from now.

I fell asleep to the sound of the humming Slurpee machine.

I couldn't wait for morning.

Chapter Nine

Seeing Is Deceiving

I awoke to the sound of Bob and Stick arguing over who was going to call and report me missing. Apparently they had not seen me sleeping on the floor between aisles. They were both in their long underwear, shivering and going on about the terrible fate which had befallen me.

"He's been abducted," Bob was lamenting as he held the phone. "The poor kid's been snatched right up."

"I wonder what they're doing to him," Stick stuttered. "I let my own flesh and blood be stolen right out from under my own nose. Now he's probably being poked and prodded like a camp-fire wiener."

I stood up and walked over to them.

"They've returned him," Bob exclaimed.

"I was never taken," I explained. "I couldn't sleep due to your snoring problem.

"Oh," Stick said as if he were kind of disappointed. "We thought you were abducted."

"I'm sorry," I joked.

"It's okay," Stick said. "I guess it's better this way."

Bob called the Bluelake police to see what they had found out about the accident. It turned out to be not much. A couple of cops had gone out to Nine Month Mound last night, but they didn't seem to think it was a plane crash or a UFO. They thought it was just a big mess. So with no planes reported missing, no one really reacted seriously to our call.

Bob decided to head back home. He wanted to pick up a Longwinded resident who apparently had once had a close encounter with a UFO. Bob figured if he brought in an expert, people would take him seriously. He promised he would be back later in the day.

Stick got cleaned up and then opened the store. He had thought a lot about Jenny and had finally come to the conclusion that despite the letter there was still a possibility she could come back. He told me things were always darkest before the dawn. In fact Stick claimed to be more optimistic about Jenny than ever. Of course he also believed that at any moment our store would be taken over by short creatures with big eyes and zero body hair. So life for him was not turmoil free.

I got ready for the day and then headed out to Nine Month Mound, but not before putting my letter to Rivers in the mailbox. It was up to the postal service now.

Nine Month Mound wasn't hard to find. The land between Forget and the Mount Taylor Mountain Range was fairly flat, but about halfway between the two the ground started to puff up like small little pockets of rising dough. The hot morning sun seemed to butter the entire area.

Bob had told me that Nine Month Mound had been so named due to the fact it resembled the stomach of a nine-months pregnant woman. When I finally found it I didn't think it resembled a pregnant woman's stomach at all. It was just a big sandy boulder that was better weathered than a casserole dish in a Mormon kitchen.

Right behind the mound was the crash site. I don't know what I was expecting, but what I found was much more than that. It was out of this world. There was a hole the size of a large aboveground pool and as deep as a two-story building. The area around it was littered with charred and strange looking pieces and objects. I was truly amazed. There didn't appear to be any sign of life or previous life. Just weird burnt things and a strong smell that I didn't recognize and didn't like. At the bottom of the pit was what looked like a big ball of twisted, melted, blackened metal. It really didn't look man-made.

I cautiously climbed down into the hole. I had seen enough UFO movies to make me a little jumpy. I kept waiting for someone, or something, to jump out at me. I carefully touched the big twisted object. It was so charred I couldn't tell what it might have once been. It did sort of resemble a small craft of some sort.

I was a bit baffled.

I pushed on it and a hissing noise shot out. I've never moved faster in my life. I climbed out of that hole like a delinquent deacon being chased by a church hall monitor. Dirt flew all around me as I clawed my way to the top.

Once out of the hole I dared to look back. Whatever it was sat there silently now. I walked around the site a few more times, stopping once to pick up a small piece of the wreck and examine it. It was about two inches long and sliver. It looked to be a metal bar, or perhaps the end of a really big key. I stuck it in my pocket to study later.

I got back in my car and headed for home. I didn't know what to think. I certainly didn't believe that aliens had landed, but something strange had crashed down there. I couldn't wait for someone else to figure out what it was.

Chapter Ten

Strong Wind

Forget got its name for a couple of reasons. Stick had told me that originally when they put in Highway 62 and laid it right over Witch Road, the crossing was called Forget because it was the point that four roads did get together.

Fourget.

But soon after the little trading post was established people started claiming Forget was so named because it wasn't a very spectacular establishment. Most people driving past hardly took notice of it, and those who did stop seemed to forget about it later. I thought this explanation made more sense. Because although four roads did meet right in front of our place only three really went anywhere.

Highway 62 went south to Sterling or north to a few small towns and then into the next state. Witch Road went west to Bluelake, but East Witch didn't really go anywhere. The quality of the road seemed to die about two hundred feet from the crossing. It turned into a hard dirt road that was rutted and washed out in more places than ten hands and a week's time could count. Bob had told me the road eventually took you over the mountains and down into Longwinded.

To get to Nine Month Mound you had to take Witch Road east about ten miles and then follow an even smaller and more

washed out road a couple of miles south. I was on that road coming home from viewing the crash site, when a big copper
Cadillac came racing towards me. Its headlights were flashing,
and even at a distance I could hear its horn blaring.

I pulled to the side of the road and stopped. A couple of seconds later the Cadillac skidded to a halt right beside me, its
motor breathing and huffing like a ticked off bull. The car's windows were so heavily tinted I couldn't see who or what was
inside. I didn't have to wait long to find out. The driver's door
opened like a moth spreading its dirty wing, and out climbed a
very colorfully dressed woman.

I stepped out of my car.

"Who are you?" this woman demanded.

"I'm Gray Stevens," I answered. "I just..."

"Do you know whose land this is?" she snapped.

"I..."

"It's mine," she declared. "Every bit your thieving eyes can
see is mine. Now go back to your pretty city or I'll have some of
the locals string you up."

I looked around for locals.

I only saw one.

This woman was something else. She wore a large feathery
cowboy hat and turquoise colored boots. Her short skirt left
exposed two of the leatheriest, tannest legs I had ever seen.
They looked to be the texture of barnacles. My first thought was
why would someone choose not to cover those up. Her hands
were heavy with rings the size of fruit, and her thin body clung
loosely to a beer-filled belly. She was probably about fifty-five,
but her condition made Adam look like a teenager. All of these
aspects were dwarfed by her face and expression. She was mean,
and her face advertised the fact that she probably hadn't smiled
in years. In a word, she was unpleasant. It looked as if she had
eaten the ugly stick and then helped herself to the stick of sour
and the stick of grimace. She was additional scripture in the big
book of bitter. A dull gray light surrounded her entire being and
emitted uncomfortable vibes. My mother had always told me if I

couldn't say anything nice I shouldn't say anything at all.

I remained silent.

"What are you doing here?"

"I live here," I answered.

"Live where?" she questioned, squinting her eyes and reminding me of Popeye.

"I just moved to Forget."

"Forget," she sneered. "Armpit of the state. What would you be doing living in Forget? That place ain't fit for dust mites."

"I bought it."

"You what?" she said slowly, taking off her hat and exposing her sweaty, tangled, and heavily frosted hair.

"I bought it."

"Forget wasn't for sale," she sneered.

"Well, I bought it," I replied.

"From whom?" she demanded.

"Stick," I said rather cowardly.

"You had better be joking," she hissed. She was clenching her fists and snorting out of her nose. Her cheeks puffed up, and the loose skin beneath her chin jiggled. She stepped up to me and pushed me with her belly. Then she poked me in the chest. "You're joking, right?" she spat.

"I'm not," I said, weakly holding my ground.

She poked me again.

I pretended like it didn't hurt.

"I can't believe what I'm hearing," she hissed. "If it's true there'll be blood to spill. You tell Stick I'm coming to see him," she screamed. "And you tell him that no force on earth is going to be able to help him when I get my hands on him. His skinny, underbelly-white neck is mine," she yelled.

She leaped into her car, spun around, and drove off, dust and rocks spraying me in the face as she cast her stones.

I raced back to Forget, thinking she was headed directly to the trading post. When I got there Stick was helping a foreigner heat up a hot dog in the store microwave. The woman I had just encountered had obviously not come straight here.

"Did you see it?" Stick asked.

"I did," I answered, not completely sure if he meant the wreck or the woman who had stopped me on the road.

"Well, could you tell what it was?"

I still didn't know for sure which one he was referring to.

"See what?" the hot dog heating customer asked.

"A UFO crashed down here last night," Stick blurted out.

"Here?" the customer asked excitedly.

"Not right here," Stick clarified, "about ten miles that way."

"Can you show me?" the customer pleaded.

"I ain't going to show you," Stick said. "I'm never going there again."

"Well, could you tell me?" the customer begged.

Stick pointed out the way to the persistent customer. The man abandoned his hot dog, ran out the door, and jumped in his car.

"You really shouldn't be telling people about this," I said.

Stick shrugged his shoulders.

"Has a woman been by to see you?" I asked, changing the subject.

"What woman," Stick asked skeptically. I think for one brief second he thought I was teasing him about Jenny.

"I don't know her name," I replied. "But the land that thing crashed on supposedly belongs to her."

"Kitty," Stick said.

"She practically assaulted me for being on her land."

"Nine Month Mound doesn't belong to her," Stick huffed. "The state set that area aside as a park."

"A park," I laughed. "That is the most desolate, deserted, life-forsaken land I have ever seen. It's just a big rock, which, by the way, does not resemble a pregnant stomach."

"Sure it's become a little worn down," Stick differed, "but years ago it perfectly resembled Lilly Watamyer's stomach right before she gave birth. She had twins," he added.

"Well it's a crummy park."

"It was going to be the center of a beautiful community," Stick explained. "Katford County belongs to Kitty. Her father,

Karl, had big plans. Neighborhoods, parks, stores. Big plans, but they were all squelched by the fact that there ain't no water here. Karl thought he could use Bluelake's water system but they refused. Sterling wouldn't allow him to use theirs, and there ain't no way you can truck in enough water to support a whole neighborhood."

Stick stopped explaining to yell out his little window at a new customer who was letting his kids play around with the complimentary window squeegee.

"Karl died about ten years ago," Stick continued. "He left everything to Kitty. Big mistake. Kitty is just about the most pigheaded person I know."

The description was right on.

"She owns everything around here."

"What's to own?" I asked.

Stick thought about it a moment. "Not much I suppose. Just a lot of flat dry land. The only buildings on any of this area are Kitty's ranch and our place."

"Weird," I said, commenting on a lot of things with just one word.

"Kitty's wanted Forget forever," Stick smiled. "But there is no way she is ever going to get her hooves on it. She owns all the land surrounding us."

It now made sense why she was so mad that Stick had let me buy it.

"Did she know you were struggling?" I asked.

"Sure, everyone knows we've been struggling. We ain't never been one of them businesses that collect their money in buckets."

"Well, she's not too happy about the fact that you sold it to me."

"I didn't suspect that she would be."

"She's coming to see you."

"I'm sure she is."

A man wanting to trade some old tires for a few new sandwiches came in to haggle with the proprietor. I left Stick to manage his affairs.

The Miracle of Forgetness

I walked back home and continued working on fixing up my place. I spent a full hour vacuuming the shag carpet. It was quite a task. Every couple of minutes the vacuum would pick up a coin or some small chunk of something that had been lodged in the long shag for years. Each time it happened I had to turn the vacuum over and operate on its belly until I located the object of obstruction. I had almost seventy cents in loose change when it picked up a quarter and then choked on it and died. I was baffled by the fact that a vacuum which struggled to have enough power to pick up dirt seemed to have no problem levitating coins, bolts, and other heavy metal objects.

I decided to stop messing around. I ripped up every inch of carpet in the house. My intention had been to then re-carpet, but what I found underneath needed to be shown off, not hidden. The entire house had beautiful wood flooring. I rolled the old carpet up like huge fuzzy cigars and hauled it outside to deposit it in the store's big industrial dumpster.

While walking back in I couldn't help but notice Bob pulling up to the store, lights flashing and people jumping out of his vehicle. He had raced to Longwinded and back in good time. I hurried over to investigate.

When I reached him Bob had an open map spread out over the hood of his car and was excitedly waving a pencil around in the air.

"This is the exact spot," Bob declared.

Bob had two other people with him. One looked to be just a couple years older than I was. He had wavy brown hair and enough good looks to make me jealous. The other was a Native American with a long, braided ponytail hanging down his back and a curious look on his face.

Bob noticed me.

"Gray," he said. "Have you had a chance to check out the site?"

"I did," I answered.

"And?" Bob asked, anticipation dripping from his chin.

"Something crashed down there," I offered.

"What did I say?" Bob said turning quickly to the other two.

"It sounds similar," the Native American said.

"Orvil's seen a UFO before," Bob bragged. "Spent some time in a mother ship."

"Really?" I asked.

Orvil nodded yes.

"Don't believe everything you hear," the brown-haired guy smiled.

"Darn you, Tartan," Bob complained. "Don't go polluting Gray's mind with doubt. First impressions are bound to be lasting."

I really liked Bob.

Orvil and Tartan headed inside to say hello to Stick.

"They seem like nice people," I said as Bob and I stood there alone.

"Good people," Bob confirmed. "Tartan's a forest ranger at the top of Mount Taylor. He's been a real asset to our town. He's Mormon like Stick and Orvil. He's got the most beautiful wife, blond with really straight teeth. She's about eight-months pregnant at the moment. Stomach out to here." Bob pushed his gut out as far he could. "He's a doubter though. He doesn't really believe in much besides God."

"What about this other guy?" I asked.

"Orvil's Orvil," Bob replied. "He's a descendent of one of the great Indian chiefs, Standing Water or Blowing Grass, I can't ever remember. He's also one of Longwinded's best assets. He's been there forever. Just got married about a year ago. Fairly nice wife. She owns the local Stop and Shop. Stick and her trade off goods every once in a while.

Tartan and Orvil came back out of the store and joined us. I shook hands with both of them as Bob officially introduced us.

"So should we go?" Tartan then asked Bob.

Bob swirled his finger around in the air as if rounding us up. I jumped into the patrol car with them all. Bob raced us to the scene, his wheels spinning dirt behind us, his lights flashing spastically. With all the commotion we were making I felt as if we were actually doing something important.

There was no one at the crash site when we arrived. It was late afternoon, and the low sun made the area orange and heavy. The wind had blown sand down into the pit, making our UFO look even more mysterious and menacing then before. Bob walked around, pointing out things as if he knew what each charred piece of wreckage was.

"That must be some sort of steering device."

Neither Orvil or Tartan said much. Finally after Bob ran out of explanations for every scattered object that he really knew nothing about, he prompted Orvil to tell us his UFO story.

"I was much younger," Orvil began. "Our family lived in a small bungalow on the top ridge of Mount Taylor. We were also boarding Sitting Duck at the time."

"Who?" Tartan interrupted.

"Sitting Duck," Orvil answered. "He was a hermit my father sort of adopted. He was the sickest person I ever knew. My father named him Sitting Duck because like a sitting duck upon the naked water illness struck him. He was always whining about a sore spleen or lazy liver. No illness escaped him. He was sick, sick, sick. But because of his glass eye he was a lot of fun to be around."

Orvil stopped to contemplate the better days.

"Anyhow, I was coming back from the doctor with Sitting Duck," Orvil continued. "We were walking up Lazy Man's Trail eating frog jerky, when a bright light started to come up over the horizon. It threw us off because the sun was going down behind us. Sitting Duck thought it was just his new medicine kicking in but me, I was scared! Seconds later a big, egg-shaped thing with what looked like Chinese writing on the side zipped over us. Sitting Duck passed out. I stood there frozen as a cold-hearted cactus at the North Pole. This thing circled back around and stopped right above me. It split open like a watermelon, and this syrupy juice came down upon me and snatched me up."

Bob was smiling a proud, this-settles-everything type smile.

"So what happened?" I asked, intrigued as to just how this odd story ended.

"I don't remember," Orvil said. "Next thing I knew it was a few hours later and I was lying in my bed. My mother was running a warm washcloth over my face, trying to wipe off this sticky substance. Sitting Duck had found me up in a tree and carried me home."

"What happened to him?" Tartan asked.

"He died a couple years later while crossing Millrod Stream during a particularly heavy runoff."

"No," Tartan laughed. "What did the space people do to him?"

"Nothing, it was me they wanted. See this," he said, pulling his long braid to the side and showing us a scar right behind his ear.

We nodded yes.

"Sitting Duck dropped me when he was carrying me home."

"And," I prodded.

"The aliens could have tripped him, making it look like I got this gash from a rock and not one of their probes."

"Makes sense," Tartan joked.

Bob flashed him a mean look. Apparently Bob didn't want Tartan corrupting me with sarcasm.

"So, does this," I pointed at the site, "look like a UFO crash to you?" I asked Orvil, as if being snatched up by a flying watermelon made him an expert.

He was quiet for a moment. He looked at the melting sun and frowned. "This certainly wasn't a human accident."

I looked at Tartan and shrugged.

A big station wagon came racing up the road. It stopped a couple of feet away from us. The man whom Stick had given directions to earlier got out of the car. A woman who I assumed was his wife got out of the passenger side, carrying a couple of plastic grocery bags. They both scurried to the site and began picking up pieces of wreckage.

Bob had a fit.

He lectured them for a couple of minutes and then confiscated their bags. Orvil tried to explain to these people what had happened here while Bob radioed the Bluelake police department, informing them that someone needed to come out and guard the site.

We all got back in the car and followed the station wagon looters out. Bob waited at Forget until he saw a Bluelake cop come up Witch Road and head out to Nine Month Mound, then he left for Longwinded with Orvil and Tartan. I went home and laid out my Sunday clothes. Church was on the horizon.

Chapter Eleven

The Wise Man
Built His Church
upon the Lawn

Bluelake was alive on Sunday. Tourists and locals wandered the sidewalks, filled the restaurants, and congested the streets with their RVs and boat-toting trailers. Blue flags announcing the coming of the Bluelake parade and fair hung from the street lamps on Main Street and made me glad to be right here right now.

Church started at eleven, but I figured it would be wise for me to sort of sneak in late. I didn't want to have to stand around by myself waiting for the service to begin.

Arriving late turned out to be a bad idea.

The church parking lot was completely full, and like plastic beads on a string, cars lined the neighborhood streets behind it. I had to park about a half a mile away and hike in.

It struck me as I was walking up to the building that there was no one outside. Not so much as one typical late arriver. Things were quiet. The only sound was that of the big American flag flapping in the wind, its pulley occasionally clanging against the pole.

The Miracle of Forgetness

The chapel was completely surrounded by a thick, lush lawn, and there was only one sidewalk that cut through the green and provided a way to the church.

The church itself was shaped like a large, two-story rectangle, with a funny looking A-Frame, Swiss-chalet-like roof covering the front half of it. The whole thing was rather brown and practical looking, reminding me of the bad suit my father used to wear on Sundays. It was at the roofed end of the rectangle that the lone sidewalk and this odd looking chapel met.

Halfway up the sidewalk I realized just why there were no other late arrivers. The building was cleverly designed to ward off people who worked on Mormon standard time. Thanks to a creatively planted sticker bush and a single sidewalk, all members were forced to walk past a huge bay window which the entire, on-time congregation faced. The window occupied almost the full wall behind the podium and made you the focal point of every person in the building. I could see the back side of the person speaking and the eyes of the whole Bluelake Ward bearing down on me as I walked quickly past the window to the front door. It was completely embarrassing and reason enough never to be tardy again. Next week I would be looking out, not in.

I made it past the window and to the front door. Thankfully there was no one in the foyer. I peeked in the chapel to search for an open spot. The place was packed. Like a windy Sunday School teacher, people went on.

There was not a single open seat. The back of the chapel was opened up to the overflow area—that too was filled. It looked like a regional conference. I sat down on the orange couch in the foyer, pleasantly resigned to sit and listen to the meeting from a private vantage point. A small black knob sticking out of the wall adjusted the sound coming into the foyer. I turned it up just in time to hear the bishop asking a Brother Hutton from the congregation to go out and fetch the late arrival.

That was me.

Seconds later a skinny man in a loose suit came out into the foyer and brought me in. It was the single most humiliating thing that had ever happened to me. I started to seriously reevaluate my jump back into activity. Had I wanted this? Had I brought this on? The memory of all that had kept me away came flooding back. The joy of just sleeping in on a Sunday and then getting up and doing nothing flashed vividly throughout every bit of my lukewarm being.

Once in the chapel, a family with at least twenty kids inhaled, creating an open spot on the third row. After I was seated, the bishop welcomed me from the pulpit.

"You must be Gray."

I nodded yes.

"Well, Gray," the bishop said, "I hope that everyone here makes you just as comfortable as they can."

The little four-year-old next to me hugged me with his sticky arms and gave me a wet kiss. The audience ohhhed.

I sat there blushing like an unspoiled piece of fruit.

We had the sacrament and then the bishop took the stand again. He was a friendly looking guy. I recognized him as being the bald man on the riding lawn mower whom I had seen the day I came into Bluelake. He was constantly smiling and seemed to make everyone feel comfortable and wanted. The crowd was completely quiet and attentive as he spoke. There was not so much as a whisper or a cry from any member or baby.

The bishop was wearing a bow tie and suspenders, and he looked as if he could be a spokesperson for something traditional and needed, like oatmeal or firewood. Every time he spoke it sounded as if he were just about to laugh or smile.

"Before we get things started here," he said, "I'd like to have our newest member come up and say a few words."

I was being summoned to the stand. Like dirt from a hard day of sweaty outdoor work I could feel everyone's eyes on the back of my neck. This was just great. I had wanted to go unnoticed. I had hoped the numbers of a large ward would make anonymity possible. I reluctantly stood up and stepped out of one kind of pew and into another.

People began whispering.

Just great, I thought. It wasn't as if I had put a lot of thought into myself this morning. I had made sure I was presentable in case the ward had any eligible girls my age, but I had not gone overboard on primping. I guessed that my hair must have been messed up, or perhaps my shirt was not properly tucked in—something was prompting these people to whisper about me. This was not the start I had envisioned.

I stepped up on stage just in time to see a young girl coming up the other side at the same time. I looked at the bishop standing at the pulpit. He looked at me. He looked at the young girl on the other side of him. He looked confused.

I suddenly realized that I was not the new member he had been referring to. Apparently this young and, I immediately assumed, eight-year-old girl was the ward's newest member. I turned as if to go back to my seat.

"Now hold on a second," the bishop said to me. "Lindy here can wait a moment while you say a few words."

"I really don't..."

Lindy started to whimper. She wasn't happy. I was cutting into her precious few minutes of new member glory.

"Now Lindy Buswidth," the bishop scolded. "You can stand here a couple of minutes and let Gray say a few words. You're glad he's in the ward aren't you?"

Lindy started to cry.

"I'll just sit down," I said, desiring nothing more at the moment.

"Nonsense," the bishop said. "Lindy has had a problem with sharing, but now that she's eight I think she can act a little more grown up."

"Really, I..."

The bishop signaled me to take the pulpit. I sheepishly did so. Little Lindy stood there weeping as I adjusted the microphone. A family of late arrivers was coming up the sidewalk behind me. The entire congregation looked past me and out the window to see who had made the mistake of coming late. Once the tardy family had passed the window I began.

"My name is Gray Stevens, and..."

Lindy picked up the volume. Low moans escaped her like heat off a black desert road. I felt awful. I had ruined an eight-year-old's grand entry into the Church. For the rest of her life Gray Stevens would be an ugly scar on her.

Lindy started to wail.

I looked out at the audience. A couple of them were looking at me like I was some sort of mythical meanie who had magically appeared at their meeting with the sole purpose of ruining Lindy's moment. I wrapped up quickly.

I stepped away from the pulpit and pushed the stepping stool up so that Lindy could better reach the microphone, but she wouldn't move. She just stood there sniffling and crying and looking at me as if I had just told her I had mistakenly backed over her dog with my car.

A big woman wearing a large floral dress that zipped up in the front stormed onto the podium. She took Lindy's hand.

"I hope you're happy," she snipped, pulling Lindy off the stand and back to her seat.

I walked back to my seat. The small child who had hugged me earlier had worked a tiny glob of Playdough into the pew where I had been sitting. I didn't care. I wanted nothing more than to end my reign as center of attention. Sitting seemed the sensible way to do so.

I sat.

This young child didn't like the fact that I had just cut him off from what was no more than an ounce of smashed in, unusable Playdough. He whispered to his brother, who whispered to his sister, who whispered to his other brother, who whispered to his mother, who in turn gave me one of those mother looks that I had thought I had out grown. She sent a message back via off-spring.

I tried to ignore the whole family by listening intently to the speaker. It quickly became impossible to ignore them. The small boy next to me stuck his hand underneath me, rooting around for his clay. It was a bit too personal. I jumped a couple of inches off the bench and then came down on his wrist. He stuck his bottom lip out and then sent another message down to his mother.

We were playing telephone.

She sent a message back. I hoped it had gotten garbled in the process because "You're a green man with no mayonnaise" was both rude and nonsensical.

The first speaker finished up, and then a couple of young girls sang a song about the color white and what it meant to them.

The concluding speaker lulled us all to sleep with engaging discourse on genealogy and the power of well-organized microfiche. He bragged about how many roots he had and then went on and on about how genealogy was not an option, it was a duty.

"We must do our duty. This is one duty we can all enjoy. Let's embrace this duty. Duty calls."

It seemed like an awful lot of duty to me.

As soon as sacrament meeting was over I stood up and tried to make my way out of the place. I felt I had endured enough for one week. Unfortunately no one would let me leave. People approached me and spoke to me like we had been lifelong friends. It appeared that I had endeared myself to a lot of the members by making little Lindy Buswidth cry. Lindy, I discovered, had made a few enemies in the ward during her first eight years of life.

A very short elderly woman came up to me and began holding my hand. Every once in a while she would pat my sleeve. It was sweet. Disturbing, but sweet. She didn't say anything to me, and it didn't appear that she would be letting go anytime soon.

Members continued to come up to me and introduce themselves.

"Gray is it?" a big man with a square body and short arms asked.

"It is," I replied.

"I'm Tom, the elders quorum president," he said as if I had just won something. He stuck out one of his short arms and shook my hand. "I see you've met Enis," he said, referring to the little old lady on my arm.

"Well, we haven't exactly met."

"She likes you all the same," he said, his shirt untucking itself as he shifted about.

"Good," was my only reply.

"Listen," Tom said, "I need to know if you're the kind of guy that likes to home teach?"

Enis patted my arm.

"What do you mean by *like*?" I asked.

"Oh, that's a good one," Tom laughed. "I can tell you're going to do just great here. I'll whip up a route for you and have it to you by the end of church today."

"No really," I tried to interject, "I'm not sure it's such a good idea to..."

"Big ward, lots of families," Tom said as if he were new at English and these were the only five words he knew.

Tom walked off with the rest of the crowd. I looked down at Enis and smiled. She wore thick eyeglasses that made her silver eyes look like ball bearings and magnified the wiggly wrinkles that grew around them.

The bishop came up and patted me on the back.

"Great to have you here, Gray," he exclaimed, his nose whistling as he breathed. "Great to have you here."

"Sorry about coming up to the podium," I said.

"Sorry, nothing," the bishop hooted. "Church works best when it's a bit chaotic."

I didn't necessarily agree, but I nodded anyway.

"Listen," the bishop said, "you're going to fit right in here. Look you've only been here an hour and already Enis likes you. That's good."

Enis used her free hand to pat the bishop on the stomach.

"Maybe you can get that uncle of yours to come back to church."

"I don't know," I said. "Stick doesn't like to leave the store."

"We all know about Stick," Bishop Withers pointed out.

"Heard he saw a spaceman," Enis spoke up, her tiny voice hardly audible over the bishop's whistling nose.

"I don't think it was a spaceman," I explained.

"That Stick," the bishop laughed. "He's one funny fellow. Oh well, gotta go."

The bishop walked off to help a couple of struggling kids close the partition between the chapel and the overflow.

Enis didn't give me a chance to slip out of church. She pulled me from the chapel and led me straight to our gospel doctrine class.

Our teacher, Brother Wendell Scatty, a forty-year-old single, droned on and on about how polygamy seemed like a tough practice to live. He then listed the things he had a firm testimony of and the things he wasn't quite sure of yet. He seemed like a rock solid Saint. His lesson went rather well except for when he made a comparison suggesting that the robes of heaven would be as soft as a baby's bottom. At that point a Sister Lee, who had one of her tiny children on her lap, spoke up, asking if he could change his comparison. She just wasn't comfortable with the word "bottom."

"Soft as a baby's forearm?" he threw out.

Sister Lee nodded her approval.

Enis sat by me the entire time and then escorted me to my priesthood class afterwards. By the time she finally let go of my arm I was a little bit sad. Enis had been a nice security blanket. She hadn't said anything to me besides, "Heard he saw a spaceman," but we had bonded. Sure, I didn't even know her last name, and she smelled strongly of soap, but she had been a nice support and had given others the impression that I must be okay.

Our priesthood lesson was on labeling others. Brother Call, the teacher, gave a rather sterile performance. He ended the lesson by relating a personal story. I guess some years ago when he was a youth, Jonathan Call had been involved in one of the ward's roadshow plays. The play was about Church history. It was a musical about life in Nauvoo entitled "Here's to You, Nauvoo." It was an allegorical play where all of the buildings and fixtures of Nauvoo sang about life in the 1840s. They put all the parts in a bowl and then let the kids draw to see who would play what. Well, Jonathan picked out the roll of "The River Ferry." He then spent the next ten years of his life trying to live it down. It was a powerful lesson in labeling.

I left church quickly after priesthood. I'm not sure what I was hoping to avoid but I felt a certain urgency to leave. As I was walking to my car I noticed a deacon-aged boy following me. I weaved between a couple cars. He weaved right after me. I picked up my pace. He picked up his. I had no idea why he was following me, but just for fun I decided to start running. This poor little kid with the enormous cowlick and big teeth took off after me.

I won.

I reached the car well before he could catch me. I could hear him screaming now.

"Brother Stevens, Brother Stevens," he yelled with a lisp.

I stood by my car waiting for him to catch up to me. When he finally did I couldn't help but notice just how big his teeth were. His two front ones were long and brittle looking. They stuck out of his gums like a couple of stark white sticks of chewing gum. He wore a red handkerchief around his neck that made him look like a Russian Boy Scout.

"I'm Glen," he lisped, still breathing heavily from his run.

"I'm..."

"Gray Stevens," he interrupted. "I was sent by the bishop. I'm a member of the appointment patrol." He spun around to show me a diamond shaped badge with the words "appointment patrol" embroidered on it sewn crookedly onto the handkerchief.

"Appointment patrol?" I asked.

"It's a real big ward," Glen said, displaying his verbal difficulty with the letter r. "The bishop sends us out to remind people of after-church appointments. There's five of us, and we're kept pretty busy."

"I don't have an appointment," I explained.

"Bishop had to bump his one-thirty to Wednesday. I guess Sister Milar's having trouble with her feet again. She barely made it through sacrament meeting. He'd like you to fill the void."

It sounded so ominous.

I followed Glen back to the chapel. He gave me the skinny on the ward, or more fitting, the fat. Bluelake Ward was one giant ward. It could have been three healthy wards, but they refused to split because no one wanted to be in the ward that didn't end up with Bishop Withers. The members here were obviously quite content, and quite stubborn.

Bishop Withers had been bishop for some twenty years. He had been called when the ward had grown from a branch to a ward. Glen said people never wanted to leave the ward because of him. He was a contractor by profession and had designed and built the chapel. The big bay window was his baby, and according to Glen it had all but put an end to stragglers and lazy Mormons.

The bishop had two passions. His wife, Selma, and the Bluelake Ward. He cared for the Bluelake First Ward like no one else. He wanted it to be the perfect ward, a place John the Beloved could stumble upon and declare, "There is nothing for me to do here."

We reached the church and Glen led me to the bishop's office. A row of children and adults sat outside waiting for their turns. Due to a lack of seats I stood. I had five minutes until my appointment. I felt confident I wouldn't be seen on time.

"Do you like the ward?" a young mother sitting by me asked.

"I do."

"Isn't Bishop Withers great?"

"He seems like a real nice person," I replied.

"A real nice person, that's sweet," she said. "I think you'll come to find he's more than that. He built us a spare room on our house."

"That's nice."

"Mild weather is nice," she mumbled.

"Excuse me?" I said politely.

"Well, it just seems to me that you don't fully understand what a great job Bishop Withers is doing."

The whole "Wonderful Bishop Withers" thing was beginning to creep me out. Sure he was a nice guy, but these people seemed a tad too tied to their priesthood leader.

"I'm sure I'll come to understand," I conceded.

"There," she cooed, "was that so hard to say?"

I moved over and stood against a different wall.

This young mother whispered something to her young child. He then came over to me.

"Once when I was born I had thrush," he informed me. He looked over at his mother who motioned him to go on. "Bishop Withers gave me a blessing and my mouth got better."

This was just about enough. I would have walked out right then if another young boy with a red handkerchief around his neck hadn't popped into the waiting room and instructed me to go on into the bishop's office.

I had no idea what to expect. Bishop Withers seemed like a nice guy, but the way he ran things didn't exactly sit right with me. The members seemed extremely dependent. The most my bishop back in Phoenix had ever done for me outside of normal bishop stuff was bless our house after my sister Maria swore she had seen a small elflike person in her closet.

Bishop Withers met me at the door. He shook my hand warmly and offered me a seat.

"Well?" he asked, once he too was seated.

"Well, what?" I replied nicely.

"Did you enjoy yourself?"

"Enjoy" seemed like too strong a word, but I nodded, "Yes."

"Would you be willing to accept a calling?"

Again my head bobbed. I really did want to get my life back on track. And despite the fact that the people here seemed a little off, I knew I had to persevere.

"Good, good," the bishop replied. He then wrote down a few words and continued questioning me. "Do you and Stick get along?"

"We do," I answered.

"Stick doesn't exactly like me," the bishop said.

The Miracle of Forgetness

"Well, he's not in the majority with that opinion," I commented while taking a good look at the bishop's office. It was a small office, sparse when it came to furniture, but thick with wall hangings. There were more framed pictures on the wall behind him than I felt a normal wall could support. Pictures of temples and Christ and catchy sentimental little sayings were staring down at both of us.

His large desk had more knickknacks on it than a table at a gaudy garage sale. Paperweights, mugs, little statues with #1 bishop written on them, and items I couldn't easily identify littered the lacquer-covered, dark wood desk.

Aside from the desk there were only four chairs, one of which I was now occupying. Each chair had a padded green seat and a small embroidered pillow on it which read "Repentance is a direction."

"Sometimes I wish the members here would feel a little more like Stick," the bishop went on, acting a lot more mellow than I had previously seen him act.

"You don't want the members to like you?" I asked.

The bishop shrugged. It was obvious that he was not unaware of how weird some of his members were when it came to their feelings towards him.

"I told Jenny to leave Stick," he said, rather abruptly. "Dumbest thing I ever did. Jenny ran off with what we all thought was a real sharp guy. But he turned out to be a total..." The bishop seethed a moment, searching for the perfect word. "A total weirdo. Who knows where Jenny is now. The Paul guy she left with is in jail somewhere."

"Too bad," I said.

"That's why Stick doesn't come to church," the bishop said. "He's not exactly my biggest fan."

"He really liked Jenny."

The bishop stood up and faced the wall. He glanced at a couple of the pictures hanging there then walked over to the far wall and cracked open the window. Summer air leaked through the opening and scented the room. He sat back down.

"I've got a calling for you," he finally said. "We're an awful big ward, which means that sometimes we get the blessing of creating callings."

"Yeah, I don't remember my old ward having an appointment patrol."

Bishop Withers smiled.

"Gray, I want you to be in charge of getting your uncle back to church."

"That's it?" I asked. "That's my calling?"

"How gentle God's commands," the bishop replied.

Gentle was right. I thought I was going to be burdened down with some calling that everyone else had rejected. This seemed like a responsibility I could handle. I might not be able to accomplish it, but I could at least give it a go. I silently kicked my heals.

"I've always felt bad about Stick staying away," the bishop went on. "You know, the one lost sheep theory and all. Your moving in has reminded me just how much I messed up with him. I really blew it."

Bishop Withers talked to me about my inactivity and how important I was going to be to the ward. I wanted to believe him. I wanted to feel like I was vital to this gigantic family, even if the faithless part of my heart said that a ward which had to make up callings didn't really need me that badly.

At exactly 1:50 the bishop looked at his watch and informed me he had a ten till appointment.

I shook his hand and left. Strangely, I felt truly happy to be in the Bluelake Ward. I don't know what it was. Perhaps the bishop had painted the walls with a mind-numbing latex paint which messed with your mind. Or maybe there was a speaker system that subliminally bombarded us with brainwashing messages. Or maybe it was just that this ward produced such an atmosphere of comfort that even its abnormal members couldn't bring me down. Either way I was happy to be a part of it.

I walked right across the grass instead of using the sidewalk. I wanted to feel connected to the land. The chapel protruded out of the center of the lawn like an ugly growth, but Bishop

The Miracle of Forgetness

Withers had been wise to surround his building with grass. The moat of green made his monstrosity pleasant. And the circle of lawn made the chapel a bull's-eye for God.

I felt as if His aim had been fair today.

Chapter Twelve

Money in Buckets

Forget was a zoo when I got back from church. There were cars all over and people milling about like wound toys. I thought at first that something bad had happened, but as it turned out people were just flocking to Forget to see the UFO.

The word was out.

Stick was so busy helping people he didn't even notice me come in. The store was packed with people, and a line had formed at the counter where Stick was doing his best to serve his fellowman. He was selling off drinks, maps, and gas at a rapid rate.

I had already fought with Stick over the fact that I didn't think we should be open on Sunday. He reasoned that there might be some people who needed gas to get to church. I tried to debate him further but it was no use. He had been open on Sunday the last twenty years, and no silly relative was going to change things now.

Stick finally spotted me.

"Gray," he hollered. "Could you sack for just a second?"

"I'd love to but it's Sunday," I joked.

Stick snarled.

I quickly walked up to him and bagged the few items he had just rung up.

The Miracle of Forgetness

"You would have left Peter to die in the mud," he commented.

"Who's Peter?" I asked.

"The guy from the Bible," Stick scoffed. "Didn't you just come back from church?"

"I did."

"Well, people in the Bible didn't walk on Sunday. Thought it was a sin."

I was fascinated by the doctrine of Stick. He had quite a mind for scripture.

"I can't believe all of these people," I commented between customers.

Stick was in heaven and far too busy to talk to his relative at a time such as this. I had never seen anyone work a counter like Stick was doing. He could yell out his window, ring up a sale, and give directions to the UFO site simultaneously. He seemed to have as many arms as a Hindu god.

I leaned around for a few more minutes before Stick said...

"Bob's out at the site," I could tell he was frustrated by the fact I was just standing around. My presence also reminded him that he didn't want my help even if he needed it. Stick felt passionately that family shouldn't work together.

I took my cue.

I figured a nice leisurely drive out to Nine Month Mound might be a good calm Sunday activity. I was wrong. The site was even wilder than the store. Cars were all over and people were pushing Bob and a Bluelake cop around, scrapping to get their hands on a piece of the infamous UFO. I jumped out to help Bob. People did not take kindly to our trying to stop them from obtaining a chunk of another world.

"People, people," Bob reasoned. "This is evidence. Do not disturb the scene."

No one heard a word he said.

I had to beat a tiny piece of something out of an older woman's hands. I said a small prayer immediately afterwards, asking God for forgive me for being so rowdy on a Sunday.

In the middle of all this a big van pulled up to the crowd with two regulation looking white cars behind it. A round man with thick hair stepped out of one of the cars and began to push people aside as he strode up to Bob. The van doors opened and seven men in fatigues spilled out and began assembling a wire-like contraption and digging holes. The round man was handed a bullhorn.

"Drop everything you have," he said. "Anyone leaving the scene with anything other than the bodies God gave them and the clothes on their backs will be arrested."

Everyone dropped the few things they had been able to get a hold of. I even saw Bob quietly pull something out of his pocket and drop it to the ground. I was glad I had left the little souvenir I picked up earlier at home.

"Now if everyone will please clear out we will assess the situation," the round man said. "Chances are this is no more than a prank."

People got back into their cars and drove off. Some parked down the road a way, waiting to see just what these government people were up to. I stayed next to Bob. After everyone was gone the round man approached us.

"Bobby."

"Jay," Bob mumbled.

It was obvious by the way Bob had said Jay's name that he knew, and didn't particularly like, this person.

"I hear you witnessed this thing," Jay said.

Bob simply nodded.

"I heard you believe it's from another planet," Jay laughed.

Bob just stood there.

Jay was about the same size as Bob. His body, however, was more of a perfect sphere than Bob's. Bob's body seemed to dip and climb—a hills-and-valley type build. Jay's hair was literally as thick as hardened molasses. It looked as though he had a dense black plug sealing off the top of his head. Bob did have a mustache and Jay had none. They sort of looked like a westernized Tweedledee and Twedledum standing next to each other.

"Listen Bobby," Jay mocked. "I don't like being dragged out here on a Sunday. The state doesn't have time to go chasing every wacko's supposed sighting of a UFO."

I could see why Bob might not like this guy.

"I'm Gray," I said, hoping to break up the tension and sticking out my hand.

"I thought I told you civilians to clear out," he replied.

"Gray's with me," Bob jumped in.

"Well, you can leave also," Jay snapped. "This is no concern of yours anyway. Don't you have something to do back in Longwinded? Certainly someone's horse must be sick or something."

"Listen, Jay," Bob said. "It's no secret you and I don't get along, but regardless of that something crashed down here."

"It was probably just some kids from the community college," Jay said condescendingly. "They dug a hole and burned something inside it. We'll just gate it off and get to it when and if we ever have the time. It could be years before I get around to this."

"I saw the crash with my own eyes," Bob snapped.

"It's a pity," Jay tisked. "Things would be so different if we had a credible witness." Jay turned and walked away from us.

I thought for a moment Bob was going to lunge after him. Instead he turned to me and asked, "Have you had lunch yet?"

"No," I answered.

"Good," Bob said. "Dot invited me over and I'm not exactly comfortable eating alone with her."

"What about this?" I motioned, waving my arms around.

"Jay's competent," Bob said.

Bob was a far nicer person than I.

Chapter Thirteen

Dining with Dot

Lunch was not yet ready when Bob and I arrived, so we sat on bar stools while Dot finished some of the final preparations. Dot's home was a nice, average tract home. The inside was conservatively decorated. The only real color anywhere were the few pictures hanging or sitting around the living room. Most of the photos were of her dog, Sissy, a fluffy little white thing that did nothing but whine.

Dot lived right in the middle of Bluelake, behind the Sizzler and north of Tickdale Elementary School. The distance between her place and the crash site had given Bob and me the opportunity to talk as we drove over. Bob filled me in on Jay, Dot, and anybody else who popped into his mind.

Apparently Bob and Jay had been lifelong rivals. Bob had grown up in Longwinded, and Jay had been raised in Sterling. The hobby of calf roping had brought them together. Jay hated Bob from day one because everyone kept comparing the two of them. Don't they look alike, don't they speak alike, don't they eat alike. They were the same height, about the same weight, liked the same things, and both of their names were only three letters long. Eerie.

Well, when they got older both of them went into law enforcement. But whereas Bob aspired to nothing more than patrolling Longwinded, Jay wanted nothing more than to be over Bob. So far that had not happened. Bob held nothing against Jay, but he did admit the reason he had a mustache was to one up him—apparently Jay couldn't grow decent facial hair. Neither Bob or Jay had ever married, which only added to their similarities.

Dot, on the other hand, had been married six times. She married for occupation. A plumber, a carpenter, an electrician, an architect, a roofer, and a doctor, whom she claimed to marry only for his looks.

After she divorced her sixth husband, the plumber, she built herself her own home where she now lived with her dog. But all was not rosy for Dot. A short while back she went to the doctor because she had a rash on her arm. Well, the young doctor diagnosed it as a rare skin disease where one layer of your skin is allergic to another. Prognosis: each layer would eat away the other until she had no skin left.

They hospitalized Dot for a while. They tried every new treatment on her they could think of. Nothing worked. The rash spread. Finally someone had the sense to call in a world expert. Diagnosis: Dot was allergic to soap. She stopped using soap and four days later the rash was completely gone.

The hospital tried to say they were sorry, but Dot didn't accept their apology until they said it with a huge check in their hands.

I wondered why she didn't use some of that money to better decorate her home.

Dot now worked as a dispatcher for the Bluelake Police Department.

On our way over Bob and I had stopped off at Forget to pick up my piece of the crash. Bob was fascinated by it. We showed it to Dot, and she was equally impressed.

"Unnerving," she said. "It gives me the full-blown willies when I think of those aliens dinking about down here. I'm afraid to leave my laundry on the line over night."

"Used to be such a nice town," Bob lamented. I slipped my souvenir back into my pocket.

"Sure I can't help?" Bob asked as Dot sprayed a nonstick pan with cooking spray.

"You just relax," Dot instructed us.

"Dot built this house by herself," Bob said, searching for new conversation.

"You mentioned that," I replied.

"It never hurts to mention a good thing twice."

"So true," Dot agreed. "I love hearing a nice piece of news at least a couple of times."

Dot set a large ceramic bowl in front of Bob and me. She opened a new loaf of store bought white bread and dumped the entire loaf into the bowl.

"Help yourselves," she said.

I felt like a pigeon. Bob dove right in.

"I love bread," he said with a full mouth.

"I thought you might," Dot winked.

I picked up a piece so as to appear cordial. I pushed on the soft bread, removed the crust, and then began to roll it into a small ball. Miss Manners would have been far from impressed.

Dot switched some things from one oven to another. It looked as if she were fixing a rather elaborate meal. She pushed back her graying hair and dusted off her apron. She really was a strong looking woman, fairly tall, big boned, and a face that looked as if it had never frowned. Smile lines rippled up her cheeks and connected with her ears.

I finished my first bread ball just as Bob polished off the loaf. He did leave me the butts, but I passed.

Dot ushered us to the table where the three of us sat down. Dot said a small prayer blessing her dog, Sissy, and her sister, Terri, who was having a rough time with one of her neighbors.

"Amen."

For all of the preparation Dot had been going through the meal seemed incredibly simple. We were served thick hamburger patties that were brown on the outside and pink on the inside, French-cut green beans in a white sauce, and more bread. I couldn't figure out what she had been doing in the kitchen earlier. I hoped that perhaps she had been preparing some sort of elaborate dessert.

"So, Gray," Dot asked, "are you married?"

"No," I replied.

"You're what, twenty-four?"

"Yes."

"Impressive," Bob said, commenting on Dot's guess.

"I had been married twice when I was your age," Dot informed me.

I didn't quite know how to respond to that.

"This younger generation is being brought up on a whole different set of values," Bob said sadly.

I felt like I needed to apologize for not being married twice already.

"Got your eye on anyone in particular?" Dot asked as she scooped me up a huge serving of green beans.

"Well..." I started to say.

"Isn't Milt's kid still single?" Bob asked Dot with a full mouth of meat.

"Autumn?" Dot asked.

"Autumn," Bob said nicely. "Pretty girl. I never could figure why she couldn't find herself a man."

"Well, that equilibrium problem doesn't help her out," Dot stated.

"She's perfectly normal when she's sitting down," Bob rebutted.

"Really," I said, "I'm fine."

"Fine is a tall man in a nice suit," Dot chimed. "You need someone. What about the single Mavis twin?" she asked Bob.

"Stelly?" Bob asked.

"No, Telly," Dot corrected. "Stelly married Harwood."

"I don't know," Bob said while buttering a piece of bread. "Telly has her father's temper and that tattoo."

"What tattoo?" Dot asked, unbelieving.

"It's on her ankle."

"What's it of?"

"A spider or something."

"How big is it?" Dot asked.

"It's about the size of a sausage," Bob replied.

"Link or patty?"

"Patty," Bob clarified.

"Well, people who scribble on their bodies make bad mates," Dot said while taking a bite of her green beans. "These things are only loaners," she said holding her arms up and looking at her own body. "The good Lord doesn't want us back all marked up and dinged."

"Isn't she spiritual?" Bob said, pointing at Dot with his fork. "I tell you, Dot, I haven't seen you in so long I've forgotten just how spiritual you are."

"I read the Bible every night and occasionally on Saturday morning," she bragged.

"I'm surprised the heavens haven't snatched you up already," Bob said, spitting bread all over. "Gray's a Mormon," Bob informed her.

"I don't know much about Mormons," Dot replied. "I think my mail lady's one. I'm really careful about what I have sent to the house. I don't want her to have to deliver anything too racy. Mormons are rather prudish you know. I got me a post office box in town so I can receive my *Good Housekeeping* and *Soap Opera Digest* in private."

"That's nice," I replied.

"Live and let live," Dot said.

We all settled into our meals, and for a moment there was quiet. Sissy started scratching at the back door, so Dot got up to let her out.

"Isn't she something?" Bob asked me at her absence.

"She seems very nice."

"Dot and I met at a Bluelake singles dance a few years back. She would have married me if I had a profession she's needed. She's always been square with the law." Bob grabbed the last piece of bread and stuck it in his mouth.

"Wavramadafagotus," he muddled.

The Miracle of Forgetness

"What?" I asked.

Bob swallowed. "We've remained friends.

"Oh."

Dot rejoined us.

"Delicious meal," I complimented.

"Thank you, Gray. I enjoy cooking for others," she went on. "Someday you'll find yourself a wife who will cook and cook and cook until everything in your closet seems like it was sewn for little people."

Different people had different views of marriage.

"I don't know," Bob broke in. "I've been a bachelor all my life. It really isn't that bad."

"Well, I'd like to get married eventually," I said.

"What about Hazel Dornt?" Dot said excitedly. "She'd be perfect for Gray here."

"I don't know," Bob cautioned. "She's a little bit intense."

"Nonsense," Dot said. "She's perfect."

"Really, I'm all right," I begged.

"Listen, Gray, this is the girl for you. She's blonde, beautiful, and just about your age."

"She's intense," Bob sang.

"Phooey," Dot spat. "When a man lights a person's house on fire because he can't be with her the world thinks it's romantic. But when a woman does it everyone jumps all over her."

"Really," I said with conviction, "I'm okay. In fact I'm writing a girl right now."

Bob looked around for a hidden pen and piece of paper.

"Not right now, now, but I'm corresponding with a girl that I really like."

"That's sweet," Bob said.

"Well, it couldn't hurt to keep your eyes open," Dot suggested.

Dot served us cherry flavored popsicles for dessert, which we ate out on her front porch. The sounds of Bluelake in the late afternoon drifted nicely through the air. And the small amount of heat in the wind caused Bob and me to keep a constant, valiant vigil on our popsicles.

Half of Bob's popsicle fell to the ground. (He obviously was not as valiant a licker as I.) He picked it up, dusted it off, and then stuck it in his mouth.

"Good to be alive isn't it, Gray," he mumbled.

A small kid with a big head came skateboarding down the road. He tried to be tricky in front of us and wiped out bad. People from all the surrounding houses ran out to help.

"Good to be alive," I answered back.

I absolutely loved it here.

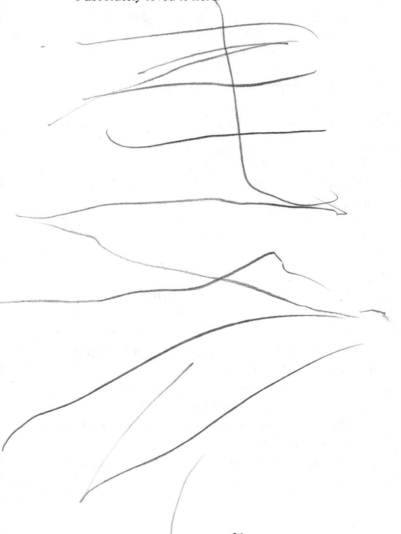

Chapter Fourteen

The Jingle of Change

Forget changed. Don't get me wrong, it was still the same barren windswept crossing it had always been, only now it was busy. People filed in and out of our doors all day long, and we had to start having food and gas deliveries made more often. Even the weathered bench at the crossing was getting some use, as small-time tour busses stopped at our place on the way to the site. People would sit on it and complain about the heat as they waited for the rest of their party to load up on convenience store necessities.

Stick began to say things like, "Maybe I didn't need your investment money after all."

I began saying things like, "Too late."

The state people had built a chain-link dome over the crash site. Folks were still allowed to walk up and look, but they couldn't get close enough to touch or take anything. Visitors were coming from everywhere. In the short time since the accident we had seen people from all over the States, two people from Canada, and a German man named Gunty who had gotten lost on his way to some other place and decided to come see the UFO before he got reoriented.

Little conversation took place around our corner of the state without the subject of the "UFO" popping up. It seemed to be something everyone liked to talk about, and some wild and highly unbelievable stories began to surface. One family swore that on the same night as the crash a little kid who seemed unusually smart was discovered rummaging through their outdoor trash receptacles. When confronted, the "Child" simply disappeared down the alley and over the park fence.

Poof! he was gone.

Another family claimed they had awaken the morning after the crash to find they now had an extra kid. It turned out in the end to just be their youngest boy, who for once had a clean face and hands. But that didn't change the fact that it *could* have happened.

Everyone seemed to love the UFO. Everyone except Kitty. Kitty Katford was livid. She hated the fact that people were crawling all over her property. The UFO could not have come down in a better place for us, or a worse place for Kitty. If the crash had occurred a few hundred yards in any direction it would have happened on Kitty's land. She then could have put up fences and walls keeping anybody and everybody out. As it was, she couldn't do a thing about curious onlookers looking on.

Kitty had come in twice to chew out Stick and me. She was mad that I had bought the place, mad about the UFO, mad about all the people around, mad, mad, mad. The second time she came in she became so upset—concerning things Stick and I really had no control over—that she began grabbing candy bars from the candy aisle and throwing them at Stick and me. She beaned Stick in the head with a king-size Snickers bar before I was able to escort her out.

Amidst all the commotion and craziness I was finding a real routine to life. Forget had become home, Stick had become family, and thoughts of Mindy rarely crept into my mind anymore. I thought about the rug girl and Rivers more than I should—given the fact I knew neither of them. But I didn't obsess over the blaring problem of life without real dating possibilities. I believed things would eventually fall into place.

The best part about the whole Forget deal was my tree. A lone living thing protruding from a valley of dirt. I loved lying on the small patch of dead grass beneath it late at night. I loved pouring any and all extra water we had on it. It was as if I were personally helping God create something extraordinary. Of course God could easily have turned the entire area into a steaming jungle had he been so inclined, but it was nice of Him to let me feel needed.

The tree stood like a lighthouse on an endless sea of sand. It was the first thing you saw regardless of the direction you were coming from. Its green leaves blinded you and marked home with a giant X. Sometimes Stick called the tree his Jenny catcher. Jenny had loved trees, and Stick felt confident she would come back someday to see the tree she had helped him plant years ago. Late at night I would lie beneath it, staring at the stars and listening to the wind run unsupervised through its branches—like a group of children goofing around while Mother Nature had her back turned. Everything was understandable under that tree.

Physics? No problem.

Chemistry? Easy.

Love?

It almost made sense.

What a tree.

I woke up early Friday to get ready just in case the rug girl did come by. She had promised she might, and at this point she was my surest thing. If I was going to get back into the Church all the way, that was going to have to include getting into matrimony someday. I needed to at least be giving this dating to find a wife thing a good go.

I was pouring a bucket of used water at the base of the tree when I saw the postman pull up to the store. I watched him speed off a few moments later. I returned my bucket to the house and then went to see if Stick needed some help.

He didn't.

Stick really wanted to make the store work without me. He liked me, but despite the fact he was incredibly busy these days he still wanted to prove he could do this without his little

nephew. I was usually happy to let him do so. I loved the freedom his devotion and commitment afforded me. If business kept
up like this, however, we would have to hire a second employee.
I needed to keep my eyes open for a nonfamily member who
wanted work.

"You got mail," Stick said as he helped a lanky kid locate a
packet of travel aspirin.

There was only one letter for me. It was in a small square
envelope with my address written in black ink. It had a stamp
with a picture of a sailboat on it pasted to the top right-hand corner.

It was from Rivers.

My hopes began to flow.

I left Stick so I could be alone with my letter. I tried to psych
myself up for what I knew would be nothing.

"You're lonely, you're desperate, and you have little or no
possibilities. This letter is going to do nothing but reaffirm those
truths."

I sat down beneath the tree and held the letter up to the sunlight—it was a rather modest envelop. I was almost afraid to open
it. Certainly she had to be in some sort of dire straits to actually strike up a correspondence with someone who had responded
to her odd ad. I mean what kind of sicko replies to a personal ad
in a ward bulletin?

Me.

I would also be surprised if she had anything other to say to
me than, "Get a life." Did she think anyone so desperate as I
could have merit? Did she live in some kind of fantasy world
where she imagined legions of worthwhile men sitting at home
thinking, "I'm rich, I'm attractive, I'm competent, I'm loving,
and I only go out with girls who have the tenacity and class to
advertise themselves in the church bulletins."

I ripped open the letter and read it.

It was flawless.

The tree looked over my shoulder and read along—at the letter's conclusion we were both pretty impressed. Rivers told me

all about herself. She told me about California. And she explained the whole bulletin ad thing. Apparently, one of the young women she was currently teaching had dared her to put the ad in the ward bulletin. It was supposed to be an experiment to see if people actually read the programs. She was amazed someone so far away had responded. She was actually amazed that anyone, anywhere had responded. She hadn't expected her ad to produce anything but a few laughs, or perhaps a couple of raised eyebrows. So what was supposed to be a silly lesson in curiosity had proven to be a chance for me to now know a girl I never would have met otherwise. This could be an okay thing.

Besides, I really did feel something more than just correspondence when I thought of her. I reread her letter a couple of more times. I was so distracted by it I almost missed the rug girl pulling up to the store.

Almost.

I stood up and tucked Rivers' letter into my back pocket. I didn't want Angela to think I spent my days waiting around for her, so I walked around the other side of the store and pretended like I hadn't noticed her and was just walking in. I was hoping she would see me and yell out my name. At the one moment when she might have seen me she looked down, flipping on the gas pump.

Shoot.

I walked into the store and out the back door to give it another go. I walked slowly and whistled this time. She sort of turned to look at me, but before she could see who I was, she became distracted by a passing car. I walked into the store and out the back again.

I came back around the store sort of clapping my hands and humming. I was walking extremely slow this time, but Angela was so busy looking the other way she still didn't notice me. I stopped and took a good long look at the front of the store. I tried to make it look like I was evaluating my investment.

Angela still wasn't looking.

I was just about to bend over and begin looking for a pretend lost contact when Stick, who had been observing my behavior from inside, slid open his little window and yelled out, "Would you look at the boy before he becomes permanently stupid."

Angela turned around and looked at me. My face red, her brown eyes shining. I just stood there, rendered lifeless by the embarrassing remarks of my uncle. Two seconds later her gas tank reached its maximum intake and the pump snapped off. I watched helplessly as she attended to her hose.

This relationship needed work.

I walked up to her. She smiled in turn, her teeth bleached white with mercy. I then followed her into the store. Stick made the whole situation that much easier for me.

"It's you," he said bluntly to her.

She nodded uncomfortably.

"Gray's been talking about you," Stick continued. "He really likes your hair." Stick winked at me as if he had just helped me out.

After she had paid I followed Angela back out to her truck.

"Sorry," I apologized.

"Don't be," she soothed.

"I mean I did mention your hair, but it wasn't in some sort of weird context. You just happen to have nice hair. I'm always envious of people with shiny hair."

"Yours is kind of shiny," she said, referring to my black mop.

"Well, I guess envious is the wrong word."

"Kinship?" she asked, sounding as if she were blessing me after a sneeze.

"I don't know," I replied. "You just have nice hair."

She looked at me with her head crooked.

I opened her door and she climbed in.

"Listen," I said boldly, "I know you don't know me, but I can't let you just drive off without asking."

"Asking what?" she played along.

"Would you be interested in doing something, sometime, with me?"

"I'm pretty busy," she replied.

The Miracle of Forgetness

That was not the answer I had wanted or expected.

"Sure," I backpedaled. "I mean rugs don't sell themselves."

"I'm only supposed to come this way once, maybe twice a month," she explained.

"The whole world needs rugs," I pointed out.

"I'll try to come back next Friday," she announced. "Try not to talk about me too much in the meantime," she smiled, touched my arm, and then got in. I accidentally shut her hand in the door as I closed it for her. She screamed out in Spanish. I quickly opened the door and apologized.

"I'm so sorry, I didn't..."

Her eyes burned for a moment; then like cooling coals, the glow left them.

"Don't worry about it," she said.

She closed her own door, and I watched as she drove off towards Sterling.

I went back home and read my letter from Rivers a few more times. I composed a new letter for her, packaged it up, and drove to the Bluelake Post Office to mail it.

I figured I needed to nurse both of my slim chances.

Chapter Fifteen

A Body without a Head

I worked really hard to fix up my house. It was in good condition, structure wise, but the finished aspects of it were groovy and more outdated than whitewall tires. The kitchen table had a lazy Susan, the master bathroom was done completely in avocado, and there was even an intercom system hooked up between the store and the house. Stick used it occasionally to summon me over. He treated the thing like it was a CB.

"This is... Ten four. Over."

That afternoon, while painting the dark wood paneling in my living room white, Stick called me over to the store. He said he had something to discuss.

Discuss was an interesting word. During the short time I had been here Stick and I had enjoyed many a good conversation. Stick loved to talk at me. He loved to tell me how things were and how they should be. He wanted me to know that he was more than just your average, full-time clerking cowboy. Yes, he wanted to make it clear to me his noggin contained thoughts that were both progressive and insightful.

He also liked to share his views about God. Stick saw God in everything from the sand outside to the shine in a freshly mopped floor. The only place he had a hard time recognizing his Creator was in church. This was largely due to his hateful feelings

towards Bishop Withers. I hoped our talks would help him come
around. At the moment I knew of no other way to fulfill my calling than to simply listen to Stick yammer.

I walked over to see just what Stick wanted to discuss. There
were customers in the store milling around, but he was free to
talk. He leaned against the counter and tipped his cowboy hat up.

"I was thinking," Stick pondered. "Do you think Adam had
more than one wife?"

"Adam who?" I asked honestly.

"The Adam."

"As in Eve?"

"None other," Stick replied.

"I guess I've never given it much thought," I said, pulling up
a stool and sitting down behind the counter by Stick.

"I think about these kinds of things all the time," Stick
bragged.

"Why would I need to know if Adam had more than one
wife?" I played along.

"It's doctrine," Stick reasoned.

"It doesn't seem relevant to my making it back."

"I'd hate to make it back and not know who to hug on the
other side."

"Hug them all," I said. "What could it hurt?"

"It's just not as personable."

Stick stepped out from behind the counter to help someone
locate the motor oil. He then returned to his spot back by me.

"Do you ever clean out under this counter?" I asked, looking
at the piles of junk hidden underneath the countertop.
Apparently Stick thought that since the customers couldn't see
back behind the counter, he didn't really need to keep it orga-
nized. All kinds of junk was crammed into the cubby-like holes
and shelves.

"I know where everything is," Stick defended.

"What's this?" I asked, pulling out a molded sandwich
wrapped in paper towel.

"It hasn't been there long."

"Still," I laughed.

"I don't need a second mother," Stick said, grabbing the sandwich from me and throwing it into the overflowing trash can next to me.

"I'm only trying to help."

"I think you're just trying to steer the conversation away from doctrine," Stick bantered. "People like you have a hard time explaining their testimonies when they're faced with such deep questions."

"Really, I don't care. I would think you should be more concerned about food rotting at your feet than whether or not Adam said 'I do' more than once."

"There's going to be questions," Stick informed me.

"Questions for what?" I asked.

"God's not going to just let you walk into heaven."

"I'll write the answers on my hand," I joked.

"I hadn't thought about that," Stick replied seriously. He looked at both of his hands. I suppose he was contemplating whether or not his tiny palms provided him with enough space to write down all the answers.

A couple of customers had made up their minds about what they were going to purchase. They brought their goods up to the counter to pay.

"Adam had to have more than one wife," one customer said. Apparently he and his missus had been listening into Stick's and my conversation. "My sister married her forth cousin and they have a kid with no ears."

Convincing argument, I thought.

Stick politely rang these people up. As soon as they were gone he continued his train of...not thought exactly, but his lips did continue to move.

"Some people say the craziest things. No ears, what does that prove?" Stick said disgusted.

"Bad genes," I replied.

"Ha," Stick said. "My sister married her third cousin and all their kids have ears. Third cousin," Stick reiterated.

"Three's a lucky number."

"Well four's only one more than that."

This "discussion" needed to end.

"Do you want to come with me to the ward activity tonight?" I asked.

"I can honestly say no," Stick replied.

"Would you come anyway?"

"What is it, a dinner or something?" he asked.

"I think we're building a float for the Bluelake Parade."

"I got to work the store."

"You could come late."

"I got to wait for Jenny," Stick stated.

"She's not going to return tonight," I said. "No one returns to a long lost love on a Friday night. It's just not wise. Friday night people are usually out and about, hard to catch at home. Now early Tuesday evening is the perfect time for Jenny to appear. You're usually free, I mean who has plans on a Tuesday?"

"That makes a lot of sense."

I was glad *he* thought so.

"So what do you say? Will you come?"

"I got to wait for Jenny," he said once again.

I headed back home and then to the church, alone.

The parking lot of the church was filled with people working on what looked to be a nearly completed float. Children ran around like bright colored roaches, and parents stood in groups, talking and working. I walked around a few minutes looking for someplace I could best assist.

The float had been made in the shape of a temple, and members were now gluing on the final pieces of crepe paper. It was actually very impressive. There was a big sign on the front of it with letters spelled out in bright purple crepe paper. The sign read "Forever Can Be Forever."

Bishop Withers slipped up next to me. "The elders sort of messed up," he informed me. "I figure what the heck, it's still true."

"I assume it was supposed to say 'Families Can Be Forever.'"
Bishop Withers nodded.

Enis McCaffy spotted me and came over and grabbed my
hand. She patted me once on the lower back and then once on
the arm. I was happy to see her.

I tried to help with the finishing touches on the float, but
Enis made working difficult. People spotted my handicap and
were kind enough to just let me watch. Tom, the elders quorum
president, pulled me aside so he could talk confidentially to me.
I guess he didn't consider Enis to be a third ear.

"Ready for a home teaching family?" he asked.

"I guess," I said, wanting to be an active participating member, but desiring not to be a home teacher. There were just too
many ways to fail at it. It wasn't the kind of calling you could
just punch in for on Sunday morning and then sign out again
three hours later. It required everything from being a decent listening ear to knowing how to fix dishwashers and trim hedges.
And the only really honorable way out of a home teaching
assignment was for the family you taught to move away from the
ward. But should that ever happen, you as their home teacher
are always the one called upon to pack up their entire existence
and load it into a hot truck while they and their children stand
around eating the very pizza they claim they bought as a thank
you for your trouble. Yes, there is nothing like carrying a hide-
a-bed down two flights of stairs and through four doors that
were designed to let through nothing bigger than a twin-sized
mattress, only to be rewarded with three cold pieces of pizza
that every other person there had personally inspected and
declined.

I wasn't giddy.

"I'm only going to give you one family," Tom said. "Well,
actually the bishop said you were in charge of your uncle
already. But besides him I'd like you to see Ned."

"Ned who?" I asked.

"Just Ned."

"Doesn't he have a last name?"

"He does, but he won't tell anyone what it is. Apparently he doesn't like it."

"Do the Church records have his last name?"

"Nope."

"That's weird, don't you think."

"Nah, Ned needs no other name. He's just Ned. I suspect you would have to wrestle his birth certificate away from him to truly find out." Enis patted Tom on the belly as if she were proud of him for finishing his last sentence.

"Is he here?" I asked.

Tom pointed him out and told me his story. Ned was an inactive. The only time he ever came around was at church activities. He lived right off Witch Road on the east side of Bluelake. Ned had been the head janitor at Tickdale Elementary School up until a couple of years ago when he retired. He was a very recognizable figure around town for a couple of reasons.

About seven years back, the Bluelake Chamber of Commerce made up T-shirts to celebrate the lake's fictional birthday. The shirts said "Happy birthday to a beautiful lakie."

Well blame it on the stupid saying printed on them, or the uncomfortable poly/rayon blend, but either way the shirts didn't sell. Sure Mable Bleat, the chamber of commerce's president, had bought two so as to support the cause, and there was a single out-of-town visitor who bought one because his car was acting up and he needed something to wipe off his dipstick with. But that was about it. They even tried to give them away with radio promotions. Be the eighth caller and the shirt is yours.

No one called.

One thousand nine hundred and ninety seven T-shirts, sizes large and extra large, with no one to wear them.

So Ned worked himself a deal.

The city sold Ned the remaining shirts for a couple hundred bucks. Now Ned wore nothing else. He figured he had upperwear until his dying day. To adorn the lower half of himself Ned would buy a good number of jeans every time Sears ran a decent sale on them.

The ensemble was complete.

Ned had joyfully eliminated the problem of having to decide what to wear every day, which freed up his mind and allowed him to make fewer trips to the Laundromat. Most members believed the only thing keeping Ned from coming out to church, besides his tobacco problem and his addiction to bingo night at the Elks club, was the fact that Ned simply didn't have a thing to wear other than his standard uniform.

Nowadays, Ned was a landmark. Tom said you could spot him all over town due to his familiar orange T-shirt. Ned spotting was a popular local custom.

And if one quirky, fame-inducing personality trait wasn't enough, Ned was also known as the rock man. Ned collected stones.

He had lined his garage walls with cheap shelves and placed rocks upon every inch of them. Understand, the fruits of his hobby were not necessarily impressive. Ned didn't own one single valuable rock. He just had a giant assortment of ordinary rocks, the kind you might find in an empty dirt lot or lying in the gutter. Sure he had a wide range of sizes (his collection ranged from shoe pebble to field boulder), but there was not a single magnificent stone among them.

Whenever the mood hit Ned just right he would open his automatic double-car garage door and let the neighborhood wander around and look at his rocks. People loved to stop and talk with Ned as he sat on his lawn chair in the middle of his garage drinking milk and waving at passing cars. Few could resist stopping to view his stones.

Ned was the rock man with the orange shirt. Ned was my home teachee.

"Ned," Tom yelled.

Ned heard Tom and climbed down from the float.

"Ned, this is Gray," Tom introduced.

"Nice to meet you," I said, extending my hand.

Ned was a friendly looking man with a large stomach and little hair on his head. He seemed like a perfect person never to wear a T-shirt. The orange shirt that had become his icon was far from flattering on him. He had blue eyes which seemed to clash terribly with his shirt, and hair grew on his arms like the deep shag carpet I had ripped out of my home.

Ned shook my hand.

"Gray's going to be your home teacher," Tom said.

"Great," Ned said. "I've got some real needs at the moment."

"Well if I can help..."

"Do you know much about rocks?"

"I've seen a few in my lifetime," I said.

Ned looked at Enis, who was smiling.

"Gray's seen a spaceman," she informed Ned.

"Say, were you involved in that?" Ned asked.

"Gray lives at Forget with Stick," Tom explained.

Ned suddenly became very interested in me. "Any chance of you getting me a piece of the wreck," he salivated. "I'd waver from rocks for a chunk of spaceship."

"The state's got it all locked up," I informed him.

"Those paranoid babies. Well. I worked for one of the schools," Ned told us. "I guess it's time to pull a few strings."

Enis patted Ned on the chest.

"Come out to Forget and I'll show you the site," I offered Ned. "I also have a little piece of the wreck I got before the state locked it up."

"I'd love to see that," Ned drooled. "I heard there were no bodies," he added.

Tom put his hands up over his ears as if he didn't want to hear this conversation.

"What's the matter, President," Ned scoffed. "Don't you believe?"

"There's no such thing as UFOs," Tom said.

"How do you explain George Sniffter's alfalfa field then? Something had to have trampled that weird message into it."

Tom laughed. "Reverend Bluth said he saw George's boy, Larry, drunk and riding the tractor recklessly through the fields late at night."

"Well, George told me Larry said that wasn't true."

"I think I'd believe the reverend over Larry."

"Siding with the church of the devil," Ned said disgusted.

Enis frowned.

"Devil," she whispered.

"What about you?" Ned asked. "Do you think there are UFOs?"

"Something crashed down there," I said. "And I have no idea what it was. So I guess it's unidentified."

"This one will work," Ned said to Tom, referring to me. He then walked off, returning to his float work.

Tom handed me a piece of paper with Ned's address and phone number, then scurried off after him.

Once the float was finished we all just stood around drinking punch and eating homemade sugar cookies some of the members had brought. We were all waiting for the bishop to return so he could officially christen the float. He had run off a few minutes earlier to grab something from his office.

The bishop's wife, Selma, went to look for him but couldn't find him. The ward started to worry. It was highly unusual for Bishop Withers' whereabouts to be unknown. The appointment patrol was sent out to locate him. Ten minutes later all five of them returned empty-handed.

Selma calmed people down by telling us that most likely Bishop Withers had just run home to pick something up. This didn't make too much sense, seeing how his car was still here. We did a ward search. Ned kept telling folks to leave no stone unturned.

Nothing turned up.

I kept thinking the poor man had simply slipped away to find a moment of privacy. I really felt for him. All these years of having everyone so dependent upon you that a couple of minutes of unscheduled absence sends everyone into a tumultuous tizzy could really wear a person down. My bishop back home used to slip out of weekday meetings to go play golf and receive inspiration. Apparently the Spirit was stronger on the green. No one ever tried to track him down or tear the neighborhood apart looking for him. I wouldn't be surprised if Bishop Withers had just taken off running, never to return.

Selma told us all just to go on. She was sure the bishop would turn up. She then left to see if she could locate him elsewhere.

Tom ended up having to christen the float. He slammed a bottle of carbonated apple cider against the bottom of it as festively as he could. Glass flew everywhere. A small piece hit Lindy Buswidth in the cheek, and another piece gave Jonathan Call a nice sized cut on his right hand.

The whole evening had turned into a real downer. People tried to cheer, but everyone who wasn't pulling glass shrapnel out of themselves was bummed it hadn't been Bishop Withers who broke the bottle. Everyone went home slightly dejected. Our full-bodied party had lost its head.

The store had already been closed for an hour when I got home. Stick was in my house cleaning up his late dinner dishes. Since the discovery of Jenny's letter Stick had become my roommate. He figured if Jenny had left the note in the house then maybe she would come directly back there instead of to the store. He also didn't like the idea of sleeping alone when there were aliens running about.

I didn't mind his company. He got up early in the morning and came home late at night. He didn't touch a thing in the house except for a few dishes and a couple items in the guest bathroom. He didn't even use the sheets on his bed. He just unrolled his sleeping bag and slept in it on top.

I sat down at the kitchen table and watched Stick scrub his chili pot.

"You missed a great activity," I jabbed.

"I heard," Stick replied.

"Heard what?" I asked.

"Bob told me the bishop turned up missing."

"Bob?" I exclaimed. "How would he possibly know that?"

"Bob knows all," Stick declared. "He's more aware of people's lives than anyone I know. I think Dot called and gave him this news."

"How did Dot know?" I asked incredulously.

"A guess a couple of members called 911 looking for help in finding great Bishop Withers," Stick slurred, showing his dislike for our bishop.

"So Bob called you?"

"He did," Stick said.

"Amazing."

"I guess you don't fully understand Bob," Stick commented. "He has always been the best source of information around this part of the country. He knows everyone, remembers everything, and makes most folks just open up and talk like a large-mouthed woman at the back fence. Bob loves to gossip. He's very interested in others. He knows what's going down long before things start to fall."

"He lives two hours away in a secluded little town," I argued.

"Geography means nothing to Bob."

I'm sure it didn't.

"So Bob's been talking to Dot a lot lately," I observed.

"Bob's always liked her," Stick said. "Dot just couldn't handle him being anything more than a friend. I think Bob would like it otherwise. He makes the single life look so glamorous, but deep down he's just as much in need of a warm companion as you and I are. I guess this UFO thing has helped to rekindle his interest in Dot."

"So what did Bob say?" I asked.

"He was just calling to let me know Bishop Withers had deserted the flock."

"He didn't desert anyone," I laughed. "He probably just slipped home to use the bathroom in private."

"In Albuquerque?" Stick said passionately.

"What are you talking about?" I asked.

"Bob said that Dot heard that your Bishop Withers bought a one-way ticket to Albuquerque. He went directly from the church to the bus station. He had already packed himself a few bags."

"You're kidding?"

"Premeditated desertion ain't nothing to kid about," Stick said.

"There must be an explanation," I thought aloud.

"There's an explanation all right," Stick spat. "He couldn't take it."

"Can you blame him?" I asked. "I mean all those years as a bishop. Poor Sister Withers."

"Selma's strong," Stick said.

"Could you be a little more callous?" I asked, disgusted.

Stick retired to his bedroom while I tried to drink things better. I couldn't fall asleep for two hours thanks to the caffeine. I was back off the wagon. In that time I cleaned out the entry closet, wrote another letter to Rivers, alphabetized the few spices I had, and cut my own hair.

When I finally fell asleep I hardly remembered anyone else's problems besides mine. I think I was comforted by that.

Chapter Sixteen

A Cornered Kitty, Sauced and Frisky

About five o'clock the next morning Stick and I were awakened by a huge crashing noise that came from behind the house. Stick thought he was a goner.

The invasion had begun.

I rather enjoyed watching him try to get out of his sleeping bag while in a state of panic. He did more harm to himself thrashing about than a dozen probe hungry Martians could have ever inflicted upon him.

I threw on a shirt and rushed outside. The aliens had landed all right. There amongst rubble and dirt sat Kitty Katford's copper Cadillac. She had slammed into, and through, our back fence, completely destroying the south side of it. I rushed around the car. Kitty was strapped in and unconscious.

Stick finally stumbled out of the house once he realized the threat wasn't real. He then began swearing and screaming about how he was going to teach Kitty a thing or two about operating a motor vehicle. I informed him that his lesson in driving etiquette might have to wait, due to the fact Kitty was out cold.

I ran to the store and called 911. Bob answered.

"Gray, is that you?" he asked.

"It is," I replied. "What are you doing answering this phone?"

"I just came to pick Dot up from work."

"At five in the morning?"

"I like to get up early. You never know what the sun's going to bring," Bob philosophized. "Besides this is when Dot gets off. She promised me breakfast if I drove over this morning. I'll tell you what, she makes the best scrambled..."

"We need some help!" I interrupted.

"What do you need?" Bob said, suddenly very official.

"Kitty Katford just crashed into our wall out back. I think she's pretty badly hurt."

"Emotionally or physically?" Bob asked.

"Physically," I yelled. "She's out cold."

"I think I would be an emotional wreck if I ruined a neighbor's wall. But then again I'm pretty concerned about what people think."

I hoped he could see what I was thinking at the moment.

"Can you send an ambulance?" I demanded.

"We're right on it," Bob informed me. "I put out a call for one the moment you said someone was hurt."

"Why didn't you just say so," I complained.

"I could tell I needed to talk you down."

I couldn't imagine feeling lower. I hung up the phone without saying good-bye.

Seven minutes later the paramedics arrived. They pulled Kitty out, stuck a bunch of needles into her leathery arms, put her into the ambulance, and then prepared to take off. Kitty seemed a lot nicer unconscious. No fuss, no trouble, quiet.

The paramedics asked if either Stick or I would like to ride along. Stick declined; he needed to open up the store in a couple hours. Oh, and of course the fact that he passionately hated Kitty with every newt-skinny fiber of his body might have had a little something to do with his decision. Me? I figured I had nothing better to do, so I hopped in.

When we got to the hospital they rushed Kitty off while I filled out forms with information I didn't really know. I then waited as if Kitty were one of my own.

The hospital waiting room was very bleak. Another man was in there waiting for someone to come out of something. He kept pinching his forehead and mumbling something about God messing up when he included appendixes. While he paced the floor, I flipped through a copy of *Entertainment* magazine. The issue there in the waiting room was over two years old, its articles outdated and terribly unentertaining.

Every couple of minutes the vending machine in the corner would make a whirling sound and then rattle until it grew silent again. I gauged my wait by counting the machine's mechanical seizures. I lost count somewhere after seventy-two.

It was late afternoon before I got a full report on Kitty. She wasn't too bad off. She had a minor concussion, her right arm was bruised, her left knee was cut up, and she wouldn't be able to walk well for weeks. The hospital told me she would need to be looked after for a little while. And seeing how she was now out of any real danger and the hospital needed the bed space, could I please take her home immediately.

I could hear Kitty screaming orders and threats at people.

"Immediately," the doctor begged.

"What about the concussion? Shouldn't that be watched for a few days?" I asked.

"That really is the least of her worries. It was a minor concussion on a very hard head," the doctor explained. "It's her knee that's going to give her trouble."

Back in some far hall I could hear Kitty screaming something about what she was going to do to a certain nurse if she ever touched her again.

"Really she's not my responsibility," I reasoned. "I just need to talk to her about repairing our wall."

"Please take her," he pleaded.

"I don't even have a car here," I said.

"Well, someone's got to get her out of here." The poor doctor looked like he was about to faint.

I needed a ride. I thought about the Church and the chain of command. I had heard the formula my entire life. When in need call your home teacher.

I didn't have one yet.

If you can't get your home teacher call the elders quorum president. I did what I thought was best. I called Dot and got hold of Bob. Within minutes he was over at the hospital talking about how he and Dot had spent the day and telling me stories about some of the mean things Kitty had done to people around here.

When they finally wheeled Kitty out to us she was furious that Bob and I were there.

Livid.

Enraged.

She'd come undone.

The nerve of us being there to escort her home. Like a tight piece of elastic she sat in that wheelchair poised to snap at us. But when it came right down to it she had no choice but to let us help her.

We took her out of the hospital and lifted her into the backseat of Bob's squad car. Kitty was ordering us around the entire time. She knocked Bob's hat off with her foot and pulled my hair as I set her down.

When we were finally on our way I asked her, "So do you have someone to help you out around your place?"

"No," she snapped.

"Could you get a friend or someone to come assist you?"

Bob looked at me as if I had just said something mean. Kitty stayed silent. Apparently she had no friends.

"I guess I could come over every day and sort of help you out," I offered.

"No!" she snapped again.

"I'm just trying to help," I said.

"Kitty doesn't let anyone into her home," Bob whispered out of the right side of his mouth as he drove.

Kitty heard. "What are you doing here anyway, Bob?" she asked harshly.

"I had a little breakfast with Dot and..."

Kitty laughed. "Now there's a cute couple," she commented sarcastically.

"Thanks," Bob said naively.

"You've got to let someone help you," I said, bringing the conversation back to where it, sadly, needed to be.

Silence.

Bob flicked on the sirens to scare a few birds that were sitting in the road up a ways.

Again silence.

I knew what needed to be said. I needed to offer Kitty a room at my house. She was lonely and incapacitated. She really needed to be at the hospital still, but she had blown it, and now I seemed to be the only person who could help. I had no idea why she wouldn't let me just come take care of her at her home. I imagined unaccounted for prisoners-of-war locked up in her basement or some other deeply disturbing secret.

"Kitty, you could come stay with me for a little while. I mean until you get back on your feet."

Bob looked at me like I was crazy.

Silence.

Kitty really had no other option. She was cornered.

"Don't go thinking that this means I like you or can tolerate any of you," she said. "Idiots, absolute idiots."

I took that as a yes.

Stick must have called a wrecker to come take Kitty's Cadillac away, because when we got to Forget her car was gone and most of the rubble had been cleared. Bob drove through the now missing wall, pulling right up to the back door of my home. He almost hit my tree in the process.

"That thing's getting huge," Bob observed.

I tried not to look too proud.

I carried Kitty in and set her up in the guest room. I figured Stick could sleep just as easily on the big ratty couch in the family room as he had in there.

Kitty fought me every step of the way. I was carrying her too high. I was carrying her too low. I set her down too hard. Our pillows were too lumpy. The room was too dusty. I was too stupid to even be considered human.

Kitty was too much.

I wanted to shut her up by saying she was too mean, too loud, and too bossy, but I was too chicken.

"What about food?" she asked.

"What about it," I replied.

"I have to eat," she screamed.

"We'll get you some food."

"What about smoking?" she asked.

"Absolutely not," I said.

Kitty growled.

"You must allow me an occasional drink and cigarette," she snapped.

"I don't know where you'd get one," I said, plugging in the small TV I had bought earlier in the week. I decided to put it in Kitty's room so she would have something to do. I gave her the remote and walked out, closing her door behind me.

Bob was now in the kitchen spreading cream cheese onto Ritz crackers.

"Do you mind?" he asked, referring to the fact that he was helping himself.

I shook my head.

"You're crazy, you know that don't you?" Bob said.

"You mean about Kitty?"

Bob nodded.

"We couldn't just leave her alone," I reasoned.

"*You* couldn't just leave her alone," Bob replied. "Do you mind if I take some of these crackers for the road?" he asked.

"Take what you'd like."

"I'd stay and eat but I've got to get back to Longwinded," Bob said, referring to the job I never saw him doing. "When the cat's away." Bob took the cream cheese, the crackers, one of my dish towels, and a knife. "I'll get you the knife back," he said. He left smiling.

I walked over to the store to tell Stick about our new house guest. As I had predicted, he didn't take kindly to the situation.

"You let that drunken fool into your house?"

"What else could I do?"

"She'll drive us both mad."

I shrugged my shoulders

"What's the deal with her not letting anyone into her home?" I asked curiously.

"Have you ever seen the ranch?" Stick asked.

The ranch he was referring to was Kitty's spread. It was located about five miles away from Forget on the way to Sterling. It was a long way off the main road but anyone driving that way couldn't help but notice it. It was big, rambling, and weathered. I always thought it housed a number of people, but I guess only Kitty lived there.

"I've seen it from the road," I answered.

"No one's been in there since Karl died," Stick explained. "Rumor is that Kitty had her father stuffed and she doesn't want anyone to see him propped on her couch where she still pretends he's alive."

"Sick," I said.

"Kitty's not real well in the head."

"I hope she gets better soon."

"Kitty's never getting better," Stick insisted. "I just hope she doesn't kill us both in our sleep," he said, turning from me to ring up a customer.

I hoped that as well.

While waiting for Kitty at the hospital earlier that day I had gone next door to Radio Shack and picked myself up a phone. The young boy who sold it to me claimed it was the best cordless phone they had. I felt so lucky. I went home, plugged it in, and then fixed Kitty and myself some dinner.

I had to feed Kitty as if she were a caged lion. I would drop her food off and run. She would then berate me with insults and complaints, throwing hatred around as if she were a major league pitcher with dead-on aim.

The Miracle of Forgetness

At six-thirty that night my new phone rang for the first time. When I picked it up no one was there. At seven-fifteen it rang again. Again no one was there. At seven-forty it rang once more. And once more the line was silent.

I kept hoping it was Rivers. Maybe she had found out my number and was now calling just to hear my voice. Each time I picked up the phone I tried to say "Hello" as nice as I possibly could, just in case it actually was her.

"Hello."

"Hello there."

"This is Gray."

At nine fifteen when Stick came home he informed me he had called twice, but for some reason I couldn't hear him speaking to me."

"Why were you answering it so funny?"

"I thought it was someone else," I replied. "So you only called twice?"

"Twice," Stick said, ready to talk about something else now.

Twice. That left one unaccounted for ring.

Hope rings eternal.

Chapter Seventeen

Mob Rules

I got to church early on Sunday. I wanted to make very sure I would not be walking past that window late again. Things were completely chaotic. The bishop was gone, the first counselor, Todd Plot, was gone, and the second counselor had decided that with the disappearance of the bishop his position was dissolved. The ward now had no real guidance.

The Relief Society president, Sister Lark, tried to get things under control, but apparently people didn't care for her as much as they did Bishop Withers. I found out later that the members had always doubted Bishop Withers' wisdom in putting Sister Lark in as Relief Society president. I guess a few years back, she had been in charge of the ward baptisms. She was pretty good at getting things arranged and helping families plan their blessed event. But it was the behind-the-scenes which was ugly and people took offense at. Apparently Sister Lark was not draining the font immediately after the weekday baptisms. She would keep it filled and then sneak her kids in and let them swim around in the font for awhile. She saw no harm in this. There was no way her husband's job as a bus driver was ever going to afford them the money to put in their own pool. Besides, to her it was a waste of water to just fill the huge font up for a single baptism. She was simply drowning two birds with one stone.

The Miracle of Forgetness

No one would have ever found out about their swimming escapades it if hadn't been for the water wing the custodian found stuck in the drainpipe. Questions ensued, and Sister Lark sang. She lost her position, but surprisingly six months later she was put in as Relief Society president. Faith in Bishop Withers had wavered at the move, but people had since come around slowly. I mean if Bishop Withers approved...

Now, however, was a different story. The bishop was gone, and people were having to reevaluate their perspectives. And most of their reevaluations brought them to the conclusion that Sister Lark had no say.

Sister Lark gave up and sat down.

Sister Gent then took a turn at the microphone. Sister Gent was our ward bulletin coordinator. I had heard that when Bishop Withers issued her this calling, he had informed her there were no menial positions in the Church. In fact he had said the calling of ward bulletin coordinator was just as important as bishop. Sister Gent took that information literally. She had since been bossing people around with her bulletin authority. Now with the bishop missing she saw her chance to step up to bat. She began trying to quiet people from the pulpit.

"Brothers and sisters," she ordered.

"Sit down, Loretta," Sister Buswidth yelled. Sister Buswidth hadn't quite forgiven Sister Gent for accidentally putting her name down as Sister Widthofbus in the program a few months back.

"When the bishop called me as bulletin..."

"We know," Brother Scatty called out. "The bishop's gone."

Everyone hushed. The truth had reared its ugly head and realization was now showing off its unsightly legs. The bishop was gone.

Sister Gent walked off the stage and Tom, the elders quorum president, went up and gave it a go. People did settle down for Tom, but it was apparent that nothing was going to get accomplished today at church. Tom directed everyone to go home and have a special fast for their circumstances. The members were not exactly gung-ho about the spontaneous fast part, but people seemed capable of following the go home rule. The good sister sitting next to me frantically rooted through her purse and pulled out a pack of wintergreen Lifesavers. She unwrapped the entire package and desperately put them in her mouth as if the mere thought of a fast left her starved. I just stared at her.

"What?" she garbled with a full mouth as she got up to leave. "Breath mints aren't food," she rationalized, making it clear to me she hadn't broken the fast we had all just been asked to start.

The building cleared out fairly quickly. I was soon sitting alone in the chapel, watching the last of the people wander past the large bay window on their way to go home. They all looked dejected, saddened and fast weary from their first five minutes of no food.

The empty chapel was kind of nice. It was the perfect place for me to reflect. I did so in earnest.

I couldn't understand why I was so happy here in Bluelake and Forget. Nothing had gone right, but regardless, I was okay. I had a paranoid uncle and a crazy woman living with me, but I didn't mind. Back home in Phoenix I had tried having a room-mate for a short time, and I just couldn't do it. A normal guy my same age and with similar interests had driven me nuts. But for some reason I could tolerate Stick and Kitty so far.

I had a smashed up back wall and a UFO crash site within walking distance, and I was fine. And yes, Forget was the furthest thing from beautiful. But still, when I got up in the mornings, the nothingness of it took my breath away. Like a last minute reprieve from doing the Thanksgiving dishes, I always felt lucky here.

It made no sense.

It wasn't as if I were some deep thinking, really together type person. I ran shallow a lot of times. Friends and excitement were the important things in Phoenix. I spent my entire days just trying to find things to do at night. Now I wanted nothing more than to go home and see my tree.

What was happening? I had thought I was so much less than this.

In Phoenix I woke up scared almost every day, afraid my life was going nowhere. Here I slept in late and woke happy to be exactly where I was, which by most worldly measures was nowhere.

The most frustrating thing about all of this was that I could see God everywhere I looked, but when I moved to approach him he would vanish around a distant corner. I simply wanted some answers. Was this too much to ask? I wanted to know if I had stumbled into something genuinely good. Or if I had turned into a giant dolt, the kind who found pleasure in sparkly objects and eating handfuls of raw sugar.

I looked up at the small board by the organ. The little wooden sign that announced the hymn numbers hung almost empty. The bottom row was the only one with a head for numbers.

314.

I pulled out a hymn book from the book sheath connected to the pew in front of me. I wasn't a big fan of hymns. I had a real hard time finding a tune. Every Sunday when we were told to sing I was reminded of this problem. I also had a horribly short attention span when it came to singing some of the songs. Did some numbers really need to be five verses long? My mother used to tell me that the best stuff was often hidden in the last verse.

Well hidden.

If most congregations were like the ones I knew, the best stuff needn't worry about ever being discovered. It always seemed to me that the singing of a forth or fifth verse was just a going-through-the-motions type exercise. The words could make no sense at all and people would still sing them.

"Put your shoulder to the wheel and sort of lean. Rest yourself while your brethren doth strain."

314.

I was at page three hundred and twelve when I began to hear whimpering coming from the foyer. I got up and went to investigate. There in the foyer stretched out on the orange, boxy looking couch was Tom. He was obviously unhappy about something because he was crying like a model with a face full of morning acne. I was a little embarrassed for him. Not that I wasn't completely accepting of grown men that cry; I just had a few prejudices when it came to dealing with grown men who cry when I'm around. What could I say?

Tom noticed me standing there. He sat up and tried to compose himself. I stood there and tried to emote sincere compassion. Both of us were fairly convincing.

"Can I help?" I asked.

"I can't do this," Tom confessed.

"Do what?" I said, sitting down next to him.

"I've got to lead them."

"Lead who where?"

"I've only been a member for two years," Tom informed me.

"What is time anyway?"

"I told Bishop Withers I couldn't do this," Tom cried. "I told him but he still said I was capable. Capable," Tom said again. "Can you believe that?"

"I think you're capable," I said.

Tom's square body went ridged, and his short arms began waving around. "You think I'm capable because the bishop believed in me."

"Actually..." I began to say.

"You know perfectly well I couldn't lead these people if I had a flashlight and a phone card."

I had no idea what he was trying to say.

"Bishop Withers should have called someone else to be elders quorum president," Tom continued. "There are plenty of people in this ward to pick from. Mark Flatly has seven kids and his house is always clean."

I patted Tom on the back.

"You want to go with me to visit Ned?" I asked.

Tom looked at me with wet eyes. He recognized a request that he could easily fill.

"It's not your job to single-handedly pull this ward through this crisis," I said. "We'll all make it."

The Miracle of Forgetness

"I can't even keep my yard maintained," Tom said.

Tom needed to take a long vacation. Darn that Bishop Withers.

Tom and I had a nice visit with Ned. He showed me around his rocks and told me all of his petty reasons for not coming to church each week. Apparently there were a few inner-church conspiracies which I had previously been unaware of. Ned was most concerned about the current prophet having said something nice about the pope.

"John Taylor said that the church in the last days would become so corrupt that God will have to strike down everyone forty and older."

"Where did you read that?" I asked.

"My brother heard it from his neighbor who works at BYU."

Well, that settled everything.

After Ned had revealed all the current secret combinations, he started to go on and on about how bored he was during the day and how he never had anything important to do. Sure, the rock collecting kept him busy, but he needed something new. If only the moon would turn to blood.

I offered him a job at the trading post. He accepted, feeling it would suffice until the Millennium.

I thought that was most gracious of him.

Chapter Eighteen

Cutting the Rug

Next Friday came and went with no sign of Angela. I figured she had stumbled upon someone much better than I. On the good side, I had now gotten another letter from Rivers, and I had sent another as well. I was beginning to feel more and more for this girl I only knew in word.

We didn't have church the next Sunday because things still hadn't been worked out. It hadn't actually been canceled, it was just that no one showed up. The Saints were labeling it a cooldown week. It was rumored that the stake president would be there next week to straighten things out. I sincerely hoped so.

Wednesday evening Angela stopped by. She was returning from a rug run and had decided to stop off and surprise me.

I was surprised.

She caught me off guard and out in the back singing to myself as I hoed the would-be garden I had just begun working on. The cool evening wind carried her voice to my unsuspecting ears.

"Gray."

I spun around. "Angela."

"Gray," she repeated, her hair straight and long.

I didn't know whether I should hug her or shake her hand. My surprise-visit etiquette was rusty. Without touching I invited her into my home, where she sat on my couch while I cleaned up. We then decided to ride into Bluelake and catch a movie at the drive-in theater. We were going to make a night of this surprise.

The Bluelake Double Feature Drive-in was busy. The mild summer evening was attracting people to the big screens like blue-collar workers to a complimentary snack wagon. I was unfamiliar with both of the films that were now showing so I let Angela pick. She settled on a movie titled *Jodi—a True Story*. It seemed like a pretty safe title. It was not rated, and I just assumed it was some sort of uplifting, against-all-odds, true account of a remarkable individual named Jodi. Gandhi, Florence Nightingale, Jodi.

Angela and I found a good spot and parked. I rolled down my window and clipped the small corded speaker onto the glass. I turned the volume up and sappy pre-show music spilled into my car like sticky soda.

"So this movie's supposed to be good?" I asked.

"My brother thought so," Angela replied.

Cars began pulling up around us and boxing us in, shifting and moving around like a poorly played game of chess. The Bluelake Drive-in was not laid out very well, and we were soon pinned in by three rows of cars.

"I'm hungry," Angela suddenly insisted.

"Should we go get some snacks?" I asked.

"I'll wait here," she informed me. "But get large things," she instructed. "Their small sizes are really small."

"Do you want anything in particular?"

"Snacks," she said as if I were stupid.

I stepped out of the car, hoping she would be kinder once I returned with food.

The snack bar was crowded. People stood in line like ants, stepping slowly forward, willing to carry off ten times their body weight in popcorn and chocolate covered raisins. I took my place.

The sticky floor and the spinning pretzels in the glass case on the counter were a good distraction. The sky turned from dusk to dark as I stood there waiting. I could see the two big screens come to life as Mother Nature dimmed the lights.

I was missing the previews.

I finally made it to the counter. A young boy with a breaking voice and crooked paper hat took my order and served me to the best of his ability. I trudged back to the car, carrying a troughful of junk food like a husband hefting his bride over the threshold.

Angela seemed glad to see the snacks.

I settled into my seat to watch the movie. After Angela had her fill she put her arm on mine and lightly brushed my hand with her beautiful fingers. Like a sorcerer concocting her spell she added a pinch of hope and a dash of possibility. My vatlike soul seemed to bubble and brew at her touch. She had seemed a little short with me earlier, but maybe she was just hungry. Perhaps she had some sort of condition that required her to eat before being civil.

She smiled at me, making it easy to forgive and forget.

I turned my attention back to the movie. I should have stayed focused on Angela. The giant screen was making it obvious that this was no G-rated movie. In fact what the camera was projecting at the moment was definitely not PG-rated, well beyond PG-13 rated, and considerably less wholesome than your average R.

"What kind of movie is this?" I asked, embarrassed.

"My brother really liked it," Angela replied.

"What kind of brother do you have?" I asked, trying to keep my eyes off the screen.

Obscenities pumped through the sound box and assaulted our ears. This "Jodi" person was certainly no Mother Theresa. I turned the sound down, looking around at all the cars that were pinning us in.

"I can't believe this."

"What?" Angela asked.

"This movie."

"We don't have to watch," Angela said in sultry voice.

I looked at her and started to worry. This was not how I had perceived the night turning out. I thought tonight would just be a

good getting-to-know-her period. Talk, laugh, and gauge whether
or not there was anything to us. Sure, I liked Angela all right, but
I didn't feel comfortable trapped in a car with her watching some
movie about some overly friendly girl named Jodi.

"We should leave," I said.

Angela shifted closer.

"More snacks?" I asked, hoping she would send me on
another errand far from the big screen and miles from the inti-
macy this particular spot was providing.

Angela shook her head no in reference to more snacks. She
had obviously had her fill of food and was now looking for
desert.

I fumbled for the door handle. I'm not sure what Angela had
in mind, but suddenly I wanted nothing more than to be back at
Forget talking to Stick about things so unimportant they
seemed grand. I pulled on the door handle. It was locked.

I unlocked it.

Angela had her head on my shoulder now. I reached to pull
the door open, but before I could do that something outside of
the car caught Angela's attention. She sat up quickly and
honked the horn.

"Marice," Angela screamed, obviously familiar with someone
in one of the vehicles in front of us.

The occupants of the cars around us began to scream and
holler at us, mad about their movie being interrupted. Angela
climbed over my lap and crawled out my car door, scrambling
like a messy egg.

She ran up to a truck one row in front of us and leaned in
its open window. A girl about my age jumped out of the truck
and hugged Angela. They obviously knew one another. Angela
ran back to me and bent down into my open door.

"Its my best friend," she told me. "I haven't seen her in
months."

A guy in the car right next to us yelled at us to shut-up.

"I'll talk to her a few minutes and then be back," Angela said
nicely.

I nodded.

Angela leaned in and kissed me on the cheek. She then walked back to the truck and hopped in. I put the sunscreen up in the windshield of my car, then leaned back in my seat and contemplated life for the duration of the film, thoughts of Rivers and Angela dominating my brain. This was not the evening I had imagined.

At the movie's conclusion Angela rejoined me. We drove home to Forget where she kissed me again and then went on her way. It was a nice kiss, the kind that causes the brain to forget the legions of imperfections and fields of impossibility. Now I had no idea what to think about her. She left me feeling like a deer, staring at the bright lights of an oncoming truck.

Splat.

As a woman she disabled my senses. Things like bad movies and feisty tempers got lost in the intoxicating rattle and hum she emitted. A glimmering strand of dangerous fascination ran through her like a gleaming fish in a clear stream. And when life caught her just right she stood out like clean tinsel against a dark green Christmas tree. Of course after one date she had shown some troubling attributes as well. My mind whispered, "Run away from her." Unfortunately my heart was much more of a loud-mouthed, selfishly persuasive debater, and he was taking the pro-Angela argument.

I liked Angela. Of course I was thinking I liked Rivers also.

Dating bliss seemed mildly illusive at the moment.

Chapter Nineteen

Rug Burn

Friday. Time worked differently here at Forget. The uneventful moments seemed full, making the hours fly by. I had spent my days doing home improvements and helping Stick train Ned. Now to complete my home teaching I simply had to wander over to the trading post, pick up something to munch on, and say something kind of inspirational to the two of them.

Stick and Ned seemed to get along well. The only complaint Stick had was that Ned always liked to hog the glory by telling folks about the UFO. Stick felt he was the authority on the matter and all questions should be directed towards him.

Kitty was getting better in one sense and worse in another. She was constantly giving Stick and me a hard time. I had never known anybody so stubborn and mean. I kept thinking she would soften up as our hospitality filled her with kindness. No such luck. She just kept getting meaner and meaner.

She would call Stick on the intercom for everything, yelling and demanding her every whim be served immediately. Stick eventually lost his top and ripped the intercom out of the store. Kitty then started pestering Stick every five minutes with her mobile phone. Stick was helpless, and just how much longer he could put up with her, I didn't know.

Stick wasn't the only person Kitty bothered. When she

wasn't all over Stick, she was right on top of me. I had to tell her over and over again that I wasn't her maid and that the only reason I was even letting her stay was because my guilt reserves would overflow and flood my entire spirit if I turned her out now. She would always sort of fold her face up and oink whenever I said this. Apparently it made her happy to know she caused me guilt.

She was a difficult person to live with.

There were only two people Kitty got along with. One was Ned. I guess Ned had always thought Kitty was kind of a sultry beauty. And Kitty thought Ned was kind of perceptive for feeling that way. Consequently, she went out of her way to ignore him so she wouldn't ever have to treat him unkindly. The other person Kitty got along with was Orvil from Longwinded. A few years back Kitty had gotten really sauced and crawled into one of the culverts right off Witch Road in Bluelake. Well, she got herself nice and wedged in. She was discovered the next morning when one of the local farmers was irrigating his field. I guess Kitty was stopping the flow of things. No one could get her out. Everyone gave it a go, pulling and pushing on Kitty like they had always desired. Finally, just when all had given up, in walked Orvil.

Orvil was down from Longwinded doing some swapping with Stick when he heard about the trouble. Remembering the time he, as a child, had gotten his mother's medicine ring stuck on his large toe, and remembering almost as vividly the remedy that had ensued, he grabbed a couple of bottles of Windex and rode out to rescue Kitty. He sprayed both bottles of Windex all over Kitty and then stuck his legs into the culvert and began pushing with them. Finally after a dozen good pushes there was a giant sucking pop and Kitty was free.

Forget the culvert burns and Windex rash, Kitty was, for once in her life, thankful. Orvil's boots and she had connected. Consequently she tolerated him like no one else.

Orvil had come by a few days earlier and was somewhat delighted to discover Kitty was staying with us. He spent the entire afternoon reading medical textbooks out loud to her. It was the only time I had seen Kitty acting human. Orvil read those textbooks like he was some sort of Native American sage. Never had I heard words like "eczema" pronounced so nobly. Kitty ohhed and hummed in all the right places; she was quite the attentive listener.

When I mentioned Orvil to her after he had left, she simply said, "It's none of your business. But if you must know, had it been another time and place things would have been different."

Things were plenty different enough already.

Orvil had told me I had a lion's share of Indian blood running through my veins. I guess he was impressed I had taken Kitty in. He also gave me a small leather band to wear around my wrist. The band was something he had been given by his now deceased father. He made me promise never to take it off.

I hated it.

I had never been a fan of wrist wear. Watches and rings drove me wild and made me so claustrophobic I almost went insane anytime I wore one.

Shackles.

Before my mission Mindy had bought me an expensive gold "Choose the Right" ring. It was the worst thing she could have given me. Not only did I feel that anyone who invested in a gold CTR ring had essentially "chose the wrong," but I just couldn't stand it on my hand. It was like a tiny prison that pinched all my nerves. I finally traded it to one of my companions for two tubes of American toothpaste. There's a sucker born every minute.

Now I had Orvil's little leathery loop that made me continuously uncomfortable, but I couldn't remove for fear of offending a friend. I think the worst part of it all was that every time I looked down at my wrist I reminded myself of my Aunt Wilma who always wore one single bracelet.

My whole life I had been compared to my Aunt Wilma, who owned a pet shop in Arkansas somewhere. It was a comparison I never felt comfortable or agreed with.

I remember when I was seventeen, about two years before my parents passed away. I was taking Mindy to the prom, and I brought her over to our house for the traditional pre-prom pictures. My grandmother, who was staying with us while she recovered from hip surgery, helped me feel more comfortable about the whole prom night by declaring to the world (or at least Mindy, who at that time was my world), "With a little curl in your hair you would look just like your Aunt Wilma."

And then my mother made things even worse by saying, "Doesn't he though. I tell you every time Gray wears a sweater I swear it's Wilma. It's unsettling."

It's a good thing that as an awkward, acne-riddled seventeen-year-old I was brimming with self-confidence.

Now here I was reminding myself of Aunt Wilma once again.

I was tugging on that black leather band, standing outside by my tree, when Angela pulled up. I had not spoken to her since our movie date. Since then I had, however, thought a lot about her. She confused me. She frightened me. She bothered me. But despite the rough spots I felt like pursuing her. She could be moody, but couldn't I, through my own gray nature, make those moods less fiery and more mellow? I knew that I was probably letting her looks govern my interests. But at the moment I viewed myself as a small town in need of a ruling class.

I pushed back my hair and wandered over. There was one other car filling up at the moment. I tried not to let its presence rattle me. I needed to appear cool. I blew on my hands and dusted off my shirt sleeve, acting as if I had just been doing something sort of manlike.

I walked right up to her and waved a goofy, by-the-hip little wave.

"Hello," she said, her dark eyes tired.

"Hey," I replied cleverly.

We stood by each other for a couple of uncomfortable seconds.

"How's the rug business? I finally asked.

"It's okay," she answered. "We're real busy right now."

"Yeah, we are too."

I was really wowing her.

"I like your shirt," she said, it matches your green eyes.

"This thing?" I scoffed, while smiling inside. The shirt comment was a definite flirt line. You don't just say, "I like your shirt," to anyone. Shoes were the only compliment item that could not be construed to connote interest.

Her gas tank gurgled, advertising its full stomach.

She walked inside and paid while I waited outside. She then came back out and announced...

"I'm done with my deliveries."

"I just got done fixing my sink," I disclosed in return.

"I mean we could go do something," she explained. "Make up for that bad movie. If you want."

I was all for that. I figured dating her would be better in the daylight.

Angela pulled her truck around to my house, and we drove my car into Bluelake. Angela seemed different today. It was as if she were wearing at the corners, and the person she had presented to me so far was beginning to fray. While we talked I could see the things I liked about her rub thin, as the things I had convinced myself to overlook were punching at my heart like big fists on a soggy drum. I thought maybe it was just me and all the analyzing I had been doing about her, but as I sat here with her now I was certain she wasn't the one for me.

I just knew she wasn't.

I admit, I was looking for the perfect person. By that I didn't mean perfect figure, perfect height, perfect treatment of me. I meant perfect for me. If those other attributes came with that, then so be it.

I just knew somewhere out there was the one woman I should be with. I guess that was the reason I had never tried very hard at love. I always figured the girl who was destined to be with me would work her way though the layers of people I knew, surface, and marry me. Nothing flashy, just pure unadulterated predestination. I had thought Mindy was the one simply because we had clocked in enough time together. I knew her, she knew me, we could a have been a happy family.

But no.

Mindy was not my 'meant-to-be,' which really messed things up for me. Now here I was twenty-four and I had no idea who my perfect counterpart was. Chances were I had met "Miss Perfect" some time ago when I was dating Mindy. I had overlooked my one and only.

Just great.

Now I had a lifelong quest to complete and I was starting twenty-four years too late. I looked over at Angela. I closed my eyes for just a second and quickly opened them back up. She still wasn't the one. I guess I'd have to try and make her work.

We went to one of the small cafes along the lakeshore. Angela ordered a sandwich with cheese and tomatoes only. I ordered a salad with pink, undercooked pieces of chicken on top of it. Angela thought I should call back the waitress and insist they re-cook my chicken.

I would rather have died.

I hated restaurant conflict. I had eaten many an undercooked burger and brown lettuce salads because I didn't want to make waves. I just knew whenever I complained the waitress or waiter simply took my meal back into the kitchen and stepped on my burger or put dirt in my salad.

Angela waved the waitress down.

"His chicken's pink," Angela told her.

"Chicken's supposed to be pink," the waitress returned.

"When it's alive," Angela said, cocking her head.

"Do you want me to take it back and cook it some more," the waitress asked, looking bothered.

"No, really," I said, "It's okay."

"Well, make up your mind," she said. "I have other customers."

"Cook it," Angela demanded, the fiery side of her surfacing like a propane flame.

I sunk down in my seat and let the waitress take my meal back for a second try at cooking it.

Angela picked at her sandwich while I waited for my salad. I watched her intently as she nibbled. She really was a beautiful woman. So beautiful in fact that I began feeling self-conscious. Men would pass our table, look at her, and then look at me in amazement. I held up my spoon and looked at my reflection in the back of it. I was put together all right. Sure I was no 'everybody's ideal,' but I was also not bad. I had been complimented on almost all of my features at one point or another in my life. I just couldn't remember being complimented on the entire package at once.

"Gray, you've got the most beautiful green eyes."

"I've never seen such thick black hair."

"What a classic nose."

Just once I would like someone to say they had never seen such a completely perfect package. The eyes went with the shoulders.

My salad arrived for the second time. I don't know if it was just me, but the chicken now looked cooked and dirty. I picked all the pieces off and set them on a napkin next to my plate.

"I'd demand a new salad," Angela said.

"I'm fine, really," I said.

Angela said something so softly I couldn't hear it.

"What?" I asked.

"Nothing."

I thought nothing meant nothing so I stabbed myself a forkful of salad and blew on it, hoping I could remove any chicken dirt.

Angela watched me put the food into my mouth. She tried not to say anything, but ultimately she couldn't resist.

"Order another salad," she tried to say nicely but failed.

"This is all right," I replied.

She watched me chew and grimace.

"It's not all right," she argued.

"It's fine," I said, taking another bite.

Angela exploded. My rug girl was coming unwound. She said something loud in Spanish and then threw her sandwich down. She stood and yelled at the waitress. The waitress yelled at

Angela. They both stood there waving their arms and poorly making their point.

Finally the waitress grabbed my salad and ran into the kitchen. Angela sat down looking triumphant, folding her arms like a pretzel across her chest. People all over the café were looking at us. Once again I had never been more embarrassed.

"Let's just go," I whispered loudly.

"No way," Angela said. "You're getting your salad."

"I don't even want it anymore," I argued.

Angela would not give in.

The third salad arrived.

I ate it with a big smile on my face. I wanted nothing more than this date to be over. Any fond hopes or vain imaginings I had been conjuring up that involved me, Angela, and some sort of future together tucked their tails and scampered off. I had never seen anyone go from cold to hot so quickly. I could only imagine being married to her.

"Gray, honey, did you take out the trash?"

"No, I had to..."

"Why you lazy... I'll clean your clock with my bare hands. Agua, zapato, adios!"

I didn't know much Spanish.

I finished my salad and paid the bill. I left a few dollars for a tip, but I noticed Angela picking it up and putting it in her purse as we left.

We drove back to Forget in silence. When we got there I pulled up next to Angela's truck and turned off the engine. I was about to say something like, "Let's never do this again," when she grabbed my hand, pulled me to her, and kissed me. I was so startled my elbow accidentally hit the horn. Angela didn't care.

I started to struggle. I think she interpreted my struggling to be something other than attempted escape because she would not let me go. She kept kissing. My elbow kept hitting the horn. Angela finally let go. She stepped out of the car and closed her door. She then mouthed the words,

"I'll see you next week," and blew me a kiss.

The Miracle of Forgetness

She got into her truck and drove off.

I had no idea what had just happened. Well, I had a pretty good idea of what had happened, I just didn't know why.

Somewhere between the undercooked chicken and a cranky waitress named Laura, Angela had decided on me. Maybe she'd been feeling short on options, too. Maybe she had already dated every short-tempered, strong-willed, crazy guy in this part of the state. Next Friday now seemed dangerously close.

I wanted to call my sister Maria. Surely she as a woman would have some applicable advice for me. Women had to be explainable. I just knew, however, that if I called Maria she would do nothing but mess things up even further. She had been vehemently opposed to my buying into Forget, and I was certain she would do nothing but chew me out for having lunch with a girl who wasn't even a member of the Church.

I could hear Kitty inside watching TV. Either inspiration struck or all the forces of evil whispered.

I could talk to Kitty.

What the heck? She was a woman. I had been wanting to prove to Kitty that I wasn't such a bad guy. This just might be the way.

I went inside and knocked on the guest room door.

"What do you want?" Kitty demanded, the TV blaring.

"I just wanted to talk," I screamed through the door.

There was no answer. I slowly pushed open the door.

"Come in, sit down," she ordered, looking like something the cat had dragged in and then chewed on for a while.

I came. I sat.

Kitty turned off the TV with the remote.

"I knew this would happen," she sneered. "I just knew it."

"Knew what?" I asked.

"I knew you'd come around begging for money to fix your fence." Kitty's eyes burned like orange colored Christmas lights.

"Actually I just wanted to..."

"Save your breath," she interrupted. "I'm not paying. Accidents happen, and that's just what that was. An accident."

141

"You were driving under the influence and you smashed up my wall."

"I don't need the play-by-play," she snipped, pointing the remote at me as if it were a gun.

"I'm letting you stay at my house while you recover," I pointed out.

"And you want something in return for that?" she huffed. "My, but don't you bleed with compassion. Does that Mormon church of yours teach you to take people in only to stick it to them once they're well? How Christian," she slurred.

"I didn't come to talk about this," I said, trying to change the conversation.

"Prickly, prickly, prick," Kitty wiggled her fingers in front of her face. "Upon a nerve, I just hit," she rhymed, looking every bit like the Wicked Witch of the North, South, East, and West. "Did you not come in here looking for money for the fence?" she demanded.

"No."

"Did you not expect me to give in simply because you were saintly enough to take a cripple in?" she barked.

"No."

"Do you not have planned out in your greedy little mind just what you're going to buy for yourself with all of the money you milk out of me? Have you got your eye on a fast car and a couple of silk shirts?" she spit. "Perhaps you're thinking of improving this dump."

"No," I repeated.

"Well, then what on this water forsaken piece of earth do you want from me?" she moaned. "Because there is no way a fancy looking city kid like you is going to pull the wool over my eyes."

"Well..." I stuttered.

"Did you come to tell me you found more space people?"

"You're impossible," I threw out.

"Impossible!" she screamed. "I'll tell you what's impossible. Impossible is the possibility of spacemen landing here. Aliens seek intelligence, don't you know. I'm certain you and Stick planned this, concocted this crazy fraud, perpetrated this gross hoax," Kitty ranted, spinning her hands in front of her as if she were fighting off a mess of flies. "Business is up isn't it?"

"Kitty, I didn't come to talk about this."

"Well, then what do you want from me?"

Kitty had done nothing but watch TV and sleep since the accident. She was bed bound. With the help of a few well-placed pieces of furniture she was able to hobble her own way to the bathroom, but aside from that she spent all her time in bed complaining. I brought her food occasionally, and I had moved the TV once when the glare of a lamp was detracting from the picture, but that was about the extent of my hospitality. I had wanted to help, but she just wouldn't let me. I couldn't stand to be in the room with her because of her foul mouth and mean spirit.

She had looked bad when she arrived, but here almost two weeks later she looked even worse. Her leathery tan was fading, leaving in its wake loose skin that was years away from bouncing back into shape. She lay in bed looking like a albino spotted sausage roll. Plus the accident had scared her hair almost completely white. Her eyes were sunken, like tiny black holes in the center of a very worn galaxy. If it weren't for her spastic, energetic outbursts I would have really been worried for her.

A private physician had been by twice to see her and to make sure she was healing properly. He seemed to think that she was doing splendidly in the mending department, but rather poorly in the mental department. It took every trick he had learned from his twenty years in medicine to get her simply to sit still so he could take her blood pressure.

Now as she lay there looking sad and pathetic, I thought about her question. What did I want? I had come into her room hoping that she might have some hidden insight into the female frame of mind. What had I been thinking?

"It's stupid," I said.

"I'm sure it is," she replied. "Now get out."

I got up and closed Kitty's curtains. The late-afternoon sun was making the room warm. I walked out and shut the door behind me. I would have to deal with the rug girl on my own. I filled up a bucket of water and took it out to my tree. I guess I was hoping Mother Nature might have a few tips for me.

Nothing.

My feminine side was extremely malnourished at the moment. Not even Mother Nature had time for me. I wished for one brief second that my Uncle Stick was actually my Aunt Wilma. Of course, she wasn't that much more feminine than Stick.

I would never understand.

Chapter Twenty

Felon for Love

I think the worst part about Forget was the fact that it caused me to forget that I didn't really have a future. Things were nice. Why worry? For the first time in my life I was perfectly content to stay just where I was. The problem was, where was I? My life was aligning itself within a solar system that contained no sun. The heavenly body of Angela had fizzled out and turned into a less than super "No-way."

I needed new stars to study.

Friday night I finally gave in and called my sister, Maria, to talk to her about Angela and my concerns, but all she did was worry at me about my future, or lack thereof. I had a hard time getting a word in edgewise.

"So in ten years you'll just be there bagging groceries?"

"I don't bag groceries," I replied.

"Well, what do you do?"

"I just kind of observe."

"Observe?" she huffed. "Dad and Mom are probably rolling over in their graves," she whined.

"I'm happy here," I pointed out.

"Happy? Who are you going to marry?" Maria asked.

Marriage was everything to her. To achieve any sort of recognition from Maria you had to be married.

"They have girls here," I informed her.

"You're floating Gray. You're floating and it scares me."

"I'm fine and that scares you," I bit back.

"I do want you to be happy," Maria started to cry. "Really, I do. Mom told me to look after you. That was her last wish."

"Mom died unexpectedly," I said. "The last thing she told either of us was to not let your boyfriend Scotty into the house while she was gone."

"Mom never understood Scotty," Maria argued.

"No one understood Scotty."

"He was very deep," Maria defended.

"He thought Florida was a country."

Maria "Hummffed."

The bond between a brother and sister can be something really wonderful. Or so I've heard.

"My life's never been better," I said. "I just wanted your opinion on..."

"In my opinion you are drifting," Maria butted in. "Have fun on the path of least resistance," was her final good-wishes. She hung up the phone loudly.

I was still no closer to understanding women.

Saturday morning I received another letter from Rivers, I also received a box of cookies from Angela along with a note telling me how much she liked of me. I sat out by the tree reading Rivers' letter and eating Angela's cookies. Rivers really was an intriguing person. From her penmanship to her point of view she was put together nicely. She also wrote as if she were interested in my response—lots of questions. Sadly, in this letter she went into depth about the missionary she was waiting for. I found myself actually getting jealous.

Otherwise, her letters were great. There was something about them that made them so much more than paper covered with ink. They were substantive and fulfilling, turning my soul into parchment that aged incredibly well with each new character. Again I found myself struggling with the concept of personal revelation. Which was stronger, revelation or desperation? There seemed to be more to this Rivers than just water on the brain.

Certainly I was just desperate.

There was one way to find out. I could force fate to show its hand by acting rashly.

What the heck.

I threw caution to the wind. I tugged on my bracelet, picked up my pen, and began to write back to Rivers. Three pages later I had told her everything. I figured it would be better if I just laid things on the line. I didn't want a permanent pen pal. Heck, I didn't even want to keep writing to her if the only thing I could ever hope to gain from it was a stack of letters. I would tell her how I truly felt about her and wait to see if she wrote me back. Open, honest, and slightly mushy. If it were meant to be then she would jump at this chance to disclose her own, hopefully similar, feelings towards me.

I tried not to sound obsessive or crazy, and I gave her every opportunity to simply never write me back. I raced the letter to the Bluelake Post Office before I could change my mind about sending it.

The second after I dropped the letter into the mailbox I began to have second, third, and forth thoughts. Just how dumb was I? I had a nice relationship going on and now I had blown it. I could have nurtured it a little while longer before tossing all of this onto it. There was no chance Rivers was going to get my letter and decide to seriously pursue "us." I had been open and frank when I should have been guarded and Gray. We had swapped a few letters and now I had demanded commitment and full disclosure of her state of mind concerning me.

I was a fool.

I parked and went into the post office to see if I could get my letter back. I knew it was against the law, but I thought just maybe since Bluelake was a smallish city they might bend the rules for me.

"Next," called a heavy woman with a cloth vest and bad hair.

I stepped up. "I have a small problem," I explained. "I mailed something in the box outside that wasn't supposed to be mailed."

"Next!" she said, looking over my shoulder and ignoring my problem.

"Wait," I begged, "I have got to get that letter out."

"You know," she said sarcastically, "I hardly know you, but for some odd reason I feel compelled to go outside and break the law by opening up the mailbox and retrieving your letter. That way when I'm in jail I can look over and tell my cellmate all about how good I feel because I helped an incompetent stranger out."

"So you'll open the box?" I asked.

"Next."

I waited outside for two hours, hoping to intercept the person who would come out to gather the mail. During those two hours I worked myself into such a frenzy over the letter that I almost attacked the man who finally did. I had to get that letter back.

"But you don't understand," I explained. "I've got to get that letter back."

He didn't understand. He just ignored me and continued his work.

He opened the box I had put my letter into and scooped up all the mail. I could see my letter. I don't know what came over me, but suddenly I had the feeling I had to have that letter at any cost.

He put the mail in a sack and started to cinch it up. I could still see my letter through the ever-closing opening. It was do or die time. I was never one to take the law lightly. No, I was as law-abiding as they came. Sure, I loosely interpreted the speed limit to fit my own needs. And yes, I had once copied off one of my friend's videos, but for the most part I was straight with the law.

Not anymore.

I pushed the postman aside and stuck my hand into the bag. I didn't mean to push too hard, but I managed to shove the poor guy to the ground. I grabbed the letter and took off running. I could hear the postman yelling at me, and people in the parking lot were staring like I was an escaped convict running around with a bloody knife.

I jumped in my car, threw the letter down onto the passenger's side floor, and sped out of the parking lot. I felt fairly confident that the postman wouldn't try to follow me in one of his little postman cars. I mean how effective can a car with the steering wheel on the wrong side be in a chase? I raced through Bluelake and on to Forget. I figured that if I did get caught at least I was friends with Bob. Certainly he must have some pull. For some reason this thought comforted me.

I nervously checked my rearview mirror the whole ride home.

Nothing.

I pulled up to my house, triumphant. I had done it. My glory was short lived, however. I had grabbed the wrong letter.

I couldn't believe it! I held in my hand a letter from Cecilia Warden addressed to the Raceway Orthopedic Shoe Company in Denver, Colorado. I felt like hitting myself for being so stupid. I had stolen someone else's mail. My infraction was all for naught. The whole situation was criminal. I was criminal.

I deflatedly stepped out of my car. I could hear Kitty watching TV inside, and I could see that the trading post was busy. I was glad Ned was helping Stick now. People continued to pour in from all over just to view the UFO. Our business had skyrocketed, and at the moment I saw no sign of it going down. Forget had become the hot spot, an official dot on the map. UFO headquarters.

The day was growing old. Tomorrow was Sunday and still nothing was resolved in our ward. Tom was running around like a headless chicken on speed, getting things bloody and working the members into a panic.

There was still no word from the bishop. Our ward was so lost. For years everyone had put all their faith in Bishop Withers and now he was gone. It was as if the soul of the ward had withered with the loss of Withers. The stake was supposed to be out to correct things tomorrow. I hoped they would have Bishop Withers with them because I saw no other solution to the ward's problems. They could call the ghost of Brigham Young to be the new bishop and folks would still not be impressed. They wanted their bishop back. They wanted things to be how they always had been.

I walked around my house and up to the tree. I wished that I could stand so tall. My perspective would be so much clearer if I had the height simply to look over all this. Six foot four just wasn't enough. Yes, at this exact moment it seemed all my problems would be solved it I could simply be taller and see further.

I found some boards behind the house and nailed some steps into my tree. By the time the sun was sinking I was up in its highest branches. I nailed a small piece of plywood down as a shelf to sit on.

Height helped.

From the branches of the tree I could see forever, or at least Forget. Things at the store were winding down and the streetlights flicked on, shining their big eyes down on the empty bench. Things smelled good from up here. It was as if Mother Nature were wearing her finest perfume tonight. I loved it here. Sure, there was no one to date, but I couldn't understand why it was so all important that I found a wife anyway. Maybe I was one of those people who was born to remain single. I had tried with Mindy, I had failed with Mindy. I had made a go with Angela and had ended up just wanting to be gone. I had felt something for the mysterious bulletin girl, but I had tossed my chance in the big blue bin by mailing that ridiculous letter. I had tried. I had failed.

I watched a few cars pull up to the trading post. I would have remained watching all night if I had not seen Bob pull up with his lights flashing. I climbed down and walked over to the store. Bob was inside talking to Ned and Stick.

"Gray," he said excitedly.

"Hey Bob, what are you doing here?" I asked.

"Came to see if you wanted to come to Longwinded. The Mormons are having a grand opening at their chapel tomorrow."

"A grand opening huh?"

"The grandest," Bob said rolling his r. "First time Longwinded's ever had a real Mormon chapel. And I thought that you being a Mormon, you might like to come take a look see." Bob noticed he had missed a button on his shirt. He quickly buttoned it. "I think there will be food, but I can't promise that. If you'd like we can leave tonight and you can get a little shut-eye in Longwinded."

I had wanted to make a trip to the town of Longwinded ever since I had arrived. This was perfect. I could bypass the confusion of my ward tomorrow and see Longwinded.

"I'd love to go," I said. "Is there a hotel where I can stay?"

Bob and Stick stared at each other and shook their heads.

"Longwinded don't have no hotels," Stick said disgustedly.

"That's true," Bob confirmed. "No hotels. There was a little bed and breakfast that Gwen Hatch was running for a while. But her husband, Conroy, has a real problem with sleepwalking. After he accidentally crawled into bed with a rather skittish couple from Germany, Gwen decided that maybe they ought to close up shop. It was nice of them German folks not to press charges," Bob said. "I bet Frau Minner always sleeps with the lights on now." Bob smiled warmly as he thought.

"If Conroy Hatch crawled into my bed I'd stop sleeping altogether," Stick shivered.

"I don't know," Bob continued. "He's slimmed down quite a bit. He's buying clothes from a normal store now."

"Hum," was all Stick had to say about that.

"So where do out-of-towners stay?" I asked.

"Well, you can't stay with me," Bob confirmed. "I just sold my home. I now live full-time in my RV. I got it parked right next to the station so I can be a full-time permanent cop."

"When you're actually there," I added.

"Even when I'm not there people have a feeling that just maybe I'm up the road or something," Bob said, confusing the unwanted heck out of me. He then retrieved a red popsicle from one of the nearby freezers. He ripped it open and began sucking.

"That must be extremely comforting to them," I joked.

"You can't buy that kind of security," Stick added. "I wish we had law like that around here, what with aliens and crazy things going on and all."

"Well, we have a different type of work ethic in Longwinded," Bob bragged, his mouth red from the popsicle. "Work is a four letter word to most people. Me, I spell it with five."

I thought Bob was going to spell out his version of work, but he became so involved with his frozen treat that he stopped talking.

"So where do visitors stay in Longwinded?" I asked.

"Don't worry," Bob slurped. "We'll find you a place."

Now I was nervous.

"Get what you need from you home," Bob said. "We'll leave in a few minutes."

I went to the house and grabbed a few essentials. I made Kitty a small snack and informed her that Stick would need to get breakfast and possibly lunch for her tomorrow. She was not openly happy. She wanted to know if I had any mace or pepper spray around. She went on and on about how it wasn't right for me to leave her alone with Stick.

I went on and on about how glad I was to be spending the night without either of them. My honesty went unappreciated.

Chapter Twenty-one

Stranded

 For some reason I will probably never understand, I talked Bob into taking Witch Road to Longwinded. I had wanted to explore it ever since I had moved here. Now seemed like the perfect time. I had seen the road on the map and it looked like a very driveable red line. People claimed that it was awful to travel, but how bad could it be? Bob said it was...

"Impossible."

I said, "I'm sure it's no big deal."

He said, "The road is washed out and grown over in spots."

I said, "How are a few potholes going to hurt us? Besides it might save us some time."

So, with no real preparation and at a late hour, Bob and I set off for Longwinded via East Witch. It was quite a rough trip. After you passed the turnoff for Nine Month Mound you drove on a relatively flat, bad road for about twenty more miles. Then you reached a part of the road that made you yearn for the bad flat stuff. Witch Road literally went up and over the Mount Taylor Mountain Range, switching back and forth—climbing and dipping at the most inopportune times. Bob's patrol car rocked and shook as we tried simply to keep moving forward, our head-lights blazing the way and shaking so much they created a sur-real, strobe light atmosphere.

"They used to maintain this road," Bob informed me.

"What happened?" I asked.

"They had a couple of bad winters up here and nobody could get through. So people stopped using it. The other routes are much more sensible."

Despite the rocky road the landscape I could see in the headlights was beautiful. I couldn't believe such lush areas could exist so close to something as desolate as Forget. Thick trees and loose grass grew wild and tall. Small red flowers lined the road and freckled the long patches of grass that grew carelessly in the middle. The tiny blossoms flashed within our view like ethnic fireflies celebrating the night.

The road eventually became so narrow that even if we had wanted to turn around it would have been impossible. I hoped no one else had had the lack of sense to drive this road coming from the other direction. There was no way two cars could pass each other. In fact, a skinny person with thin bones and an eating disorder would have been hard pressed to work himself between the small amount of space that was left on either side of us.

"We shouldn't have taken this road," I admitted.

"I don't know," Bob said. "It's awful neat out here at night. Just look at those stars," he pointed.

Bob was right. They were some stars, and we seemed to get closer and closer to them with each few yards we progressed.

"I haven't driven this road in years," Bob said. "It's really not that bad. Kinda makes me sad to know all this is here and I choose to always drive through that ugly Sterling. All that concrete and asphalt. I think people need to feel the earth through their toes every once in a while. I recommend it at least twice a day."

I agreed with his prescription.

"I tell you," Bob continued, smiling, "there is nothing like a splinter from a pine tree or a rash from a thick patch of ivy to remind you that God lives. Poor city folk," Bob tisked with compassion. "They think they've got it all figured out."

The Miracle of Forgetness

Bob was right. As backward as he seemed at times he really did have the right idea. I believed at that moment the rest of the world had been duped, snookered into thinking life was something more than this. I felt compelled to have Bob stop so I could simply touch the ground, but I fought the urge.

The road leveled out just beneath the top of the world. I truly felt that at any moment we would run into God, catch Him in our headlights hieing to Kolob. The night was just that spectacular. Maybe it was the thin air or the full moon, but I had never been so content.

"They call this spot the Throne of God," Bob informed me.

The sky was bigger here than I had ever seen it, and huge stars were pinned against the dark at what seemed a simple arm's length away.

"Amazing," I whispered.

"Haste to your Heavenly Father's throne and sweet refreshment find," Bob said. "That's a hymn," he explained. "It was always one of my..."

We hit a pothole and a giant snap echoed through the night. The car stopped moving. Bob pushed on the gas pedal until he was absolutely convinced the car was not going to go any further. We both got out.

Bob bent over to take a look under the car. I couldn't help but notice he was competing with the moon.

"Broken axle," he declared. "Split right in half."

"I'm so sorry," I said, feeling as if this were all my fault.

"Don't worry about it," Bob said. "I got a good mechanic in Longwinded."

"So what do we do?" I asked.

"We camp."

Bob opened up his trunk and began pulling things out of it. Then in the light of his headlights he built a fire and set up a small camp. Bob had only one sleeping bag, but for some reason he had a bale of hay in his trunk and a number of blankets. I spread some hay out on the ground and then laid down a couple of blankets. The warm fire was just enough on this mild

155

summer night. Bob unrolled his sleeping bag and started to settle in. We both just lay there under the stars, breathing in the mountain air and feeling the warmth of the world against our backs.

"Could you ask for anything more?" Bob asked.

"I don't think I could," I replied honestly.

"I wonder if any of those stars are aware of us," Bob said. "Maybe there's a couple of guys sprawled out on the ground with their hands behind their heads staring down at us from one of them."

"Or maybe there are some aliens watching us for one of their scientific studies," I joked.

Bob pulled his sleeping bag up closer to his chin. "I know there's somebody out there," he told me.

"I hope they're as happy right now as I am," I said.

Bob laughed a quiet, nonguttural laugh. "Some city folks might have a hard time settling into Forget, but not you. You've really taken a shine to this place, haven't you?"

I let the crackling fire and the scratchy music of the crickets answer for me.

"Stick likes you here," Bob disclosed. "He was getting pretty lonely being there by himself. This UFO thing has really helped out business, and I don't feel as compelled to visit him since I know you're there." Bob shifted in his sleeping bag. "I don't know how he does it though. Me, I love to be alone, but I couldn't survive without getting out and being with people. I remember about a year ago when we had a big barbecue for the folks of Longwinded. I was helping myself to some of Sister Lynn's egg firm pudding when I noticed a little shaving of mashed potatoes there in the pudding pan. Apparently someone had used the potato spoon to scoop out pudding," Bob clarified. "Well, Sister Lynn started fussing about getting me a new spoon but I didn't even mind. I was just so happy someone had been there before me. Community pudding. Someone had helped himself before me, and I was careful to leave some pudding for others to enjoy after me. It's a circle Gray, and sometimes we get knocked around by that big, sticky wooden spoon, but in the end we all seem to gel."

I looked over at Bob in his sleeping bag. He created quite a silhouette, and he expressed himself like no one I had ever known. Spoken by him, the pudding analogy seemed to make sense. I needed people. For some reason I just couldn't connect to this life alone.

Disengaged.

Bob sat up and threw a small branch onto the fire.

"Bob, were you ever married?" I asked.

"I almost got married," Bob confessed. "I don't really like to talk about it though."

"I understand."

"Her name was Chloe," Bob continued. "She was the most beautiful woman you could ever imagine. Skin like bleached milk and eyes that sparkled like cellophane under a heat lamp. I met her at the police academy in Sterling. I accidentally shot her friend, and while she was healing, Chloe and I got to know each other better. She was an angel."

Bob sighed.

"I remember one Valentine's Day when she wanted to do something special for me. She managed to get the key to my room, and while I was sleeping she slipped in and decorated the entire place with hearts and stuff. It would have turned out so nice, but she started to sprinkle glitter on my face and I woke up. How was I supposed to know it was her? I thought she was some kind of burglar. I hit her so hard in the jaw that I knocked one of her teeth out. She always sort of whistled when she spoke after that. She was one in a million," Bob said fondly.

"We planned on getting married after the academy but she got real sick and reluctantly went back home to live with her parents while she recovered."

Bob was quiet. A soft breeze blew over us and whipped the fire around. Sparks shot off into the night, competing with the stars and snapping like an uncoordinated flamenco dancer.

"Did she die?" I asked, feeling this story had a tragic end.

"No," Bob said huskily. "She fell in love with her doctor. She didn't have much time for a simple kid like me anymore. I went out to her home in Washington to try and win her back, but I only made things worse. She was embarrassed to see me." The wind blew something into Bob's mouth, and he took a couple of seconds to try and spit it out. The fire sizzled as flecks of saliva hit the embers. "Embarrassed to see me," he said again. "Can you imagine that?"

Poor Bob.

"What about Dot?" I asked, hoping to lighten the mood.

"Dot's a good person," Bob said, "but she and I could never be more than friends. I've seen her with her teeth out."

Well, that settled that.

"So I guess you can understand how Stick feels," I said. "I mean you both lost the women you loved."

"Neither Stick or I will ever understand love," Bob sighed.

"Who will?" I asked to no one in particular. "It's supposed to be this void filler, but I never feel incomplete unless I'm thinking about it. I'm fine just how I am."

"Well, you are kind of handsome," Bob said. "But that's not going to fix your lunch when you're old and unable."

I went on, ignoring Bob. "If we are these great eternal beings, then why should there be any game playing at all? Aren't there thousands of spirits invading my personal space at this exact moment who are more than capable of searching out Miss Right and pushing her towards me? They have all this time on their hands, and yet I'm expected to spend the few free minutes I have between work, church, and life to seek out that certain someone? I'm willing to work for her, if I just knew who to work for. Can't the heavens send down some sort of signal or sign as to how to go about it?"

"I did read a book once about what men need to know about women," Bob offered.

"Was it helpful?" I asked.

"Well, I didn't actually read it, but I flipped through it while I was waiting in line to buy groceries. It looked pretty long."

"I give up," I said, telling the heavens exactly where I stood and forfeiting a position I was never fully qualified for in any case. "I give up."

"Let me tell you something," Bob said, yawing. He then proceeded to repeat some sort of limerick. "There is nothing fulfilling in being the giver, if it were not for the journey, the route, or the river."

"Shakespeare?" I joked.

"No, I heard it on *Hee Haw*," Bob mumbled, slipping into unconsciousness.

I was left alone with a dying fire and a stupid impression that just maybe something somewhere had influenced Bob to tell me that dumb poem about the river.

Darn you, Mom and Dad. Here I was again with no one. Thanks to Bob that void was now wide open, and the fact that I was lacking was painfully clear to me once again. I had been so happy moments ago, but with the introduction of love, things were now confusing and complicated.

I got up to go to the bathroom. I walked off a ways and found a private place a few yards from camp. I was tempted to just keep walking and lose myself in the forest. At the moment, living as a lonely forest dweller didn't seem all that bad. I sat down on a fallen tree.

Darn you, Mindy.

Darn you, Mom and Dad.

Darn you, Angela.

Darn you, Gray.

I pulled out the letter I had gotten earlier that day from Rivers. I used the tiny light I had on my key ring to read it. As I read it the stars above seemed to shift and scatter, giddy over me doing just what I was doing. The letter. Rivers. Inspiration flowed like water through my veins. Was this the girl for me? There was something about being on the top of this mountain that made things clear.

Words I had once heard or read or sang blew in from the east, entering my head like the scent of rain and wet morning flowers.

Robert F. Smith

"We'll gather at the river...river...river...
That flows by the throne of God..."

Rivers. The words stacked in my head like heavy bricks, and each word I reread of her letter was mortar that cemented the thought.

Rivers was waiting for a missionary, I reasoned with myself.

Mindy had been waiting for a missionary, my thoughts bounced back.

This was true.

A shooting star streaked across the sky.

She lives in California, and I've never even seen her, I thought.

The wind gushed like water through my mind, leaking out of my nose and ears.

None of this made sense to me. In a couple of days Rivers would receive my letter demanding commitment, realize I was an idiot, and that would be that. It was out of my hands; I had broken the law to try and fix things and I had failed.

Things were out of my hands but not out of my head.

I couldn't comprehend how I could have these kinds of feelings for a person I had met through a church bulletin. But I couldn't deny that I did. If this had simply been a bad case of desperation the impressions I had would not have lasted this long. Inspiration was poking its nose around, sniffing the air and making me nervous.

Shoot.

Life was so much easier when I simply had to worry about myself. Easier and emptier.

Away from the fire the full moon really made things light. I didn't feel like falling asleep yet, so I decided to climb up a small rock cluster. Once I was on top of it and above the trees I could see the valley far below. I located the speck of Forget.

What was I doing out here?

I suddenly felt strongly that I needed to get home to Forget. It wasn't a feeling like I had left the iron on and I needed to race home to prevent a fire; it was more like I needed air and the only place producing any at the moment was Forget. Moments ago my lungs had been filled with thoughts of never leaving this mountain, but now I wanted nothing more than just to be home.

The urgency was so strong I considered waking Bob. But I couldn't see what good that would do while we were stranded.

Growling erupted from the campsite. I thought for a moment it was some sort of animal, but it was just Bob. I had completely forgotten about his little snoring problem. Just great, I thought, as if nature wasn't noisy enough.

I went back and collected my blankets. I found a soft spot a ways off and settled down for the night. I wanted to fall asleep so that I could wake up and go home. I needed to rewrite Rivers. I needed to plug back into Forget. I had places I was supposed to be. Perhaps if I hurried in the morning I could still make it to my ward. Perhaps if I express mailed a letter to Rivers I could tell her not to read the one I had mistakenly sent.

A small stream ran in the distance and helped lull me to sleep as I thought extensively of larger bodies of water.

Chapter Twenty-two

Dedication

I was awakened the next morning by Bob, poking me with a long stick.

"You sleep so quietly I couldn't tell if you were alive."

Despite the celestial arena we had slumbered in, I had not slept well. The ground, although soft, was peppered with tiny stones that kept poking up through my blankets. And the early morning dew had decided to show up around one in the morning. Things were wet, cold, and primitive.

Bob's clothes were wrinkled and his hair was sticking out from under his hat in all different directions. His mustache looked flat and matted, and he had beard stubble creeping up his neck.

I'm certain I didn't look much better.

"How far do we have to walk?" I asked after we had packed all of our stuff into Bob's car. "I need to get back home."

"But what about the grand opening?" Bob asked, surprised that I now wanted to skip it.

"I just need to get back to Forget," I insisted.

"Well, Orvil lives right around the bend," Bob said, a little confused. "I'll see if I can commandeer you a car."

"Which bend does Orvil live around?" I asked.

"That one up there," he said, pointing to a spot no more than a hundred feet away.

"Why didn't we just spend the night there?" I asked, bothered.

"Oh, I didn't want to be a burden," Bob said. "Orvil's wife is sort of bossy."

Orvil's home was no more than three hundred feet away from us. He had a large house that would have had ample room to house us for a night. Orvil and his wife let us clean up in their bathroom, where I was able to change into the Sunday clothes I had brought along. I wanted to be able to go directly to church when I got back home. Sure I would be late and have to walk past the window, but I needed to be there.

Orvil offered me one of his cars to drive back to Forget. There was no way I was going to take Witch Road back and risk breaking down. I would have to go through Longwinded. Bob and I thanked Orvil for his hospitality and left.

Bob scratched at his unshaven face the entire six-mile ride into Longwinded. Despite his condition, however, he was more than able to point out the sites of interest on our ride in. Apparently many mediocre and disturbing things had transpired here outside of Longwinded.

"That's where Phyllis Benderholden found that finger."

"If you look past those trees you can see a rock shaped just like the youngest Smith kid."

"Ten years ago a visitor had a heart attack right there next to that stump. Right there."

We soon pulled into the tiny town of Longwinded. The town itself wasn't much to look at, but the surrounding forest was more than the human eye could completely take in. Longwinded consisted of a few buildings, a paved road, and a nice new Mormon chapel that sat right across the road from a small, considerably older Baptist church. There were hundreds of cars parked outside the Mormon building.

I pulled up to the front door and let Bob out.

"Do you know how to get back to Forget?" Bob asked.

"By going forward?" I joked.

Bob just stood there thinking about that.

I wished Bob well with the dedication. I then raced out of Longwinded and on towards home. I had tracks to make, and I had a new found dedication of my own to attend to.

I was going forward.

Chapter Twenty-three

The Bridge

The Bluelake chapel was nowhere near as crowded as it used to be. I easily found a parking spot in the actual parking lot.

Amazing.

Sad.

Our temple float was still sitting in the parking lot waiting for the Bluelake Parade that was coming up in a week. The excitement for the parade had dwindled with the desertion of our former bishop.

Sacrament meeting was already in progress, so I rushed up the sidewalk and past the window. I could see through the glass that there was someone at the pulpit whom I didn't recognize. I walked into the building and found a seat in the back of the chapel. The overflow areas were not even open today. The members looked dejected and bitter. I tried to smile a lot in an attempt to make up for all of them.

The person speaking was our stake president, Filo Gram. I had not seen him before today, but I had heard he was a good leader. He was tall and wore big glasses which kept reflecting under the chapel lights. He was trying very hard to get us all motivated about the possibility of a new bishop.

"Next week you should have a new bishop," he said. "And it is my hope that you will sustain him as you did the last one.

Although maybe not quite as much," he added. "The Church is set up to work as a body. Each person has a responsibility. Your bishop had a reasonability, and now he has been released from that. You all have responsibilities, and none of you have been released from those. Likewise, your testimonies should be of the gospel and not Bishop Withers."

His words sounded nice in theory, but it was obvious that the bulk of our members didn't feel as he did. The stake president and Tom, the elders quorum president, were the only ones up on the stage. Everyone else had deserted his or her post. The stage was suspiciously absent of chorister, organist, and counselors. The congregation was spotty at best, and the front row where the deacons usually sat was empty except for one kid who was glumly representing the entire Aaronic Priesthood. We had gone from the biggest ward around to a crowd the size of a struggling branch.

"Because most of the class teachers are gone today," the stake president continued, "we will end this meeting after the sacrament services. However, there are a few individuals whom I would like to stay for interviews."

He then read off a list of names. My name was not among them. After the stake president had spoken, Tom got up and gave a short talk. Poor Tom, he obviously had not slept well in the last few weeks. His square body looked tense and ridged. His short arms never bent as he talked.

"You might all have heard the story about the bridge," he began. Tom looked out at the audience as if expecting a reaction. The only response he got was Sister McCaffy yawning so loudly that everyone turned to look at her.

"Well, there was this man," Tom continued. "He owned this little bridge that went across a lake and turned so that certain trains could take certain tracks." Tom wiggled his fingers down and twisted his wrist to demonstrate what a turning bridge might look like. Then he nervously went on. "Well, one day this bridge guy went to work, and while he was working a buzzer went off in his office alerting him that the track had not connected with the shore track properly. He walked down to the track and noticed the bridge track and the shore track were not connecting right. He quickly found this bar that he could use to manually hold down and connect the tracks right. He then held the track down as a train approached."

The members were beginning to listen.

"Well," Tom continued, "this man had a son whom his wife had sent over to bring him lunch or something. The son spotted his father holding down the bar and started walking across the bridge and down the railroad tracks towards him."

Tom tried to increase the dramatics by simply talking louder.

"Well, the father spotted his son and wanted to run and save him, but he realized that if he let go of the bar the approaching train would crash and kill hundreds of people. So instead of saving his son he had to hold the bar down, and his child was killed."

I had heard this story told a hundred times before, but somehow Tom told it worse than anyone. His monotone voice made it even more depressing and shocking than usual. I'm certain he was hoping for a reaction from the audience, I'm just not sure he was hoping for the reaction he got.

A frazzled Sister Lee, sitting with her four kids, burst into tears.

"That's awful," Sister Lark shouted out.

"Couldn't he just have screamed at his kid to get off the tracks?" Jonathan Call yelled.

"His kid was on the bridge," Tom said worried. "There was no room for him to get off."

It was open form on Tom. The congregation came alive. It was a good thing tomatoes had not been handed out at the door.

"There had to be a little room on the side of the tracks," Brother Scatty argued loudly. "Nobody builds a bridge without including a little extra room.

"Yeah," the members agreed.

"The train was too noisy," Tom yelled. "His son wouldn't have heard him if he had yelled."

"Well, he could have waved the boy off the tracks,"

"He had to hold the bar down."

"He could have used one hand, or leaned on the bar," Brother Flatly said.

"He could have leaned," a pregnant mother bawled in agreement. "He could have leaned."

"He didn't, I don't..." Tom tried to explain.

Sister Lee sobbed in her two cents, "Couldn't the boy just jump off the bridge into the lake," she cried. "Did anybody drag the lake for the boy?" she wailed.

Tom was growing angry.

"Did the father even know the people on the train?" Brother Flatly asked, concerned.

"No," Tom said frustrated. "That's the point."

"Well, if I had made that decision, my wife would have never spoken to me again."

"Yeah," someone yelled, "Did they stay married?"

Tom threw up his short arms as far as he could throw them. "I give up," he said, gathering his things and storming off the stage and out of the chapel. The stake president stood and tried to calm things down.

"It was just an analogy," he explained.

"Bishop Withers never told horrible stories like that," Sister Buswidth pointed out.

Some of the members started to get up and clear out. People had lost their minds. Once the migration had finished the stake president gave a closing prayer, blessing us that we all might come to our spiritual senses. He then dismissed the few remaining members and offered to give blessings to anyone who felt he, or she, needed one. It looked to me as though the stake president could use one as well.

Tom was sitting in the foyer when I walked out. I sat down by him.

"I'm quitting you know," Tom spit out before I had a chance to say anything. "When I go in for my interview with the stake president I'm asking to be released."

"I don't blame you," I said.

"You don't?" Tom asked, surprised.

"I think they need a whole new ward," I replied. "These people will never be happy without Bishop Withers. They need a clean start."

"So what should we do?" Tom whined.

"You and the stake are going to have to figure that out."

"Nobody would listen to anyone else who was called to be bishop," Tom said dejectedly. "The Bluelake Ward is completely finished."

I got up and headed out. I was glad this mess wasn't any of my affair.

It's amazing how wrong I can be at times.

Chapter Twenty-four

Interrogated

I felt bad about my ward. But I felt it was best not to dwell on it. After all, I had only been here a short while. How and why should I factor into all this? I would step back and wait for the dust to clear. I would let them pick a new bishop, and then I would act like none of this had ever happened. I wouldn't let any of this bother me. There was safety in numbness.

I did feel my future would level out despite all of this. I knew now that I belonged in Forget. The impressions I had felt last night were too strong to deny. So if I could just hang in there until someone or something pointed out what I should be doing, life would be fine.

Mapped out.

Course charted.

Yes, things were going to work out. At the moment, however, I was going nowhere fast. More specifically I was headed home going ten miles over the posted speed. I wanted to get home and write a letter to Rivers.

When I arrived, Stick was at the store and Kitty was sound asleep. Stick told me things had gone all right the previous night, except for when Kitty started demanding he fluff her pillows. Stick had to take her TV away until she apologized for treating him like a servant. Stick was now whining about how he didn't really feel her apology had been sincere.

I went home and busily worked on a new letter for Rivers. I was flipping through the thesaurus looking for another word for "nice" when an unmarked white police car pulled up to my home.

"Well this is pleasant," I said to myself, putting my recently enhanced vocabulary to good use.

At first I thought it was just Bob in a loaner, but it turned out to be a couple of people from the state department who were in charge of investigating the UFO. One was tall and one was Jay, Bob's rival. They both wore overcoats and stared a lot when they spoke.

I invited them into my home, where they sat on my beat-up old couch and drank water that I served them.

"So did you see it?" the tall one asked.

"I didn't actually see the crash, but I went out the morning after."

"And?" Jay prodded.

"It looked like something had blown up there," I replied.

"What do you mean 'blown up'?"

"You know," I said. "Like something had exploded."

"Oh, exploded," Jay said, glimpses of sarcastic excitement seeping out of his stuffed shirt. "This sounds important enough to waste my Sundays on."

I shrugged my shoulders.

"Does your Uncle Stick drink?" Jay questioned.

"Alcohol?" I asked, seeking clarification.

"Yes or no?" he snapped.

"No," I answered.

"Does he have cause to perpetrate this fraud?" the tall man asked while writing something down.

"Not that I know of."

"How's business at the store?" the tall one fired.

"Great," I replied.

"So UFOs are good for revenue," Jay said smartly.

"It hasn't hurt things," I agreed.

"Let me tell you something," Jay said, leaning in closer to me. "I don't believe in UFOs. I don't believe that the same God who created me created anyone with three arms or six legs or that flies around in some sort of saucer." Jay stood and scratched his thick hair. "And I'm not closed minded," he continued. "God may have created people with bigger livers, or perhaps a race where acne was nonexistent, but there is no way he gave the okay to create men with plate-sized eyes and two hearts." Jay drew in breath. "But maybe you think he did, maybe you pray to some sort of crystal or worship some kind of tree god. I don't know what your kind of people do, but I know it makes me sick."

I sat there silently. What kind of response could I give to something as stupid as what he had just said? Hand me my crystal and let me see if I agree with you?

"If your uncle is making all of this up," he continued, "then some serious heads are going to roll. Serious heads."

I tried to picture what a serious head looked like.

"Unlike your friend Bob," Jay jabbed, "I've got work to do. I can't waste my time on stupid pranks and country bumbles."

I didn't know how to respond to that either, so I offered them both some more water. Neither one accepted.

"We better go, but if you think of anything else we should know, call us," Jay grumbled. "I would hate to have to write you down as an accessory to the crime."

I promised I would, knowing full well I would never willingly call either of these guys, regardless of the information I might have. I didn't care if a couple of space people came by my house selling candy for some sort of "Crush the Humans" intergalactic benefit, I would not be relaying the news to those two.

I went back to writing my letter to Rivers. No sooner had I thought of a clever way to wrap up my thoughts to her, then another car pulled up to my house. I could see through the front window that it was my stake president.

I pulled my scriptures off a shelf and laid them open on the couch. I wanted to at least give the appearance of righteousness.

President Gram knocked a stake president sort of knock and

I let him in. He took a seat on my couch.

"So you're Stick's nephew?" he began.

"I am."

"I like Stick," President Gram said. "Long before Jenny, he and I used to go fishing together. We were pretty good friends. Of course that was before I told him he needed to forgive Bishop Withers."

"I can't see him ever doing that," I observed.

"Stick's stubborn all right."

"So did you come out here to talk about Stick?" I asked honestly.

"No, I came to talk about you."

"And?" I asked.

"We need a new bishop."

"I've heard," I answered, an unknown fear creeping up in me.

"The problem is, no one wants to step in and fill old Withers' shoes."

"I can't say as I blame them. People get sort of used to someone after so many years."

"Yeah, I think it might be time to disband the Bluelake Ward," President Gram said.

"What are you thinking?" I asked nervously.

I don't know why I was suddenly uncomfortable, but I was. I had no need to be scared of this man or to fear his words in the least. It was just that my heart was now pumping ten times too fast. His next words made clear as to why.

"I'm thinking of starting up a Forget First Ward and putting you in as bishop. You would all still meet in Bluelake, but you would be a brand new ward."

The thought was so absurd I couldn't help laughing.

"Seriously," I asked, "what do you have in mind?"

"I'm always serious," was his only reply.

This was the most uninspired idea I had ever heard. This part of the world made people delusional.

Stick believed Jenny would come back.

Kitty thought she was a classic beauty.

Bob saw no connection between overeating and heart disease.

And President Gram could foresee a world where someone like me could be bishop. Just how desperate was he? Certainly there were plenty of people who could be bishop here. A month ago people were shooting off at the mouth about how huge the Bluelake Ward was. Now they couldn't seem to locate a worthy male who was both willing and able to be a bishop? This was crazy and I told him so.

"This is crazy."

"I agree."

"Good," I said. "I'm glad you understand."

President Gram got up and started to pace the floor. "I was interviewing the members whom I felt would make good bishops," President Gram began to explain. "No one was right. I didn't even feel slightly good about any of them. It was as if I were interviewing cardboard cutouts. No inspiration, no vibes, no spiritual confirmation that I was heading down the right track. Nothing. Then I interviewed Tom. He told me all about you. He also mentioned how you had suggested we form a whole new ward. Wipe the slate clean and begin again."

"I was joking," I pointed out.

President Gram stopped and looked out my front window. He noticed a small crack at the bottom of the glass.

"I can fix this," he said.

Who cared about cracked glass at a time like this?

"I run a glass business in Sterling." President Gram got out one of his business cards and handed it to me. "I give all members a fifteen percent discount. Ten percent off on all tempered glass."

"Thanks," I said, taking the card and hoping the glass talk would distract him from ever again mentioning the possibility of my being bishop.

"So what do you think," he asked.

"I think the glass industry is a noble business," I replied.

"Gray," he said as if he were my father and I had just shown him a less than spectacular report card.

"No offense, President, but I don't think I could say yes to such a thing."

"And why not?"

"I'm twenty-four."

"That doesn't matter."

"I'm single," I pointed out. "Isn't it a requirement for a bishop to be married?"

"It's best that way," he answered. "Any prospects?"

"No prospects," I replied. "I am so single it's not funny. I don't even have a friend that's a girl at the moment. In fact I think I might stay single my whole life."

"Well, we'll have to change that," President Gram said with finality.

"You can't change things like that," I argued.

"I don't think we should put you in as bishop until you're married, or at least engaged. I'll give you two weeks," he said. "If you aren't engaged by then we'll reconsider things."

"You'll give me two weeks? This is insane," I said.

"I know," was his reply once again. "I can't understand why the Lord would want someone so stubborn and young to be the bishop when there are plenty of others to chose from. But then, who am I to doubt his will."

"You'd be a sensible man," I said, frustrated. "A sensible, sensible man."

President Gram smiled at me.

I was desperate. I searched my mind for some way to get out of this.

"I've been inactive," I tried.

"It's good to see you're changing your ways."

"I'm lazy."

"The Lord will change that."

"I stole a candy bar from my grandmother's purse when I was ten."

"Gray, if you don't want to be the bishop just say so," President Gram said kindly.

I caught my breath. "It wouldn't be right."

"Two weeks," President Gram said, opening my front door.

"I said no," I pleaded.

"As a stake president I've learned to hear only certain things," he said as he stepped outside. "I'll see you in two weeks, Brother Stevens."

The door shut behind him and I fell back onto my couch. What was happening? This had to be the sickest and saddest joke ever perpetrated on anyone. Me bishop? Come on. Certainly God had far more sense than this. The councils in heaven must have turned things over to a bunch of teenage angels.

"We just lost Withers, whom everyone loved, adored, and respected. What should we do?"

"You know what would be funny, let's put Gray in his place."

"Cool."

I sat there on my couch staring at the ceiling. This was so ridiculous, I didn't know why I was even giving this thought gray matter to grow on. There was no way I could ever....

The guest room door moved just a hair.

Kitty.

I had completely forgotten about my disabled house guest. Her door was cracked a bit, and I could see her listening. I jumped up to yell at her. She saw me and ran to her bed. I threw open the door just as she was pulling the covers up over her head.

"What are you doing?" I demanded.

"I needed some water," she tried to play up.

"I saw you run," I insisted. "You're perfectly capable of getting around, aren't you?

"Maybe I am," she snipped.

"Well, why didn't you say anything?" I said angrily.

"I don't need to tell you any of my business," she roared.

"I think you do."

"I guess I'll be leaving now," she oinked loudly. Kitty stood up and put on her robe. "It appears your compassion has run dry."

I couldn't believe this. Kitty was walking around the room as if nothing were wrong with her. I guess her leg had not been as bad as the doctor had originally thought.

"I can't believe you can walk."

"Get over it," Kitty said, grabbing her keys and slipping her boots onto her twisted feet. "You're a stupid boy," she said, storming out of the room and my house. She got into her newly repaired Cadillac, started the engine, and tore out. No thanks, no wave, no, "How can I ever repay you?"

This had been one weird day.

I had too much to think about.

Last night I had felt there were no voids in my life except for where marriage was concerned. Now I felt like my life had more cracks and crevices than the parched lips on a prizefighter. And the very idea of my being bishop. Come on.

I picked up my letter to Rivers and went outside. I then climbed to the highest branches of my tree. I needed a double dose of composure. From the top of my tree I could see Kitty off in the far distance speeding home. I had tried to help her. I had even thought that she might come around to the nice side. I knew now it was no use.

I finished the letter but remained in my tree, contemplating the ridiculous fact that I had been asked to be bishop.

"Forget First Ward," I huffed.

Forgotten.

"Two weeks," I scoffed.

This entire day had been crazy. I climbed down and went to the store to help Stick. I figured that my doing a little work on Sunday would make me less worthy and cause the stake president to recall his offer. I considered for a moment telling Stick about the stake president's "idea." But I didn't. I thought it would be best if no one knew. That way when I did end up saying absolutely no way, only I would know what a huge chicken I was.

Chapter Twenty-five

Dial M for Muddle

Monday was the first day of the last two weeks of my life. I got up early with Stick, and we ate breakfast together. Stick was really feeling good about his chances of Jenny coming back. I guess he had been having dreams about vegetation. He saw this as a clear subconscious message that his relationship with Jenny was becoming fertile.

That was one way of putting it, I thought.

Stick cooked up a bunch of pancakes in the shape of cowboy hats and served them to me with a pile of bacon and half a stick of butter. I dissected the butter and put pieces of it on my pancakes. I then covered everything with a thick layer of syrup.

"I could put syrup on anything," Stick said, sitting down to his plate of similar fixin's.

I didn't comment due to a full mouth.

"Mable Bleat came by the store," Stick reported.

"Did she have news about the parade?" I asked.

Mable Bleat was the president of the Bluelake Chamber of Commerce. She was in her mid forties and had more energy than a room full of sugared up toddlers. She was always thrusting her fist into the air with enthusiasm. You had to be careful about standing right in front of her because her zest for living could leave you bruised and battered. She had a pixie-cut hairdo and a tacky addiction to cow items. She always wore little cow earrings, a cute pewter cow bracelet, and a funny cow pin that said, "You udder know better." I thought all of the items looked quite nice with the leather belts and shoes she wore.

I had been bugging, courting, and manipulating Mable for a week now. I wanted her to have the Bluelake Parade end here in Forget, and she was the woman with the power to say "Yes" or "No." I thought it would be great exposure for Forget to have the celebrated event peter out at our doorstep. The idea was to have people set up booths right here next to the store so when the parade ended everyone could have a little food, fun, and Forget.

I had been waiting for word on whether or not this would go through. Word had arrived.

Stick finished chewing what was in his mouth.

"She said yes," he smiled. "She said they'll have the parade stop just a bit out of Bluelake, then folks will drive to Forget. That's where the booths and such will be assembled. She says she liked the idea of having her parade end up right here at UFO headquarters."

"That's great," I replied.

"I'll say it is," Stick gleamed. "This is the big event. I tell you what, Gray, you and I don't always see eye to eye, but I'm real proud of you for this. Yes, this here is a coupe."

"You mean coup," I corrected.

"I mean people are going to think we're something," Stick said. "We're going to be looking real pretty to all them parade goers. And just think," Stick enthused, "all them hot, tired people ending up here where we can happily supply them with parade-priced drinks and goodies." Stick thrust his thumbs up in the air, showing me the direction prices would be going.

"We're not doing this to gouge people," I said. "Besides, we can't handle much more business. This UFO thing has you and Ned running ragged already."

"That's the way I like it," Stick said, licking his lips. "Them little aliens have been the best thing that's happened to us. I always thought the invasion would bring doom and gloom, not pride and prosperity. I tell you what, the other day when Nelson Parker came in and started telling folks about me seeing a UFO, I was never so proud. I just know Jenny's going to hear about me and how brave I was. Then she'll come running home."

"Here's hoping," I said, remembering just how truly brave Stick had been on the night of the crash.

I picked up my plate and washed it off in the sink.

"I guess we better start preparing for it," I commented on the parade. "Maybe Ned can start making some signs or something."

"Ned's good with his hands," Stick said.

I guess that settled that.

I went out back to pour my dish water on the tree. I would have stopped and declared it a beautiful morning but I was distracted by the fact that someone had painted my tree orange. It was awful. My poor tree had been coated in ugly orange paint. And it wasn't as if someone had done a nice job of it. It was as if they had just flung cans of paint all over it.

"Stick," I yelled.

He ran to my side.

"Welcome to the ways of Kitty," he said, looking at our sad tree.

"Why would Kitty do this?" I said, frustrated. "We took her in, we fed her, we did everything for her. We didn't even ask her to pay for the wall she ruined, I just let her leave. This is the thanks I get?"

"Ask Bob about Kitty sometime," Stick said, walking up to the tree and touching the paint.

"Why don't you tell me?" I asked.

"Bob just has such a way with words."

"Don't sell yourself short," I said.

Stick smiled. He loved it when ever anyone used the word short to describe him.

Stick looked at his watch. He still had a good hour before he had to open up the store. "Years ago Kitty wasn't so sour looking," Stick began. "She was sort of pretty and slightly nice. Don't get me wrong, she's always been heavily spoiled, but she hasn't always had that face thing going on." Stick took a moment to grimace. "Well, back then there was nothing to do around here. Bob would come down from Longwinded, and the two of us would shoot tin cans or dig big holes."

"How old were you?" I asked, imagining they were twelve-year-old boys at the time.

"We were about your age," Stick answered.

"And you spent your time digging big holes?"

"You ever tried it?" Stick criticized.

I just laughed.

"Can I continue?" Stick asked.

"Please," I replied.

"Well, occasionally Kitty would come around to show us something her dad had just bought her. We didn't really care. If it wasn't something that blew stuff up or made a neat noise we didn't give it much notice. Kitty hated that. She couldn't stand the fact that we weren't impressed by her toys. So she offered to pay Kevin Hartman's big brother, Billy, to beat us both up."

"You're kidding?" I said.

"Nope," Stick said. "Billy beat the tar out of both of us. He got Bob while he was up in Longwinded. Bob was walking home from Beaver Lake when Billy jumped him. Poor Bob. He really got it rough. Billy got me right here in Forget. He knocked on the door, and when I went to open it he taught me a lesson in force and give." Stick stopped to feel his jaw. "This thing still gives me trouble."

"Did someone arrest Billy?" I asked.

"We thought about it, but Billy's father was a cop and Bob was entering the academy soon. We didn't want to do anything to ruin Bob's chances or get him blackballed. Besides, it all turned out well. After the deed Kitty refused to pay Billy, so he had his girlfriend, Amber, do a number on her. I'd rather feel the wrath of Billy than the anger of Amber any day. Amber was one of those glamour nail manicurists, so she had real long nails. Kitty has never forgiven us for forcing her to hire Billy who in turn had Amber scratch her up.

"People really began hating Kitty after that. No one could imagine someone doing something so cruel to Bob. Most folks thought I had it coming. But Bob? Nah. He'd never hurt a person in his life. Ever since that time though, people have been bothered by Kitty and her conniving ways. And she has just kept getting meaner and meaner, her face contorting more and more with each ounce of hate. She swears she will never forget how quickly people turned on her. Claims she's got no reason ever to treat folks kind again."

"I thought she was coming around," I said, still looking at my tree.

"Kitty's hopeless," Stick said. "I bet the only reason she stayed around here was for free food. It'd take a miracle to change her."

I was afraid Stick was right. If this was the way she treated people who tolerated her, I could only imagine being on her real bad side. Poor Kitty.

Stick headed off to get the store started, and I went back inside to get dressed for the day. I had a lot of things to get accomplished, not the least of which was finding a way to get out of being bishop without having to resort to having my name removed from the records of the Church.

I wanted out, but not out.

I wanted the stake president to come to his senses. There was no way a true and living church could function with an unorganized and struggling bishop such as I.

As I was heading out the door to go into Bluelake to mail my letter, I stepped on a bouquet of roses that were lying on my doorstep. They were from Angela. The small card with them said quite clearly that she missed me and that she hoped to see me Friday.

I felt slightly sick. I had been planning this Friday to be busy daydreaming about Rivers up in my tree, hidden from Angela and avoiding her all together. But now she had gone and done this. I couldn't just blow her off when she had gone to the effort to give me cookies and now roses.

The Miracle of Forgetness

I sent my letter to Rivers, explaining my previous letter, express. I didn't have the guts to go back to the post office where I had done my terrible deed, so I mailed it at one of the specialty mail shops in Bluelake. As I was driving back to Forget thinking about Rivers a thought struck me.

I could call her.

It was so crazy it just might work.

Everything seemed to hinge upon this Rivers deal. A girl I had never even seen, hardly even knew, who was waiting for another guy and living hundreds of miles away, held the future of my pathetic, unstable, and nondirected life. If I had no possibilities I would be out of the running for bishop. Roses or not, Angela wasn't a true consideration anymore, and I believed that despite the inspiration-like feelings I had felt towards Rivers I truly had no chance with her. One phone call was all it would take.

Why had I wasted stamps? I could know in a matter of minutes if there were anything to Rivers and me. I could then call up President Gram and inform him with a clear conscience and guilt-free mind that as much as I would love to help out, there was no way I could.

I pulled over to a roadside pay phone. I wasn't even willing to wait until Forget. I had to know now. It would be so freeing to have all of this over with. Then I could just go home and hang out by my tree. Or maybe I would help Stick stock shelves. That's what I would do, I'd help Stick. How noble.

I couldn't wait to be noble.

I found a bunch of quarters I had been saving for the Laundromat. A washer was a luxury Forget had not afforded. (Stick had done his laundry in his backroom sink for years.)

The pay phone I had picked stood alone on the edge of Bluelake. It was well used and marred by felt tip marker and knife wounds. The bottom glass panel on the right side was gone, replaced by a rough piece of plywood. Who cared? The phone worked.

I dialed California information.

I was suddenly so nervous my heart felt as if it had slipped down into my right knee.

I put the phone down and tried to gain my composure.

Don't be stupid, I told myself.

I dialed again.

"What city?"

"Sacramento," I answered clearly.

"What listing?"

I remembered Rivers' parents' names from one of her letters.

"Philip and Margaret Jordan."

"One minute."

What seemed like two days later, a voice rattled off seven digits. I wrote them down accordingly. I had the formula. Now I just needed the nerve.

I hung up and gave myself a pep talk.

I could do this. There was no reason I should feel anything. This was just another phone call during the long run of life. I'd put the quarters in, talk to Rivers, and get on with my life. If I felt anything at all, it should be glee, happiness, and relief that things were about to accumulate into nothing.

I put in more quarters than necessary and dialed.

Ring.

I could hang up and just go home.

Ring.

I could hang up, go home, and never answer my door or phone again.

Ring.

I could hang up, run, lock myself in my house, and never go out again as long as I lived.

Ring.

I could...

"Hello."

If it had not been a male voice, I know I would have passed out. I called upon every ounce of courage I had simply to utter the words.

"Is Rivers home?"

"Yes. May I tell her who's calling?"

"Gray," I answered.

"Just a minute," he said, obviously unaware of who Gray was. I was devastated.

Had Rivers not spent the last few weeks dreamily walking around her house, incessantly talking about the mysterious Gray guy from Forget? Had her mother not noticed a difference in her and in turn asked Rivers to sit down and tell her all about this new presence in her life? Did not her younger brother relentlessly tease her about how she was falling in love with some guy she had never even met while waiting for her missionary?

I could hear the phone being set down against something hard. I then heard talking in the background. It sounded as if two people were discussing something totally unrelated to my call.

I waited.

I heard a door shut, followed almost instantly by a car horn and some kid yelling something.

I kept waiting.

I didn't know what the proper period of patience should be. Had they forgotten I was there? Had he delivered the news and Rivers had simply decided not to answer the call?

Had I completely lost my mind?

What in the world was I doing?

I had to be the most demented person on the entire planet. There was no way there could be anything between Rivers and me. There was no way she could have read anything into us. There was just no way. She probably thought I was some lonely discarded single who needed a letter mate. It was probably nothing but compassion that stirred her to write back to me. She must never have received her "Daughter of God" award in Young Women and now she was trying to make up for it. She was completing a few service hours, graciously writing the poor, socially retarded boy from Forget.

I was just a box to check off.

Write a letter to a shut-in.

Check.

The other end of the phone was completely silent now. I had been forgotten. If someone did pick up the phone now I would be completely embarrassed that I had held on waiting as if I had nothing better to do.

I had nothing better to do.

I started counting, promising myself I would hang up when I reached ten. Around eight I started adding quarter- and half-numbers. After nine I began using fractions so slim they reminded me of my chances with Rivers. Once I reached ten I started over, counting only to eight this time—I had my pride. Eight came and went without so much as a single background noise or a disconnected dial tone of mercy.

I needed to hang up. I knew now I had no chance with her.

I started one final countdown, this time starting at ten and going backwards. It seemed more appropriate that way.

I was so busy counting in my head I almost missed the question.

"Gray?" a female voice on the other end said.

It was Rivers, and she sounded almost excited.

I didn't know what to say.

"Is that you?" Rivers asked.

"Hey," I replied. I admit it wasn't much of an opener, but at least it was audible.

"I can't believe you called," she said.

"Well, I," my mind was whirling a million miles an hour trying to come up with something clever to say. I settled for, "I just wanted to talk to you."

"This is so weird," she replied. "How'd you get my number?"

"I called information," I answered. "I hope I'm not bothering you."

"No not at all," she said. Her voice was wonderful. My knuckles began to sweat, and the hair on my head felt as if it suddenly grew an inch. I could feel my ribs burning, and the bottoms of my feet turned spongy and weak. I sat down on the little metal shelf there in the phone booth.

The Miracle of Forgetness

"So how's California?" I asked.

Somebody shoot me.

"Same as always," she replied.

"It's sunny here," I said.

Somebody should have shot me.

"That's great."

"Yeah," I replied.

I didn't know what to do. I suddenly had no concept of what a person said to another person during the course of a phone conversation. I couldn't even hook sentences together in my head. It was as if at that moment my being was overcome with darkness. But not the kind of darkness that had surrounded Joseph in the grove. It was more like the kind of darkness that clouds the brain after watching twelve straight hours of cartoons on TV.

A stupid fog.

I prayed for a kinder mentality to break through the black and deliver me from this darkness. I prayed for someone driving Witch Road to fall asleep at the wheel and accidentally plow into me. I prayed that black clouds would fill the sky and lightning would strike me repeatedly, sending at least some sort of spark over the phone line. I prayed for the earth to open up and swallow me, pushing me to its furthest bowels, down to the center where outcasts like the ten tribes and every fabled being from Cain to Nessy lived. I could fit in there.

I just plain prayed.

"Well," Rivers finally said, "I'd better go. It was nice talking to you."

I had been right. No chance.

"Wait," I said, hoping to resurrect some shred of something other than awful. "Don't go yet."

I had asked her not to go but I had nothing to say.

"I'm still here," she informed me.

"I just wanted to talk with you a while," I said without sounding weird. In fact I had delivered the line rather well.

Rivers picked up the pieces of this abstract conversation and began to place them. "When I got your first letter I thought it

187

was a joke," she said. "I mean the envelope was so worn, and your saying you were Gray from some place called Forget sounded like one big joke."

"I can understand that," I said. "I had similar feelings when I saw your announcement in the bulletin. Rivers Jordan?"

"It was my parents' attempt to be neat."

"It works," I said.

"I kind of like Gray," she said back.

There was silence for a few moments.

Finally I spoke, "Well, I just wanted to hear your voice. You know, see if the voice fit the letters."

"And does it?" she asked.

"I couldn't answer that honestly and still have you take me seriously," I said.

"Try me."

There's nothing like a challenge to bring out the stupidity in all of us.

"I'm mad," I said.

"You're mad?"

"I am," I continued. "I was hoping to find you flawed. Instead all I hear is someone who is much more than your letters even suggest."

"You're looking for a flawed woman?" she laughed.

"I'm looking for some sort of explanation as to why I should feel anything at all for you. Your letters have made my life one confusing mess. I dated a girl for five years and never once was I as impressed with her as I am with the person I see in your letters."

I had reached the point of no return. I had said too much. There was no way I could stop now; I had to finish this out or die. I had to make sense of a conversation that didn't have an outline. I forged ahead.

"I was hoping to call you, find the flaw in us, hang up and go on with my life."

"I can think of a few flaws," Rivers said, laughing.

"Please," I said.

"We've never met."

"Mere logistics," I responded.

"I'm here, you're there," she listed.

"Geography is just a convenient excuse."

"A good one, however," she replied.

"But certainly not insurmountable."

"I'm engaged to another guy," Rivers threw out.

"Engaged?" I asked.

"Well, he asked me in his last letter," Rivers answered.

"That's not a flaw. That's a situation," I said, trying desperately to hide my disappointment. It was one thing to seek after a girl who was waiting. But it was an entirely different thing to go after an engaged woman. Wasn't there a commandment against that? Sure, maybe it hadn't made it to the top ten list, but certainly it was one of the alternates.

"If thou shalt see a promise ring, don't thou do a thing."

"I'm sorry," I finally said. "I didn't know."

"And I didn't say yes, yet," Rivers replied.

Talk about reading too much into something. Rivers had just thrown out a line that I considered to be a five-hundred-page thesis on why there was a possibility. My stomach shifted and my chest became tighter than the budget of a welfare ward.

"Am I crazy?" I asked.

"I hope not," she laughed.

"Is there a possibility?" I ventured.

"I don't know," Rivers replied. "I only know I have a hard time reading your letters without feeling something."

"Is it good?" I asked.

"It's weird."

"Is that bad?"

"It's strange."

"So there's a possibility?"

"All things are possible."

Rivers and I talked until I ran out of quarters. We talked

about Forget. We talked about Sacramento. We talked about our letters. We even talked about Elder Higgins, albeit briefly.

It was wonderful.

For some unknown reason that neither of us could understand, there was more to us than just pen pals.

I had a hard time driving home. Normal things like driving seem so commonplace when you've just been orbiting planets.

The eclipse had begun.

Chapter Twenty-six

Me Bound,
She Determined

Tuesday evening my letter writing was interrupted by honking outside of my home. I pulled the curtain aside to find a small car with its headlights shining towards my front door. Curiously and without thinking I stepped outside to investigate. The sun was out of sight, but weak light lingered like trace aroma from a big meal. What a dish the day had been.

I walked toward the headlights, my hand over my eyes like an awning, thinking somehow this would improve my vision. I couldn't tell who it was, and before I was close enough to find out, a bag was thrown over my head, arms closed on me like a clamp, and I was picked up as if I were something other than a six-foot-four man. I tried to struggle, but this person's arms were around me so tight I couldn't move. I felt myself being pushed into the car before I could even make a real fuss. Doors shut, and a tiny engine revved like a cat on fire. I fought to take the bag off, but a strong hand came back and hit me on the head. The strike was followed by a gruff warning,

"Don't take it off!"

The voice was male and foreign to me. I tried to figure out what was going on. I didn't consider myself worthwhile enough to kidnap, but that was what appeared to have happened. This had to be a case of mistaken identity. Just about the time I started to really worry, I heard Angela's voice.

"Just hang on, Gray, we're taking you someplace great."

"Just what's..." I started to say.

"Shhh," was her only reply.

I tried to think about which direction we were headed, hoping for some chance to escape. I didn't want to be with Angela, and I certainly didn't want to be with her someplace that I didn't know my way out of.

"Can I take this bag off?" I asked.

"No!" the male voice snapped.

"It would ruin the surprise," Angela added.

I felt like an idiot. I was sitting in the back of a car, hands untied, willingly wearing a burlap sack over my head. I had the power to remove the bag, but like a courteous (or cowardly) kidnapee I obeyed my captors and left it on. The burlap was scratchy, making my outside as uncomfortable as my inside.

After some time Angela introduced me to her brother Fetch.

"Fetch?" I laughed.

A low grumbling erupted from him.

Angela said a few soothing words to Fetch, and I could hear him cool.

"He got the nickname while he was in prison," Angela informed me.

I suddenly felt really bad for laughing.

"What is this all about?" I asked nervously.

"You've been datenapped," Angela said. "Just sit back and enjoy it."

I sat back.

I didn't enjoy it.

What seemed about an hour later we turned onto a dirt road. I bounced around like an inflatable punching bag in the backseat, my feet full of sand, my head light and bothered. We made a series of turns and climbs, dips and bends, weaving and crawling across the landscape. At one point we stopped and Fetch got out to open a hidden gate of sorts. I, of course, couldn't see it, but Angela explained it to me. We drove a few more miles and then finally stopped.

"You can take off the bag," Angela announced, her voice indicating that this was all great fun.

I shimmied out of my itchy hood.

It was completely dark now, and the skies were offering little assistance by leaving only a single star on. Just like the heavens to be conservative at such a time.

Fetch turned on a lantern. Light exploded everywhere, splattering against trees and bushes, dripping off rocks and cliff walls, and blinding me.

"Some lantern," I commented.

Fetch looked at me and sneered. He then set the lantern down on an old tree stump and wondered off toward what looked to be a house.

"Where are we?" I asked, looking at Angela. She was dressed in western garb, a yellow scarf around her neck, chaps on her legs, and a straw cowboy hat on her head. She handed me a cowboy hat and told me to put it on. I did so very reluctantly.

"Partner," she drawled, sticking her elbow out to latch onto mine.

I was obviously waste-deep in a theme date, and not even the effervescent great outdoors could mask the pungent smell of it. I thought only Mormons put themselves through these sadistic rituals. I was obviously wrong.

"So where are we?" I asked again.

"This is Fetch's place."

"Why did you cover my head?"

"Fetch and his roommate don't really want their address to be known."

"Why'd you bring me here?"

"I thought it would be fun," Angela snapped, obviously unhappy because of the lack of enthusiasm in my voice.

Angela took my hand and led me to Fetch's house. Another lantern popped on inside the house, and light burst out of the windows like jumpy spirits. The house itself was covered with tree limbs as if for some reason Fetch was trying to hide it. Angela led me up some shaky temporary stairs and into this abode.

Once inside we sat down on a short couch with a long coffee table in front of it. The coffee table had two candles on it and silverware that lay rigidly upon yellow paper napkins. Fetch brought out a big bowl of chili and set it in front of us. It looked as if I was about to have dinner for the second time that night. I wished Angela would have had the common sense to take me hostage before I had eaten.

Fetch turned the lantern down low, dimming both the light and my comfort. I stared at the two bales of hay that had been placed next to the table, providing both ambiance and allergies.

"Angela..." I said, my eyes beginning to itch.

Angela glared at me, unhappy with the tone of voice I was using. I sat back defeated. Angela got up and left the room. Fetch had a weird home. It was long and skinny like a single-wide mobile home, but the west wall was solid stucco. It didn't look like a super floor plan either. The inside walls and doors seemed uncentered and out of place. It was as if his house were missing half of itself.

Angela came back into the room carrying plates with hot dogs on them. She set one in front of me and took a seat. She scooped up some chili and put it into a bowl, smiling.

I smiled back. This whole thing was stupid. I had hoped we would never have to go out again, and now here I was shanghaied and forced to be with her. I liked Angela, but I just couldn't see a world where her temper and I could cohabitate happily together.

Angela leaned her head on my shoulder as she chewed her hot dog. I could see Fetch through one of the doorways. He had on tight nylon workout shorts and a stringy tank top. Fetch was big, but he wasn't toned, big. He was probably six foot six and weighed about three hundred pounds. It looked as if he enjoyed fried foods far more than squats and pull-ups. He reminded me of Greg

The Miracle of Forgetness

Fillword, a guy I knew in high school. Greg was well known, but not well thought of. He played life so shy of a full deck that people simply couldn't deal with him. Up until our sophomore year Greg was a relative unknown—it was his costume for the school Halloween dance that year that really brought him his fame. Greg, like Fetch, was a big guy, a big guy who made the unfortunate mistake of going to the dance with a homemade costume.

Greg had taken pounds of chocolate-covered Whoppers and glued them all over his body. The adhesive balls of chocolate and a pair of short shorts were the only two elements making up his Mole Man costume. Greg had thought his idea was a stroke of highly creative genius; unfortunately, the dance chaperones experienced strokes of a far different kind.

Greg's big white body had moles enough as it was, and here he had amplified his dot-to-dot condition by permanently applying Whoppers.

I will never forget the image.

Greg, standing there in the doorway, the chaperones barking about his uncovered body, and the warm October night sending his costume downward like brown rain on a glass window. Mindy thought it was the funniest thing she had ever witnessed. I didn't have the heart to tell Mindy that her hobo costume was in my mind equally stupid.

The chaperones refused to let Greg into the dance—way too much skin. So Greg had to call his parents and ask them to come pick him up. He then stood outside the school auditorium waiting. Well, the Whoppers melted quickly, covering his body in a dark fog that brought about a sticky, spotchy modesty. Eventually Greg re-petitioned the powers that be, asking to be let into the dance now that most of his body was completely covered. A brief huddle, a few stern words, and Greg was in. Of course no one wanted to dance with him, considering the condition he was in, so he just sat in the corner drinking punch and occasionally licking himself. Last I had heard Greg was delivering mail someplace outside of Phoenix.

Now here Fetch was, reminding me of Greg. Fetch had the

195

same body and the same height. The only difference was the substitution of a hard scowl for a dazed expression. Fetch walked about as if the entire population hated him. I couldn't speak for the citizens of the world, but my first impression was not one of being positively impressed.

I choked down my hot dog and then ate a few bites of chili. Angela kept leaning on me or touching my arm. Her touch became annoying, like sandpaper on a sunburn. Once she even wiped my face for me.

"Angela," I said, pushing her back.

"I'm just trying to help," she huffed.

Fetch walked back in the room and halfheartedly refilled our water glasses. I drank as if I were actually thirsty.

Angela, sensing that the night was turning out to be far from magical, stood up and took my hand. She was ready to propel this evening forward.

"Close your eyes and open your hands."

"Angela," I whined.

"Close your eyes and open your hands," she demanded through gritted teeth.

I closed, I opened.

I felt something being placed in the palms of my hands.

"You can open."

There was a small piece of paper with instructions written on it.

"I am round, but I can help you go straight."

I wanted to cry. I wanted to demand that this nonsense cease and I be taken home. I didn't want to go on some sort of dating treasure hunt. I had dated before, and I knew from experience that the process rarely produced treasure of any sort. Insecurities and complex emotional problems were the fruit which this ritual bore. Now here things were, blossoming like a stinkweed in the dry desert.

"Angela," I complained.

The Miracle of Forgetness

She didn't take note of my discomfort; she was too busy acting as if she were trying to figure out the clue she herself had
written.

"I am round, hummm. That's a tough one."

She was right there.

"Wheels are round," she exclaimed, deciphering the code she
had concocted and pulling me outside.

I thought about Rivers as Angela dragged me through her
sadistic, getting-to-know-each-other maze. It wasn't a scavenger
hunt per se, but I was feeling plenty picked over. Certainly Rivers
was above this sort of thing. You would never catch Rivers creatively ruining our relationship. Sure she advertised herself in the
ward bulletin, but I could tell from our letters and phone call that
she was wonderfully void of the embarrassing creative date gene.
I was suddenly overwhelmed by anti-dating feelings. I would
gladly get married according to President Gram's timetable if it
meant that all uncomfortable mixing and matching would cease.
The problem was that I had to date to find the right one.

Shoot.

I just wanted that right person to pull up to my life with
everything she owned, we would mesh, and dating would be
done with. Signed, sealed, and delivered from the ugly possibility of having to spend weeks discovering there were just enough
things wrong with us to make us too scared to give it a go.

The second clue was taped to the steering wheel of the car.
The third to the back of the couch inside. The forth was cleverly buried outside next to the steps. The fifth was in a plastic bag
at the bottom of the pot of chili. It read,

"Let's face it, without me things would be pretty quiet."

Angela had really been the only one participating in this activity. She had pushed me along and tried very hard to figure out
the clues she already knew the answers to. I tried to be kind, and
at one point I even acted as if my heart were in this. But it was
just no use. I didn't want to be here, and Angela was so wrong

for me. Every second I spent with her I fell more and more in love with Rivers. I kept telling myself how absurd it was to be whipped over a girl I had not yet met in person, but I just couldn't help it. There was something embedded in the unrational part of my heart that generated a constant signal to the wishful portion of my brain, which relayed general instructions to every inch of my soul, commanding me to shiver and float like a small piece of Styrofoam on a large trembling sea. Rivers drove me wild.

Thoughts of my watery love were temporarily pooled.

"You're not guessing, Gray," Angela complained. "Let's face it, without me things would be pretty quiet." She repeated the clue as we sat together on the couch.

"Horns?" I guessed.

"Horns?" she bit. "That's not a good guess. Let's face it, FACE it," she said, growing ever more impatient with my lack of sincere participation. "Let's face it, without me things would be pretty quiet."

I agreed with that.

"Noise," I lamely guessed.

Angela threw her arms up. "Mouths," she complained. "Mouths. Let's face, as in face with a mouth. How could your face speak without a mouth?"

"It couldn't," I answered.

"Exactly," she huffed.

I could see Fetch through the doorway. He too was growing impatient with how I was handling this night his sister had put together. I decided to try harder.

"So which mouth?" I asked.

The next thing I knew Angela had her lips tightly pressed against mine, her recently flailing arms now wrapped neatly around my shoulders like a heavy wool sweater that you were embarrassed to be wearing.

I pushed her away.

Angela grrred and then tried again. Again I pushed. She flopped back into her corner of the couch steaming.

"I'm sorry," I said. "I just can't."

"What, are you a Mormon?" she sneered.

"Yeah," I replied, wondering what that had to do with anything.

"You're Mormon?" she asked again, this time a little more nervously.

I could see her look over my shoulder at Fetch. Her face was now pale, and her eyes clearly gave away the fact that something bad was about to happen. I turned to see what Fetch could possibly be doing, but before I could see anything my hat was knocked off, the bag was back on my head, and I was being dragged back out to the car. I could hear Angela saying, "I didn't know," over and over again. Obviously being Mormon meant *something* to Fetch.

Fetch was far less kind to me on the return trip home. He kept screaming at Angela for being so stupid and then screaming at me for being Mormon. Apparently Fetch didn't like Latter-day Saints. I could literally hear him fuming as steam from his hostile personality made the air inside the car stale and hard to breathe. What seemed like three hours later we skidded to a stop, Fetch pulled me out of the car, threw me to the ground, threatened to beat the life out of me if he ever saw me again, got back into his car, and sped off. I could hear Angela scream, "I'll work things out, Gray," right before Fetch slammed the door.

I pulled the bag off my head to discover that I was sitting just outside my home. I walked around the house and up to my tree. It was very late, and Forget was forgotten, asleep, turned off like an old lamp that had hours ago been yellow with life but now sat dark and lightless. I was certain that Stick had been asleep for hours. Morning wasn't to terribly far away. I was comforted by the fact he had been so concerned about my absence that he had taken it upon himself to go to bed.

I chastised myself for not telling Angela I was a Mormon sooner. This whole night could have been avoided had I just been a better missionary. I went inside and put myself to sleep, uncertain over just about everything.

Chapter Twenty-seven

Hog Wild

The next morning Stick and I were awakened by the sound of glass shattering. Kitty had thrown a brick through one panel of my big bedroom window. I suspected that it was Kitty who called all day long now but only cackled when we would pick up the phone. And late Wednesday afternoon someone released a potato sack full of desert snakes into our backyard.

Kitty had found someplace to focus her ugliness and gone hog wild. I couldn't understand why she felt such a need to hate me. I wanted to go to the police and have her restrained. But Stick informed me that the Bluelake chief of police was a distant relative of Kitty's, and he didn't have the guts to take any action against her. Apparently he preferred to have as little contact with her as possible. Bob dropped by that afternoon and promised he would keep an eye on Kitty for me, seeing how the local law was of no help.

I felt so safe.

Bob also helped me chase snakes out of the backyard. It was an exercise in futility. Bob kept hitting my ankles with the golf club he was supposedly using to fight off serpents. Most of the snakes found holes near the fence or beneath my tree to slither off into.

After the snake hunt I went to work cleaning up the broken

glass from the window Kitty had destroyed. I had let it sit all day, hoping it would magically take care of itself.

It hadn't.

I had phoned President Gram earlier and asked him if he would come out and do the repair. He told me he would send someone tomorrow and then questioned me further on my possible calling.

"Have you given things a thought?" he had asked me.

"Yes," I said. "I'm thinking of moving away just so I can get out of this bishop calling."

"That's not an option," he had told me, sounding like the dad I no longer had.

"What are my options?" I pleaded.

"You've got less than two weeks."

"I've got this parade coming up, and the UFO stuff," I listed. "I don't have time to be thinking about this."

"I'll call you Friday," was all he said.

Bob was upset I had even called President Gram at all. Apparently Bob was capable of replacing windows. He had a friend who could get glass cheap, and Bob was more than willing to do the labor. He also didn't particularly care for President Filo Gram. The reason Bob had bad feelings towards him was because President Gram didn't care much for Longwinded.

The Sterling Stake covered a huge territory. It had all of Sterling, the Bluelake Ward, and the Longwinded Branch. Bob informed me that after one little incident in Longwinded years ago President Gram had refused to ever come back.

"Some people have no tolerance for life," Bob said.

According to Bob, when President Gram was first put in as stake president he was determined to make Longwinded his pet project. He went out every couple of weeks, consistently trying to mold the people into who he believed they should be.

The members quickly got tired of him pointing out their weaknesses and faults. They considered themselves just fine as they were. They certainly didn't need some city person telling them how to run their lives. Well, just as emotions and feelings were coming to a boiling point, in came President Gram with yet another solution.

He felt that the members of Longwinded would really embrace him if he could provide them with a chapel. Longwinded had never had one, and this had always been a disappointment and a source of discouragement to the members. Well, there was no way that the Church at that time was going to build a real building in Longwinded—too few members. So, President Gram was forced to find another way.

Things looked hopeless.

Then one day while servicing a glass client of his he saw a home made entirely out of tires. President Gram was thrilled. It just so happened that his brother owned a tire dumping lot in the next state.

Voila. Free materials.

Well, without telling the members, President Gram used his own money to buy a worthless piece of land about five miles outside of Longwinded. He then had his brother truck in enough tires to build a right nice chapel.

When the members discovered what he was doing they were livid. No one wanted to attend church in a discarded tire chapel. These people had their pride. They refused to help with such a stupid, ridiculous, degrading idea. But, like the little red hen, President Gram pressed forward with the work, confident that once the chapel was complete the members would all change their minds. After all, who in their right minds would be able to deny the beauty of a building made out of Goodyears? President Filo Gram's problem was thinking he was dealing with folks in their right minds.

For a week he came up every night and single-handedly began stacking and filling tires. Well, just as he got the second wall up the entire structure collapsed on him, trapping him under pounds of rubber and dirt. Since no one had been helping, no one saw it happen. President Gram spent an entire night under those tires. He probably would have been trapped under there for years if it hadn't been for a couple of local kids who saw the tire mound and started shooting at it with their BB guns. It didn't take long for one of them to hit President Gram. Once discovered, they quickly dug him out.

Except for a rather large BB welt on his left leg President Gram was no worse for wear. Unfortunately his state of mind hadn't fared as well as his mortal coil. And when he told the Saints what had happened he received zero sympathy from any of them. The only response he got was the Longwinded zero-tact-at-all choir singing a few choruses of I told you so's.

That was it. Enough was enough.

President Gram vowed never to return to Longwinded. The huge pile of tires still sat there. It had turned into sort of a unofficial city park. A lot of local kids spent their weekends climbing and jumping on what was once going to be the Longwinded LDS chapel.

"So he never visits Longwinded?" I asked.

"Never," Bob replied. "He sends a representative."

"Is it really possible to build a house out of tires anyway?" I asked skeptically.

"Sure," Bob said. "Hyrum Whittle over in Buttercrest has a beautiful tire home."

Bob and I cleaned up the broken glass and covered the open window with a thin piece of cardboard. I promised Bob I would cancel my glass appointment with President Gram and let him do the repair. Bob whistled for ten minutes straight, happy he had gotten the bid.

I had a Bluelake Parade meeting to attend that evening at Mable Bleat's house, so I left Bob at my house and headed to town. When I returned home the store was closed and Stick was in my house talking to Bob. Moments before I had arrived Kitty had driven by and egged the front of our house. Stick was outraged by her act. Bob was outraged at the waste of good eggs.

"I say we go out to her place and soap her car windows," Stick roared.

He was quite the deviant.

"I could turn my back," Bob said, giving us the illegal go ahead.

"We can't do anything," I reasoned.

"Vengeance is fine, so saith the Lord," Stick raged, quoting his version of scripture.

"Vengeance is *mine*," I corrected.

"Is that true?" Stick asked Bob.

"I'm a cop not a preacher," Bob answered.

"It's true," I persisted.

"Well, that changes a few things," Stick said to himself, contemplating the lifestyle shift he would now have to make.

As the three of us sat around my table talking about Kitty, the parade, and scriptures, I suddenly had the strongest impression that I should fly to California and see Rivers. It probably was the fact that I was sitting around a table discussing things like vengeance and parades with two considerably older men that caused my brain to seek the higher thought. I brought the idea up for discussion.

"I'd fly anywhere to go see Jenny," Stick said.

"Why don't you then?" I asked.

"I have no idea where she is," he said. "Besides we might overlap in the air. I'd hate to miss her coming to see me."

"You're talking to the wrong people," Bob said. "Stick and I know nothing about successfully seeing women. We're the bad example."

"Well, did either of you chase after your woman?"

"I flew to Washington," Bob said.

"I just waited," Stick threw in.

"So either way, I lose."

"I waited too long to fly out," Bob lamented.

"And I've just plain waited too long," Stick said.

We sat there in silence while each of us mourned the women none of us had.

"I'm actually happier single," Bob finally said, and not very convincingly.

I spent the rest of the night pricing airplane tickets over the phone. I was going to see Rivers.

Chapter Twenty-eight

Love Is a Really Ragged River

I couldn't believe I was going to do this. Rivers would probably think I was so obsessive she'd never speak to me again. It was a chance I looked willing to take. I had bought myself a one-way ticket to Sacramento, leaving early Friday morning. I figured once I was there I could see how things went between Rivers and me and then buy myself a return ticket home when necessary. Plus, this arrangement would put me in California when Friday rolled around. I would be with Rivers and miss Angela if she did come by. I would also miss the stake president's call. He would then deem me unreliable and move on to finding a different bishop.

Three birds, one stone.

I decided not to tell Rivers I was coming. I needed the element of surprise on this one. I couldn't remember having this much anticipation over anything for quite some time.

Then Thursday afternoon I received another letter from Rivers. It was a great letter, with well-penned thoughts and filled with hope regarding the two of us. But the letter was overshadowed by the picture that had been enclosed with it.

I hadn't given Rivers' physical appearance too much thought. The gentleman who had originally given me the flyer had said she was cute. Plus, she was waiting for a missionary, so obviously others saw her as someone fit to pursue. Besides, I wasn't looking for perfect looks, just the perfect person—and Rivers felt perfect. She had a great phone voice, and the person she presented herself as in word was wonderful.

The picture she sent, however, was awful.

There was just no other way to say it. I didn't even want to think the things I was now thinking, but I was. Sure, I hadn't been looking for perfection, but I also wasn't in the market for the furthest thing from perfection there was. I think that in the course of my lifetime I had only met or seen maybe four other people who were less appealing than the picture I was now holding.

I was heartbroken.

She was everything I had thought she wasn't. Every preconceived image I had of her was shattered like hard candy on sore teeth. I couldn't believe this elder she was waiting for had asked her to marry him. And I really couldn't believe she had not said yes to him instantly. No offense to Rivers, but even an extra sweet spirit couldn't make the dish I saw in front of me edible.

I was sick.

I searched the picture for something I could like—I wanted so badly to be attracted to her. Her eyebrows weren't bad, and the top half of her left ear was not totally offensive.

I was doomed.

I couldn't believe my heart had felt so much for Rivers, and now that she had, in a sense, materialized, my entire body was looking to reject her like it would a wicked flu.

I was suddenly reminded of flying.

I couldn't go see her now. What would I say? How could I possibly disguise my self-centered, shallow, unfeeling feelings? How could I look her in the face and tell her I felt absolutely nothing for her? How could I look her in the face? Inspiration had sent me hurtling down a one-way road in the wrong direction. And fate had placed me in a Pinto with no seat belts, no airbags, and a full tank of gas. Planets were colliding.

I looked at the picture again.

Ugg.

I read the letter.

Oh.

I looked at the ticket I had picked up from the Bluelake Travel Agency just hours before.

Non-refundable.

Big deal. Rivers didn't know I was coming. I could just tear up the ticket and write Rivers, telling her how impressed I felt that she marry Elder Higgins. I would be out a couple hundred bucks, but that seemed less painful than having to go and have a face-to-face with her.

I went outside and climbed to the top of my tree. I could see that the store was busy and life was moving and circling like it always had. How was this possible? How could people be filling up their cars with gas and buying beef jerky at a time like this? Hadn't people noticed the dejected, self-loathing twenty-four-year-old up in the tree? Where was the sympathy?

I sat up there for an hour, looking at the picture and willing myself to fall in love with this person. When I finally climbed down, the only burning desire I had was to call the whole trip off. It would be unfair to both of us to take this relationship any further. I was sure she was a great person, but I had to be honest with myself. Didn't I? Why did I feel so rotten about telling myself the truth.

I couldn't see beyond the picture. I felt as if I lacked vision.

I had even tried to picture her as a celestial goddess in the next world. It was no use. Besides, the kingdom I would end up in probably didn't allow for relationships.

I went to the store to see how Ned and Stick were doing and to possibly drown my sorrows in a liter of Sprite. (I had gone Pepsi-free for almost two days now.) I would have been proud of myself if I hadn't been so sickened by my shallowness.

Stick was ringing up a customer, and Ned was out at the pumps washing a woman's windshield.

I slumped down next to Stick behind the counter. Once he

was finished with his customer he turned to me and asked, "What time do you leave tomorrow?"

"I'm not going," I informed him.

"Why not?"

"I've got my reasons," I said.

Stick tisked. "I guess you can always wait around here for her to come to you."

"She'll never come."

Ned came in the store and asked me the same question.

"He's not going," Stick answered for me.

"That's a pity," Ned replied. "I was hoping you could bring me back a couple of west coast rocks."

"Sorry," I said.

"What about Rivers?" Ned asked.

"It's over."

"Boy, it'd be a shame to end things without ever meeting. People are different than letters," Stick said.

That was the truth.

I longed for the Rivers I knew only hours ago. The one with no picture.

"You should go," said Ned. "You can't just never meet her."

He was right. I couldn't just break off our relationship without a so much as a handshake. We had known each other for only a short while, but she had left an indelible mark on my soul. At the very least I had to meet her. Maybe the picture didn't do her justice. Maybe she had been snapped on a bad day.

Maybe this was the kindest picture ever taken of her and reality was even harsher.

"California's nice this time of year," Ned commented.

I went home, packed my bag, and went to bed around eight. I had an early fight to catch tomorrow. My gut was giving me grief, and my mind refused to be talked out of this trip. Apparently I couldn't just let this go.

Chapter Twenty-nine

Seep, Drip, Trickle, Flow

Life was playing with me. I had endured a plane ride with more turbulence than a rough marriage, a rental car clerk with customer service skills so dull he couldn't cut through soft water, and now I was lost. Who knew Sacramento was so big? I missed Forget already. Whose idea was it to stick so many people this close together? Memories of Phoenix and all that I had happily left behind came rushing back to me.

I had decided to get the Rivers part of my trip over first. I would find her, find out, and move on. Then I could do a little sight-seeing, maybe drive out to the beach and spend some time lounging on sand.

I had not looked at Rivers' picture since last night. I was hoping my mind would conjure up other images and trick me into thinking she looked different than she actually did. I was praying that the power of positive thought might have the strength to change bone structure and skin tone, or at least change my eyes so that I could see past the physical. Because despite what the picture told me, I was still in love with the girl I had grown to know in the letters.

None of that mattered right now anyway—I was lost.

I got off one freeway, onto another, and off that one and into a really bad neighborhood.

I was reminded of my mother.

Once when I was about fifteen my mom took me downtown to try to find a particular pair of shoes she needed. Well, Mom made a couple of wrong turns and we ended up in a neighborhood that was less than desirable. She foolishly stopped the car and asked a couple of the rough looking kids for directions. Well, these kids were a little bit upset about having their drug negotiations interrupted so some woman could find the right color pumps. They threatened to kill us, broke out our back window with a rock, and hollered obscenities so absurd I still remembered them.

Once my mother and I were out of harm's way I began bad mouthing the ruffians and commenting on the fact that our city was going to pot. Mom immediately jumped all over me, sticking up for the drug dealers and giving me a scorching lecture on judging others.

"Maybe one of them had just lost his mother," she had argued.

I missed my lost mother.

It was funny, because on the other hand my mom had seen evil in the oddest things. She used to put up a fuss when I went to see any movie with a worse rating than a straight PG. She thought things like white flour and salt were sinister. She never wore anything that showed her knees for fear of appearing immoral and wicked. But a drunken wino could be standing in front of his dilapidated crack house and she wouldn't think twice about asking to use his phone.

I really missed her.

I was really lost.

I thought about just scrapping the whole Rivers idea. If I had nowhere in particular to go right now then I wouldn't actually be lost. I could just drive until I came to the west end of our country, lie on the beach for a few days, and then go home tan and rested. Certainly the warm rays of the California sun would be sufficient and company enough.

The Miracle of Forgetness

Who was I kidding? I had come too far to not at least take a peek at Rivers. I stopped and studied my map for a few minutes. Almost an hour later, and after stopping twice to ask directions from strangers, I found Rivers' address. I pulled in front of a house two doors down from hers and tried to collect my thoughts. I checked my appearance in the rearview mirror.

I was no Rivers.

I got out of my rental car and approached her house. It looked as if Rivers had a nice home. It was a one-story ranch style house with gravel rocks substituted for a front lawn and a brick walkway. There were a couple of cars in the carport and two small palm trees standing casually next to the road at the origin of their walkway. I walked up the sidewalk and rang the doorbell. I tried to settle the butterflies in my stomach by gulping in air. I was hoping the extra oxygen might make them mellow. No such luck. They fluttered like clothes on a Chicago clothesline.

A nice looking older woman answered the door. I assumed it was Rivers' mother. She was tall and had hair that looked as if it was molded, not brushed. Her wide green eyes gave me a once over. I was so nervous now, I could barely get the request out.

"Is Rivers at home?"

"Just a minute," she said, inviting me in.

I closed the front door and stood waiting alone in the front hall. Eventually a tall girl with beautiful hair and a nice smile approached me. I assumed she wanted to know what I was doing in her home.

"I'm here waiting for Rivers," I announced, explaining my presence.

"I'm Rivers," she announced back.

I looked at her sideways.

I looked at her right ways.

What was this? Some kind of sick joke. This girl was gorgeous. Her brown hair was so dark it was almost black, and her blue eyes were so ensnaring I couldn't pick up my feet to move away. Her skin glowed like warm sand on private beach, and God had colored this girl with his best crayons. She was perfectly drawn, all within the lines, and not a single muted shade. Where was my Rivers?

"I think there must be some kind of mistake," I said, fumbling through my wallet, looking for the picture I had. "I'm looking for this Rivers," I said, handing her the infamous photo.

This girl took the picture and looked at it. She then began to laugh.

"This is my cousin Candice, right after her car accident two years ago."

"What?" I asked, still not comprehending what was going on.

"I'm Rivers," she said.

"You... Rivers...," I stuttered.

"Me, Rivers," she laughed.

My knees went weak. Each and every one of my bones slipped out of their joints and hung there by ligaments. It was a miracle I remained standing. My eyes dilated so rapidly I began to see spots and streaks across everything in my view. The heavens were falling into my lap.

"I'm Gray," I managed to inform her.

"You're Gray?" Rivers said with amazement.

"I am."

"What are you doing here?"

"I came to see you," I replied.

She smiled a huge smile.

"Where did you get this picture?" she asked.

"You sent it to me."

"I never sent you this," she said, laughing. "I bet my brother Milo had something to do with this. He must have slipped it in before he mailed it for me. Milo's not too happy I'm writing someone besides... besides..."

"Elder Higgins," I helped.

The Great Wall fell. The pyramids crumbled. The continents scrolled together and then broke off into small, handsize chunks. All birds everywhere forgot how to fly, and gravity became confused as to just what its role was. The great Nile flowed wild, dammed only by the huge joy I now felt.

The Miracle of Forgetness

She had temporarily forgotten his name.

Like Joseph Smith when he was finally handed the gold plates, I, too, now knew there was more to this than I could have ever imagined. Rivers was the final mile marker after a long and grueling trip; she was the first taste of sugar following a lifetime of nothing but salt. Her presence was an open window on a hot summer day, and her smile was nuclear, causing my very core to melt down.

We sat on Rivers' front porch and talked for hours. Rivers was amazed I had even bothered coming after the girl in the picture. She was also, and I say this with complete humility (well, at least partial humility), Rivers was surprised I was put together so nicely. To her my shoulders went perfectly with the eyes. She had assumed I was more a male version of her banged up cousin Candice. After all, what kind of guy responds to a sacrament bulletin? My ego puffed up, pushing out the wrinkles Mindy had once inflicted and lifting me inches off the ground.

It was the best night of my entire life. There was not one thing she said that I didn't completely care about. We both had to fight not to move closer to one another while sitting on the couch. At one glorious point my left foot bumped against her left knee. It was incredible. There was definitely more to us than we had both dared hope.

I talked extensively of Forget, and I didn't embellish a single thing. I told her about Bob and Stick and Kitty. I told her about the UFO and the Bluelake Ward. I told her about my tree and about the rug girl.

Rivers was so funny, kind, and beautiful that the creation of the world now seemed simple. And the make up of the rocks and soil paled in comparison to the introduction of water. I marveled at the fact that days ago I hadn't even realized I was thirsty. She was the twelve inches of rain my parched heart had been in need of.

Love is a River.

It was eleven-thirty at night before we separated. I could hardly wait until morning when the sun would once again circle back around and illuminate the better part of this planet.

Chapter Thirty

Ships Passing in the Chapel

I have read about and witnessed many miracles in my life. Parted seas, water to wine, and the time when I was eleven and Luke Winchester caught a fly ball with his forehead during one of our little league games—softest skull I've ever seen. That particular miracle had left a lasting impressing on both our minds. But now I was witnessing a resurrection-type miracle. Yes, my future was rising from the dead. In the four days I had spent in California I was able to successfully talk Rivers into coming back with me to Forget, for a visit. She could come see the Bluelake Parade and Fair. She had said yes almost instantly. She wasn't going to school at the moment, nor was she working. So she was happy for a reprieve from the everyday norm. I figured the fair and parade would be adequately distant from any norm.

The four days in California had been great. Rivers and I had seen and done just about everything there was to do. She had shown me the sights, and I had barely noticed them due to her presence.

On Saturday she had received a letter from her elder. And on Sunday morning when I came to pick her up for church, the letter still sat unopened on the kitchen table. This was a good sign.

During sacrament meeting her ward had the Melchizedek Priesthood pass the sacrament, and I was assigned to her row.

Her hand touched mine as I gave her the bread tray. I blushed like a deacon in love. When I handed her the water tray the concept of eternity made perfect sense, and I had to walk slowly back down the aisle due to light headedness.

When I was done passing and returned to her, she held my hand and sort of leaned against me. I suffered through three leg cramps and a sleeping arm because I didn't want to move an inch and ruin the moment. Sacrament meeting had never been so fulfilling.

The talks given in Rivers' ward seemed to make more sense than the few I had heard in Bluelake. I started to feel bad about how different our ward was, but then the concluding speaker started to go on and on about how Satan lives in vinyl, leather, and occasionally busy fabrics like plaid. I was comforted. The Church really was the same the world over.

In the beginning, Rivers' parents had been a little leery of me. But once her mother found out that my genealogy, for the most part, was completely done they embraced me at an arm's distance.

"Straight teeth and good hair mean nothing if their genealogy isn't done," Rivers' mom had told her in front of me. "I'd rather date a boy with bad posture and a thick book of remembrance than the other way around."

"Who wouldn't," Rivers had joked.

I stood up straight and said a silent prayer, thanking God for a mother who had done more than her share of genealogy in her lifetime. I was acceptable to Rivers' parents because of my mom's passion for filling out family group sheets and pedigree charts. Kindred dead.

Rivers and I flew into Sterling and then drove to Forget in my car. Every time I looked over at her in the passenger's seat I wanted to shout for joy. I couldn't believe she was here with me. The flat valley was taking shape.

Once outside of Sterling, Rivers began to comment on the great nothingness of it all.

"Where is everything?" she asked.

"This is it."

"No Wal-Mart, no McDonald's, no movie theater with seventeen screens?"

"This is it," I replied again.

"It's kind of nice," Rivers sighed.

It was a gross understatement.

We drove directly to Forget. I took Rivers into the store and introduced her to Stick and Ned. As usual Stick had lots to say.

"She's tall," he said as if she weren't there.

Rivers was tall. She was only about six inches shorter than I.

"She seems a little too modern for you," Stick observed, commenting on Rivers' clothes and style.

"You're pretty perceptive," Rivers said nicely.

Stick turned red. "Well, I am a retailer," he commented. "We sort of have to have a head for these things."

"I can see why you're so successful," Rivers said sweetly.

Stick was eating it up.

"I take great pride in my work," he beamed.

Stick showed Rivers around the store while Ned and I ran the counter. It wasn't often that Stick would allow someone other than himself to actually cash people out. But he was so intent on giving Rivers a tour of the place that he didn't seem to care what Ned and I were doing. It occurred to me that I had never really seen Stick interact with anyone female besides Kitty and his customers. It was nice to see him happy.

Stick even took Rivers outside and showed her around the pumps. Through the window I watched him take one of the gas pumps out of its cradle and fill up an imaginary car. He was showing Rivers precisely how to best hold the handle.

When the two of them came back in, Rivers had her arm locked with Stick's and Stick was looking as proud as if he had just been knighted sir-worth-a-lot.

Who was this girl?

I had never seen or met anyone quite like her. She was so beautiful one would expect her to be nothing but cold toward us little people. Yet she acted as if she was fortunate to know us. She was amazing and so alive that energy spilled from her blue eyes and practically drowned all those lucky enough to be standing in the course of the runoff.

I gasped for air.

Mom and Dad had to have a hand in this.

I finally pulled Rivers away from Stick and took her to see my home. I had always liked my place, but now with the light that she shed everything looked ten years older and more outdated than it actually was. I started to make excuses for my less than spectacular castle.

"I've got plans to change everything," I explained.

Rivers put her arm through mine.

I took her out to look at my orange painted tree. She was appropriately impressed by it. We climbed to the top and sat down on the piece of plywood I had nailed up. There wasn't much room so we really had to squeeze together. Nature was very accommodating.

"What a great place," Rivers said leaning even closer to me than the tree was forcing her to do.

"The mountains look closer from up here," I observed. It was a rather stupid observation. I would have kicked myself if I hadn't been afraid of losing my balance in the process.

"I could live here," she sighed.

"What is it with you?" I asked.

"What do you mean?" Rivers asked back.

"I've never met anyone as kind as you," I said, confused. "But what would the kindest, most ideal person be doing sitting here by me? In a tree," I added.

"Wondering what comes next," she smiled.

That was my cue. If ever the truth had been made manifest unto me, it was now. Rivers was ready to shift from casual to serious. It was time for me to kiss her.

I suppressed every nervous twinge in my body and leaned over. The mood was right, the place was right, the moment was right...I was wrong. Rivers pulled away.

She pulled away!

I tried to make it look like it was no big deal.

I nervously clapped my hands. I patted her on the knee as if she were my granddaughter. I picked off a leaf from one of the branches and tore it in half. She loves me, she loves me not. I tossed the leaf and watched the two halves flutter to the ground.

What had happened? The spell had been broken.

"Rivers..." I started to say.

"Gray," she interrupted. "I'm supposed to be waiting for my missionary."

Oh, this was just great. I could think of no finer moment for her to point out what I already knew. I guess she considered she and I just to be good friends. Two pals hanging out in a tree waiting for someone to walk by so we could spit on them. She was waiting for her love while playing with me.

"Hey, Rivers, want to come up in my tree fort?"

"Sure, Gray, but I get to be the mommy."

I had tried desperately not to read too much into all of this. But after the time we had spent together in California, and with her so willing to come out to Forget, my hopes were having a hard time remaining sufficiently suppressed. The short time I had known her seemed longer than the entire span of my life. From her first letter to her present pout, I had received nothing but confirmations that we were meant to be together. And now here we were, Gray and Rivers sitting in a tree, not K-I-S-S-I-N-G.

I wanted to get mad.

I wanted to storm down from this tree and blame her for pretending to like me.

I couldn't.

Rivers was one of the best things that had ever almost happened to me. Just to have known her would be reason enough for men to fight lions and scale walls. Just to have sat by her, alone in a tree, was reward enough to please even the greediest of love pirates. I should be content.

I wasn't. I imagined Elder Higgins and hoped he was having a tough time on his mission right now.

Wind brushed though the tree and painted both Rivers and me confused.

"I'm supposed to be waiting," she said, breaking the silence.

"So, do you mind if I wait with you?" I asked, half-joking.

Rivers gazed at me. I wiped my face with my hand, thinking there must be something on it that she was staring at.

Rivers blue eyes burned.

"What?" I asked self consciously.

Her pink lips curled up at the ends and parted where they were designed to. She was the most beautiful woman I had ever seen. My heart raced, and my eyes felt like they were floating around in huge sockets of saline.

"What is it?" I asked again, feeling like I couldn't properly evaluate the mood. I didn't have to remain in the dark for too long. The clouds dissipated and the sun moved into view.

Rivers advanced, and like a military fort made out of Styrofoam I collapsed under her invading presence. I had come under friendly fire. The tree swayed and dirt from the ground far below sang hymns so beautiful that only God himself could have written them.

The entire earth harmonized. And it wasn't like one of those annoying doo-wop or barbershop type harmonies; this was like every angel in heaven being in sync.

I struggled for something to hang onto as Rivers knocked me backwards. I grabbed a small branch and hung on for dear life. Death was the only thing that could have ruined the moment.

Her lips touched mine and salvation coursed through my veins. I fought to get my other hand on something. I wanted to hold Rivers and return the affection she was showing, but I was losing my balance. My feet sprang up and Rivers flew back and into one of the big branches. I should have been so lucky.

I desperately tried to grab something to stop me from falling. My backside slid off the board and my weight threw my body out of the tree. I flew through the air like a spastic octopus, hitting the ground feet first. I felt my soul give, and the last thought that went through my head was just how stupid I must look to Rivers up above.

Unfortunately it was far too late to put on a brave face.

Chapter Thirty-one

Focus on the Feet

Physically I was all right, one sore ankle and a couple scratches. Mentally, however, I now knew God did not want me kissing Rivers. I hoped the time would soon arrive when He would feel differently.

Rivers thought she had killed me. I was happy to shake it off and find her crying over my beat-up body. She helped me into my house, and then Ned took her to the hotel in Bluelake where we had made reservations for her.

She called me that night and we talked for hours.

"Sorry," she kept saying.

"It's all right," I repeatedly replied.

"I wanted to kiss you."

"I wanted to be kissed."

"I'm going to write Elder Higgins and tell him."

"I'm glad."

"I think I'm falling in love with you."

"Really?"

"It's weird."

"It's great."

"I know, but..."

"But what?"

"We barely know each other."

"So?"

The Miracle of Forgetness

"Oh, Gray."
"Oh, Rivers."
"This can't be."
"It is."
"Amazing."
"Isn't it though?"
I never knew love could be so concise.

I took Rivers to the crash site the next morning. It had been a while since I had been out to Nine Month Mound, and things were a whole lot crazier now than before. There were big crowds of people and more than a couple of vendors selling things like alien fry bread, alien trinkets, and alien T-shirts out of the backs of their cars.

The actual crash sight was completely fenced off, but I could see that people had slipped pieces of paper and little notes through the wires. I stuck my fingers though the fence and picked up a little scrap of paper that was lying near the edge. The note read...

Come back you forgot me.

Rivers thought the entire thing was comical. There was one state policeman there keeping an eye on things. We wondered over to him. He informed us that a big specialist team was coming out later in the week to determine what really had happened here.

"If this is a UFO, these folks will be able to tell," he said.
"How's that?" I asked.
"They went to school for this stuff."
"UFO school?" Rivers asked.
"Some school in Tennessee," the policeman answered, bothered by our questions.

Rivers and I walked off and went over to one of the vendors selling alien fry bread. It was sort of like regular fry bread except for...well, it was exactly like regular fry bread except it cost a few dollars more. We sat on the hood of my car eating the sweet, honey-covered bread and watching people view the site.

"So Stick saw this happen?" Rivers asked.

"He did. Bob and he were right here when whatever it was crashed down," I said.

"When do I get to meet Bob?"

"He'll blow in here soon."

Rivers took a great big bite of her bread. Honey dripped from her lips. God was testing me.

"Did I ever show you my souvenir?" I asked, reaching into my pocket to retrieve my crash sight memorabilia and knowing full well I never had. I handed it to Rivers.

"What is it?" she asked.

"I have no idea. I picked it up the day after the wreck. Stick thinks it's part of a giant key."

"Weird," Rivers commented. "Does anyone else have any other pieces of the crash?"

"Not that I know of," I said, swallowing the bite of bread I had in my mouth. "One guy from Buttercrest claimed to have a piece of it, but it turned out to be just a spatula he had wrapped in tin foil. There probably are a few people with some pieces, but they fenced the site off before too many people could really steal stuff."

"How come they let you keep this?" Rivers asked, handing me back my unknown object.

"They don't know I have it," I bragged.

"What are you going to do with it?" she asked.

"I think I'll give it to Bob. He's really been fascinated with it."

After we finished our fry bread we drove to Bluelake and had lunch. Alien fry bread isn't really all that filling. The entire town was pumped and ready for the big parade tomorrow morning. The parade would officially kick off the Bluelake Fair. Through the front window of the restaurant I watched two tough looking men fix a pothole. Excitement and the smell of burning tar were in the air.

The Miracle of Forgetness

Rivers seemed to genuinely like Bluelake. She kept talking about how this was the kind of city she could settle down in. I kept feeling she was being a little too accommodating to my dreams. I couldn't believe that I had existed for twenty-four years without her.

After lunch we drove to the actual blue lake. Rivers and I swam for hours and then spent some time walking along the shore. She had great feet. The rest of her was great as well, but I tried to keep my mind focused mainly on her feet. It was safer that way. We hung around the lake until the sun was gone.

When I dropped her off at her hotel, her hair was still wet, and her face was brown from the sun.

"Big day tomorrow," I said.

"Nothing like a parade," she joked.

Rivers stood there waiting for me to kiss her. I couldn't do it. Sure I could have done it. There was nothing I would rather have done at the moment. But the last time her lips had touched mine I fell fifteen feet. I figured those looking out for me on the other side would let me know when the time was right. I prayed they would hurry and let me know that the time was right now.

Nope.

Rivers slipped into her room and I headed out. I had a parade to prepare for.

Chapter Thirty-two

Parade of Fools

The morning had arrived. Parade day. Both Stick and I got up extra early so as to have enough time to accomplish our parade day schedules. Stick opened the store, and I headed into Bluelake to pick up Rivers and help the Saints get their float moving.

After I got Rivers, we headed over to the church. A few members were there milling around our temple float. No one really knew what to do next. A fight broke out among two members who both felt that they personally would make the best person to pull the float through town. Finally after a nice round of heated words they decided to draw straws. Sister Buswidth had a fit. She started in on how drawing straws was form of gambling.

"So is life," Brother Scatty snarled.

Sister Buswidth withdrew to go and pray for their souls.

Jonathan Call found a couple of rough sticks on the ground and put them in his hand. He then asked Wendell Scatty to draw. Brother Scatty pulled one of the sticks out of Jonathan Call's hand so fast that it left a trail of splinters in poor Brother Call's paw. Wendell found this to be a small satisfaction; Brother Call had won. The temple would be toted by his automobile. With wounded hand Brother Call triumphantly attached the float to his vehicle.

The Miracle of Forgetness

No one was excited. This whole parade was nothing but a huge reminder of how bad off the ward was without Bishop Withers. Sister Selma Withers had left town to go and spend some time with her sister in Utah. She was not handling the desertion by her husband well. Everyone kept waiting for Bishop Withers to show up and apologize for his absence. Of course, each day he was gone seemed to lessen the possibility of that happening.

Tom walked around the parking lot looking as if the entire weight of the world were on his shoulders. He didn't smile and only spoke in short, mumbled sentences. Sister Lark had gone into hiding, vowing she wouldn't come out until she got some respect. I didn't expect to see her soon. Sister Gent, the ward bulletin lady, was still running around acting as if she were in charge. Things had really gone from bad to rotten.

Now here we were, having to pull our float with the misspelled saying on it through town and act as if everything were all right. Look at the Mormons, happy, smiling, and falling apart at the seams.

Brother Call started up his car and slowly pulled the float out of the parking lot and into the street. The rest of the members got into their cars and followed him to the start of the parade route.

Main Street Bluelake was bustling. It looked as if every business in town had put together a float for the parade. Somewhere some crepe paper makers were rolling in it. People were pushing and honking and demanding that they get their rightful place in the supreme float order. All the Mormons jumped out of their cars and swarmed onto the temple float. Bishop Withers had asked us to dress up as pioneers so as to represent our pioneer heritage. Well, Bishop Withers was gone, and most members were wearing shorts and T-shirts. A few people had neckerchiefs on, and little Lindy had an ankle-length dress on with her hair done up in braids.

The members started arguing about who got to sit where on the float. Enis McCaffy got pushed off by one of the impatient thirteen-year-old girls.

The pioneer spirit was alive and well with us.

Rivers and I decided to skip being on the temple float altogether. We went down route a bit and set up our lawn chairs. The parade would make it to us eventually. Finally we heard a gun go off and could see the entrants beginning to move. The Bluelake Parade was coming.

I hoped I would survive.

I wasn't big on parades. One of my earliest childhood memories was of a parade I had seen in Phoenix. I was only eight, but I remember vividly just how hot it was and how my father forced me sit on his shoulders as he stood. He wanted me to see everything. Even now I could still smell his Head and Shoulders shampoo and remember the embarrassment I felt at being so old and being made to sit on my dad's shoulders.

I wanted desperately to get down, but Dad insisted I stay up there so I could see things better. This line of reasoning did nothing for an eight-year-old. For one thing I felt I was tall enough to see the sights on my own two feet. And for another thing I knew there was nothing I wanted to see anyway. The only thing that did catch my attention was the local grade-school bully, Timmy Knollmiller, coming my way with a couple of his friends. I knew that if he spotted me on my dad, I was a dead man.

I scratched at my dad's ears, but he refused to let me down. I pulled his hair. He pinched my ankles. It was hopeless. Luckily one of the parade floats caught fire and Dad had to let me down so we could run for our lives. Yes, the image of a parade was not one I particularly cherished.

Now here I was joining the good folks of Bluelake by lining Main Street and patiently waiting for the parade to pass us by. I looked at Rivers. Somehow this parade seemed better than any I had ever attended.

Finally the first float reached us. It was shaped like a huge globe and had a plethora of screaming kids around it. I couldn't help notice that whoever had made the float had put North America in the wrong spot. It passed us slowly and was followed by a couple of kids on tricycles waving American flags and pedaling as fast as their little legs could.

Behind them was the Bluelake Police Band. A hundred grown men and women in uniform playing instruments like piccolos and triangles. They stayed in perfect sync until one of the kids on a tricycle in front of them tipped over. The kid scraped his knee and ran to the sidelines. The capable men and women of the Bluelake Police lacked sense enough just to stop. They walked right over the tricycle. Finally a large man playing the flute tripped over it and fell to the ground. Those behind him followed like domino shaped sheep.

The parade came to a temporary halt while people picked themselves up and tried to regain composure. Once it started moving again, the parade showcased a number of floats from local Bluelake businesses.

The "Pizza Platter" float had actual employees on it who tossed actual pepperoni slices at the folks watching. The "Weight Whippers" float came next. It was shaped like a big scale and had a real-life heavy woman and a real-life thin woman on it. One was "before" and one was the "after." The "Before Woman" kept snatching flying pepperoni from the Pizza Platter float and eating them.

After that came the Bluelake High School Marching Band. Right behind them was the high school drill team, "The Dancing Wasps." Neither the band nor the Wasps had their hearts in this. It sounded like each member of the band was playing a different song, and the Dancing Wasps just sort of swayed as they walked. The queen wasp did keep throwing her baton up into the air, but only once did she actually catch it.

"Impressive," I commented to Rivers.

"Unlike any parade I've ever seen," Rivers replied.

Then came our temple float. Somehow between the start of the parade and the present, it had taken a beating. The spires were bent, and there were bald spots where some of our pioneers had picked away the paper. Rivers and I tried to wave loudly to show our support. Jonathan Call waved back with his splintered hand, and the few Primary kids on the float stuck their tongues out and made noises at us.

I felt proud to be associated with them.

Right behind our float was the "United Christians Unitarian Oasis of Love" float. The people on board kept throwing things at our temple and participants. I saw an object hit Enis McCaffy in the head. Enis had been loosely strapped to our float to prevent her falling off again. After she got beaned in the head she waved and smiled. I wished we all could be more like Enis.

Little Lindy took off one of her shoes and threw it at the United Christians. They in turn bombarded the Mormon float with anything they could find to throw. Tommy Stern, one of the United Christians, had a cooler full of ice cubes, and he wasn't holding back. I heard later that the ice chest had "supposedly" been holding sodas. But I saw no sodas that day. Oh no. I believed it had been pure unadulterated premeditated bombardment. It was just too convenient to have a cooler full of ammo at your disposal. Tommy, like the rest of us, had known the order of the floats, and Tommy had come prepared.

A couple more entries drove through, and then the mayor passed by in a vintage car, waving at the masses. He was followed by the official Bluelake float. Steering the float was Mable Bleat, the chamber of commerce president. Bluelake's entry was shaped like a big sailboat. At the top of the boat, in a tub like a crow's nest, stood a very old lady with a sash over her shoulder that read "Miss Bluelake." She waved a tired, stooped-over-in-pain-and-discomfort type wave at the people below. Folks cheered for her and for the fact that this part of the festivities was coming to an end. I began worrying about the parade actually making it to Forget. Everyone was hot and tired, and the enthusiasm level had plummeted drastically in the last half hour.

"How old is Miss Bluelake?" Rivers asked.

I didn't know. I had heard that Bluelake had an official female debutante. But I had no idea she was so well aged.

A heavy man standing next to us answered Rivers' question for her.

The Miracle of Forgetness

"She's almost a century," he said, butting into our business.

"Isn't it about time for her to step down?" I asked.

"Never," this large man insisted. "She was crowned the first Miss Bluelake. She won the title the second year, the third year, and the fourth. The fifth year no one else even bothered competing. So instead of making it a competition we just do it with our one contestant. Every October, Bluelake throws a big pageant to celebrate our perpetual winner. We go through all the motions with just her. Same show, one beauty. Of course the swimsuit competition was eliminated from the festivities years ago."

"Of course," Rivers replied.

The float after Mable's and Miss Bluelake was from the "High Stackin'" Sandwich Shop. Their entry was shaped like a huge hoagie, and on top of it was the owner's daughter singing "God Bless America" with a portable microphone. She kept putting the microphone too close to her mouth. Feedback filled the air and pieced our ears.

The entry before the last float was Ned. He had apparently taken a wrong turn and ended up driving along the parade route. Trapped between floats and unable to get off on any of the roped off side streets, he tried to act like nothing was wrong and just followed the float in front of him. He waved an embarrassed wave to Rivers and me. I didn't think Ned should be embarrassed in the least. He and his outfit were as much a part a Bluelake as any of the entries I had seen.

The last float was a creation from the Bluelake Post Office. The man I had taken the letter from was at the center of the float holding up a piece of mail. I shrunk down in my chair and tried not to be noticed.

"What's the matter?" Rivers asked.

I told her the mail theft story. She laughed at my discomfort. We picked up our chairs and carried them to my car. We needed to speed off to Forget to make sure Stick was ready for the oncoming parade.

The plan was for the parade to stop, pick itself up at the end

229

of Bluelake, and then all entries would drive to a spot just before Forget. There the parade would resume again, ending a block later at the doorstep of our store.

When Rivers and I got to Forget, Stick was ready. He had the store so straightened and cleaned, even the cheap prepackaged things we sold seemed to shine. He had also cleaned out beneath the counter. He was a little upset that Ned hadn't come in yet to help him out. But once we explained Ned's parade problem, Stick was okay.

A couple of little booths had been set up on Witch Road right next to my house. A few businesses from Bluelake had kiosks there and were preparing to sell their goods to the parade people. Things almost looked festive.

It seemed like an awful long time before signs of the parade were spotted from Forget. I knew the moment I saw the first float that this had been a bad idea. Apparently the parade had run into a few problems between Bluelake and here. For one thing, when people had reached the end of the run in Bluelake they had just put the pedal to the metal and increased their parade speed from two miles an hour to sixty-five. And whereas anyone with common sense would have stopped, gotten all the people off of their float, and then driven on, most of the floats just took off, speeding along with unfastened participants clinging to crepe paper and cardboard for dear life. It took a few unfortunate accidents to make people aware of the problem. I guess folks were falling off floats like crazy as their designated drivers callously sped on.

Luckily no one was seriously hurt, but it took a few minutes to bandage people up and get things in order. By then the wind had decided to pick up, blowing floats to and fro, stripping them of their paper and pride. I watched all kinds of colorful paper blow off the approaching parade.

By the time the parade got right in front of Forget, things were pretty pathetic. Kids were crying, people were complaining, and the floats were falling apart left and right. The two kids on the tricycles were being pushed by their mom and dad. Both the kids sat limp on their trikes, trying to smile. The Bluelake Police Band shuffled by like old worn out cards, finally collapsing right in front of the store.

The Pizza Platter had run out of pepperoni to throw, so the employees just stood there dispensing dirty looks. Miss Before and Miss After were sitting down on their float. Miss Before still waved while Miss After worked on a sandwich she had bummed off the High Stackin' float.

Entry after entry drove by, tired and mad about having to come out to Forget. It had seemed like such a good idea. Finally the last float came to a ceremonial and much needed halt. It took four men to get poor Miss Bluelake down from her post.

With the parade completed, people seemed to be more charitable. I forced Stick to give all the parade participants free soda, and people milled around the few outside booths talking and going on about what a desolate place Forget was. There was lots of talk about the UFO and how this year's parade seemed less celebrated than last year's. All in all, I felt everything was turning out pretty well until Miss Bluelake collapsed right in the center of our festivities. She just fell over like a deflated punching bag. Everyone rushed to her aid. Since I was sort of the host I propped her up and tried to see if she was breathing.

She was.

I held her in my arms and fanned her as spectators looked on in worry. Finally she began mumbling something.

"What?" I asked kindly.

"My legs hurt."

Mayor Lockhurst plowed through the crowd. He kneeled down by Miss Bluelake and took her hand.

"Cecilia," he pleaded. "Don't leave us now."

"I'm not going anywhere," Cecilia snapped. "My hips hurt, that's all," she continued. "I've been standing on my feet all day in bad shoes."

"What about the special shoes we gave you money to buy?" the mayor asked.

"I never got them," Cecilia moaned, resting her head in my

arms. "I asked them to express me a pair, but they never sent them to me."

"Cecilia Warden?" I asked.

"Yes," she whimpered.

Oh, this was just great. I held in my hands the owner of the letter I had stolen. The letter that was still sitting on my kitchen counter. I had meant to re-mail it, but since it didn't seem directly related to me, I had forgotten. I was the most self-centered person I knew. I had since mailed two or three letters to Rivers, but I still had not bothered to put back the piece of mail I had taken. Now Miss Bluelake lay in my arms with a bad hip because of my gross oversight.

I patted Cecilia on the hand.

The mayor had someone pull up his car. We carefully lifted Cecilia into the big back seat. The mayor raced off to the Bluelake Hospital.

"This is awful," Jonathan Call said.

Miss Before broke out crying.

The Bluelake High School band began playing "Taps."

"Cut that out," Ned yelled.

Everyone was grieved.

"We should be with Miss Bluelake," someone shouted.

The crowed ayed.

People unhitched their floats and jumped into their cars. Within a matter of minutes Forget was deserted. Rivers and I stood alone, looking at the cloud of dust the stream of racing cars had created.

I made Rivers wait outside while I ran inside and got Cecilia's letter. I tried to wipe off any fingerprints I may have gotten on it with a kitchen towel before I shoved it deep into my front pocket.

We went straight to the Bluelake Hospital. The waiting room was jammed, and people were overrunning the hospital gift shop trying to find some token gift for Cecilia. What do you get the person who has everything but a complete hip? Ned had settled on a big box of chocolate cigars, each wrapped in foil with a label that read "It's a boy."

The Miracle of Forgetness

Ned proudly showed them to Rivers and me. "Cecilia loves chocolate," Ned informed us. He then opened up the box of cigars and took two out. "I'm sure she won't miss a couple of these," he said, slipping them into his back jeans pocket.

"Who's counting anyway," Rivers said.

"Exactly," Ned said, smiling. He opened the box back up and took out a few more for himself. "Exactly."

It was obvious that people really cared for Cecilia Warden. Everyone sat in the waiting room swapping stories and talking about the little things they particularly liked about her. Mayor Lockhurst was busy telling us about Cecilia's problem with immigrants when the doctor came out and informed us we were now welcome to come in and visit her. Two by two, people went in to convey their sorrows.

Rivers and I found this to be the perfect time to slip away. We left the hospital, stopping only to deposit my stolen letter in a post office box next to the information counter. I was glad to be rid of the evidence.

We spent the rest of the day painting the inside of my house. By the time we were finished Rivers was speckled and tired looking. I had to fight every urge in my body to stop myself from kissing her. Heaven still had not delivered the okay.

When I dropped her off at her hotel she stood there waiting for me to make my move. I did nothing.

Once again, Rivers slipped inside her room, bringing a very long day to a very short close.

Chapter Thirty-three

Truly Twisted

When I returned to Forget it was pitch black outside. No stars, no moon. A heavy wind was stirring and moaning through the darkness. The sky was creaking like an old rocking chair under the weight of a heavy being. The two streetlights at the crossing were having to work overtime to ward off the heavy black that pressed down upon them. I could barley see all the floats still sitting there like big mounds of mis-shapen ugly. They cluttered up Forget like trash at a city park. I hoped people would have the courtesy to come and collect their creations first thing tomorrow.

I thought about the parade. What a day. I couldn't believe I had had a hand in hurting Cecilia Warden. I should have mailed that letter the second I discovered it wasn't mine. Now I had a home surrounded by floats and a gut filled with guilt because of it.

I thought about Stick. For some reason I had really grown to love him. We didn't spend too much time together, and our talks were, well...different. But he had become the uncle my father never let me know. I knew without a doubt that I was supposed to be here.

I thought about Rivers. Of course lately there didn't seem to be a shot of thought traveling through my brain that was not somehow connected to Rivers. Late last night I had begun a diary, and in it I had written down all the impossible things about Rivers' and my relationship. The list was depressingly long. Despite all the cons, however, we were working. We seemed to have achieved the perfect relationship. The last couple of days I had even begun thinking about marriage. I was almost positive that Rivers would give me a yes. The problem was things were just too neat. It was as if the first twenty-four years of my life and been scattered, painful, and confusing. But with an injection of Forget, everything had come together. There was magic in this dry soil.

I said a long prayer thanking God for everything and begging him to give me a sign concerning the Rivers/bishop ordeal.

I fell asleep to the sound of violent wind, and with no answer.

About two-thirty in the morning I was awakened by Bob. He shook me awake, scaring the sleep out of me.

"Bob?"

"Shhhh," he said loudly. "Stick's sleeping."

"So was I."

"I can't get over how quiet you sleep," Bob replied.

"What do you want?" I asked, rolling over to go back to sleep.

"I've got something I need to tell you."

"Can't it wait?" I complained.

"It can't."

I sat up and rubbed the tired out of my eyes. "How'd you get in here?" I asked.

"I made myself up a key," Bob explained. "Hope you don't mind. You never know when there might be an emergency or something."

The wind outside howled amazingly loud.

"What's going on out there?" I asked.

"It's just windy," Bob answered.

"So what do you want?" I asked dejectedly.

"I figured something out," Bob said.

I sighed. Bob was probably going to tell me that he had just discovered that sugar was bad for your teeth or that there was a Washington state *and* a Washington, D.C.

"The state department's coming to investigate the site tomorrow," Bob informed me.

"I already knew that," I said, figuring this was his discovery.

"They're going to determine once and for all what that was that crashed down there," Bob pointed out.

"So?" I asked.

"That crash has done a lot for Forget," Bob stated.

This was true.

"What are you saying?" I asked. "Are you admitting it wasn't a spaceship?"

"Don't get me wrong," Bob said, "I still believe in aliens. I'm just saying that if it isn't a spaceship out there, Jay's going to do his best to make it look like Stick and I, and you, perpetrated some sort of fraud."

"That's silly," I said, while feeling that Bob was actually making some sense.

The wind rocked the windows of my house.

"I've made a few calls," Bob said.

"And?"

"Well, I kept thinking that somewhere there had to be record of some sort of plane going down."

"Was there?" I asked.

"No."

"So you don't know what it is?" I asked.

"I know," Bob said smugly. "It took me a while but I found out. Actually it was your little souvenir that gave it away."

Bob sat down on the end of my bed. His weight made the mattress tip to the right. The small lamp by the side of my bed was the only light on. Its dim light made the room eerie and small.

"Dot helped me," Bob exclaimed. "I had her call a few people with one of those fake voices that she's so good at. I tell you, she gets me all the time. Her Richard Nixon impression is right on."

"Bob," I said, steering him back on track.

"Did you know Todd Plot?" Bob asked.

The Miracle of Forgetness

"The Mormon?" I replied.

Bob nodded. "He and Stick were pretty good friends. Todd's a gruff one, but he's always been a good support to Stick. I can see past his faults on the merits of that alone."

I hadn't thought about Todd since he left his wife.

"Todd flies planes," Bob threw out.

Todd did fly planes. I couldn't believe I had not made the connection. No one had seen Todd since the day of the wreck.

"So it was Todd?" I asked.

"I thought it might have been for a moment," Bob said. "I mean Todd's been missing for some time now. That's why I had Dot call up Todd's wife, Cloris. Dot pretended to be a crisis center worker taking surveys of what different people did to make their marriages work. Well, just as I suspected she would, Sister Plot opened up. Spilled her guts like a glutton with an open belly wound. Cloris told Dot everything. Seems Todd had a real hard time communicating his feelings. I think that was as much their problem as anything. Although Sister Plot was giving a lot of her time to that sewing club she's president of. It's hard to keep a marriage solid when you're going different directions."

The sky outside lit up with lightning. Thunder cracked just seconds later.

"So?" I said, prodding Bob on.

"When Todd left he was mad. Spitting mad. According to Sister Plot he was punching holes in the wall and blaming her for everything from the First and Second World Wars to the fact that milk prices were so high.

"Sister Plot took off out of there. She drove over to Bishop Withers' house to see if he could come settle Todd down. But when the good bishop and Cloris returned, Todd was gone. And not only was he gone, but he had taken half of the furniture and most of the valuables."

Bob stopped.

"Do you have that piece of the wreck still?" he asked me.

I leaned over and picked it off my nightstand. I handed it to Bob.

He looked at it and laughed. "This little thing has bugged me," he said. "I can't tell you how many nights I've laid awake thinking about this."

"It's pretty weird," I admitted.

"Yep, it looks right unworldly," Bob agreed. "But there was something about it that struck me as being familiar. I thought for a while that maybe the space people were just putting deja vu thoughts into my head, but then I finally figured it out."

Lightning struck what must have been just a few feet away from Forget. The light next to my bed went out. I could also see from my windows that the crossing lights had gone out as well. Wind beat upon my house like a big butcher on tough meat.

"This is a huge storm," I said unnecessarily.

"Wild country," Bob replied. "I've seen people lifted off the earth and put down in the next state over."

Bob fumbled for a little cop flashlight hooked to his big cop belt. He pulled the flashlight off, turned it on, and held it up to his face as if he were telling a scary ghost story.

"I live in an RV," he said.

That was scary.

"Consequently, all of my needs are in the space of twenty feet," he continued. "Well, last night I was watching a late made-for-TV-movie about an adoption gone horribly wrong. What a movie. I don't usually cry," Bob said. "But I'm not made of stone either," he added. "Anyhow I had just made myself a couple cans of ravioli when I noticed something unusual in my kitchen. At first I ignored it, but then the possibility became so crazy I jumped up and took a good look at it.

"I called Dot at the dispatch and had her make a late night call to Sister Plot. It was hard getting Sister Plot to believe that Dot was the crisis center calling back at two in the morning, but eventually we got our answer."

"Answer to what?" I asked.

Bob handed me back my souvenir. He then unbuttoned his shirt pocket, pulled out a silver object, and handed it to me along with his flashlight.

"I brought that from home," he said.

I held the object in my hand, shining the light on it. I read the word.

"Kenmore."

I held it up to my space souvenir. It was almost a perfect match. Mine was charred, melted, missing the K and the last e, and the remaining letters were unreadable, but it had at one time been the same thing.

"Kenmore?" I asked.

"Cloris Plot's heirloom refrigerator," Bob answered. "I pried that off my ice-box."

I didn't know whether I should laugh or cry. I couldn't believe it. The hype, the fright, the confusion, the T-shirts and souvenirs, the hysteria and the fact that our business had quadrupled in the last month was all due to, and because of, a refrigerator.

"Todd must have pushed it out of his plane," Bob said softly. "And the way it exploded like that, he must have filled it full of gas or something. It was Sister Plot's favorite."

"I can't believe it," I whispered, commenting both on the answer and the fact that Sister Plot had an heirloom refrigerator. It seemed like a rather odd thing to pass down to your heritage. A legacy of cold condiments and crisp lettuce.

"Well, believe it," Bob said sharply. "And tomorrow the state's going to discover that it's not a UFO, and then they'll come after Stick and you."

"And you," I said defensively.

Bob chewed on the end of his mustache. The small flashlight he now held up gave me a perfect glimpse of his big nostrils and hairy upper lip.

"So we'll just tell them the truth," I suggested.

"Truth doesn't always work around here," Bob said.

"So what do we do?" I asked.

"I'm not sure yet," Bob answered. "That's why I came to see you."

Bob turned off his little light. We sat there in the darkness as both of us thought things over. The wind outside was getting extremely punchy. It kept coiling up against the house, slithering rapidly down through the chimney, and rattling the windows like an irate snake. The piece of cardboard covering the hole in my bedroom window pulsed with each gust. The house seemed to move with each direction the wind chose to dance.

It was so dark I didn't even see Bob lean up to me and whisper in my ear,

"Kitty's outside."

I had no idea how he knew this, but I took his word for it. I quietly slipped out of bed and put on my pants and shoes. Bob tiptoed down the hall to wake Stick. I grabbed a flashlight from one of the kitchen cabinets and went to the front door. I threw the door open, the wind rushing in strong and confident. I shined my light in the direction of my outside bedroom window. There was Kitty, caught like a not-so-dear in the beam of my light. She had her ear pressed up to the cardboard covering the hole she had made in my bedroom window. She had been listening. I didn't know if she could have even heard anything Bob and I were saying over this wind, but I knew I had to find out. Kitty ran to her car. She jumped in, flipped on her headlights, and raced off.

I ran back inside, grabbed my keys, and then took off after her. Her car handled higher speeds better than mine did. With the heavy wind blowing against me I couldn't get my car to do more than sixty-five. Just as I thought I was going to lose her she turned off the road and sped to her house.

I had her now.

When I pulled up to her place she was already out of her car and inside. I got out and cautiously approached her front door. I hoped Bob had the sense to follow me. I did not want to be here alone. The night was unnerving enough. Now here I was standing before a house that looked to be a theme park for psychos and pursuing a woman who seemed to have no sense of boundaries.

I missed my mother.

The Miracle of Forgetness

A gigantic tumbleweed whipped past me. With the beam of my flashlight I watched it fly off into the dark sky. Lightning flashed above the Mount Taylor Mountain Range. I should have been home dreaming about Rivers.

Kitty's front door was wide open; it gaped like a slack-jawed mouth, the door blowing like a loose lip. It looked like a trap. I shined my light in front of me and then stepped inside slowly. Like jittery crickets my nerves hopped around my stomach.

"Kitty," I screamed. I could barely hear myself over the wind.

Thunder and lightning struck twice. My ears began to ring in protest.

"Come on, Bob," I whispered, hoping he would arrive soon and help me out.

From what I could see of it, Kitty's home looked to be rather nice. Huge pictures in gaudy frames hung on the walls, and there seemed to be an excess of throw pillows scattered around. The wind was filling the place like a thirsty lung and causing things to shake and wobble. The darkness made it appear to be the perfect house for someone like Kitty to haunt.

"Kitty," I yelled again.

The roof rattled with the wind.

I had decided to turn around and go back outside when I heard Kitty growl.

"Don't move," she sneered.

I turned to find Kitty pointing a shotgun at me. She was standing next to one of the walls, her ratty hair hanging in her face and her big nostrils meshing in the weak beam of my flashlight and giving her the appearance of having only one big one. She looked jumpy and crazed.

"You know there are laws about breaking into people's houses," she yelled. "I could shoot you nice and legal."

I didn't reply.

Kitty circled back around me and shut the front door. The wind roared angrily, upset about being shut out.

"It's just you and I now," she hissed.

"Kitty I just wanted..."

"I know what you wanted," she interrupted. "You wanted to sneak a peek at the crazy lady's house. You wanted to tell all your friends that you got inside. Ha, ha, ha, ha, ha."

"Bob's coming," I informed her.

"Bob," Kitty laughed. "The incompetent boob. He's like gum in the gears of life. The only way he ever accomplishes anything is by messing up. I can't believe he was able to figure out the UFO."

She had heard.

"But I'm glad he did," Kitty squealed with delight. "Now when Bob and Stick get here I'll take you all in to the Bluelake Police Department and turn you over as the criminals that you are. I can't believe the three of you would have the nerve to perpetrate such an ugly fraud on the good people around here."

Wind threw something up against the east wall of Kitty's home. I had never heard Mother Nature so angry. She was loud and violent tonight. All of nature seemed to be falling apart.

"After I turn you in," Kitty continued, "then maybe people will begin to see me in a different light. And with you and Stick in jail, the state will have to repossesses Forget. Then I'll buy the whole thing for a couple stinking dollars and make a dump out of it. It would be an improvement don't you think?"

Kitty was foaming at the mouth. I hoped the different light which people would soon see her in was a dark one. She was ranting like a doomsday prophet on the last day of 1999. And the wicked weather outside made her espousings even more sinister and unsettling. Lightning and thunder kept hitting the ground like bratty gods, but there was still no sound of rain. Darkness flickered around the large strings of lightning, giving the whole scene a strobelike effect.

I prayed for Bob to hurry.

"We didn't push that refrigerator out of the plane," I argued.

"So what?" Kitty argued back. "You had an accomplice."

I needed Bob's help. I needed to buy some time.

"Why do you hate me so much?" I yelled loud enough so she could hear me.

"Don't start thinking you're all special and singled out. I hate everyone. No one's ever given me an ounce of respect or kindness. Everyone loved Karl. But not his ugly daughter Kitty. Poor Kitty, sad Kitty, lonely, pathetic, mean Kitty."

"I tried to be nice," I offered.

"You stole the land that belonged to me right out from under my nose. Forget should be mine. Stick would have had to close up shop if it weren't for you."

"I didn't know," I countered.

"You're all the same," Kitty squealed.

Nature turned things up a notch. Large fists of wind pelted Kitty's home. Kitty began to unravel. She was nervously looking over her shoulder and twitching at every creak and crash.

She waved me into a corner with her gun. She was loosing control of the situation and she knew it. The storm had taken over the wheel.

A huge ripping sound roared just outside of Kitty's house. Kitty jumped a good two feet into the air. The gun began to shake in her hands. Seconds later one of Kitty's trees came bursting through the front window. Glass flew everywhere, and Kitty screamed like an injured monkey with bionic vocal chords. I raced to the front door but it was too late.

The wind ripped the entire front part of the roof off and sucked it into the dark sky. A huge rush of air swooped down into the house and began twirling things around. Kitty shot at the wind a few times and then dropped her gun in fear.

I didn't know what to do. The house began splitting apart. Walls moved and objects bigger and heavier than I were being blown about like puffed wheat in a wind tunnel.

I stared at Kitty, she stared at me.

She put her hands over her ears in an attempt to shut out the deafening noise the wind was making. I watched as she was lifted off of the ground and sucked out of the house.

In an instant she was gone.

I would have felt great grief for her except I seemed to have my own problems at the moment.

I was going to die.

Wind streamed up my nose, sucking the life out of me. It encompassed me, lifting me into the air and grasping me so tightly that I felt as if every vital organ in my body was suddenly going to start popping like hot corn on burning coals. I lifted my heavy arms and flailed desperately, grasping for something to hold on to. The elements wouldn't hear of it. My feet flew off of the ground. It felt as if someone had a hold of me by the ankles. I saw the ground back away, and I knew I was done for.

My mind started to go.

My spirit shriveled as the wind dried it out. Like a giant hand it had swooped down from the sky and plucked my body from off the earth. I was lifted higher and higher. Miles seemed too small an increment to measure my height. The wind flung me around like a scarecrow, my spirit spinning like straw. Then in what seemed to be only a second of time, the wind threw me towards the ground with such force I could feel my bones swelling.

I hit something. The ground seemed to push up over me as the force of my fall pushed me deeper down. I had landed in water. It was thick and surrounded me like dogs on a piece of meat. Biting, snarling, thrashing.

I was drowning.

I could feel the cold liquid filling my lungs. It was no use. I was a dead man. I put my hands to my side and let my body just sink deeper. My eardrums pounded and pulsated as the pressure became too great for them to bare.

I thought about Stick. I thought about Bob. I thought about Rivers. I considered my life and the tragic end it had met. No wonder the Rivers deal had come to me wrapped up so neatly. She was a present I could never hope to open.

This was it.

My hands went numb, and an odd sensation shot up my arm. Then, like a warm pickle spear being violently shaken, my body started to convulse.

Darkness started to fill my eyes, as light and warmth became

The Miracle of Forgetness

nothing but fond memories. My mind continued to blacken.

Death appeared on the horizon. He stuck his large, hairy arm out as if to shake my hand and welcome me into the next world.

I put my hand forth and then politely declined.

Chapter Thirty-four

The H20 Savior

I heard a voice. It seemed to call to me. Like angels welcoming me to the other side.

"Look, Cid," the voice said. "Some dumb kid's floating here in the water."

I could feel hands grabbing me. My body ached as they tugged. They pulled me from the water and laid me out on the deck of their boat. I could feel the early morning sun shining upon my face. Heaven could be no less subtle.

"Is he dead?" Someone asked.

I felt a couple of kicks in the side. I tried my best to moan.

"He's alive," a voice exclaimed.

I couldn't open my eyes. I couldn't move my arms or legs. I was unable to do anything but listen to these people carry on about how bad I looked.

"I've never seen anyone so pale who was still living."

I kept slipping in and out of consciousness. But every once in a while I would get my brain to remain focused so that I was able to understand what was happening. They raced the boat to shore and then laid me out in the back of a truck. Whoever had found me had children with them. I could hear the kids begging to ride in the back with the body. The parents consented.

The kids kept daring each other to touch me as we drove to the hospital. I wanted so badly to open my eyes. I wanted to speak as if from the dead. One of the kids found a screwdriver and started prodding me. He kept getting braver and braver, jabbing me harder and harder. He began pushing the screwdriver with so much force I thought he was going to puncture me. I used everything I had in me to simply twitch my arm. The kids began screaming. Suddenly none of them wanted to be in the back any longer.

They started pounding on the back window of the truck cab and screaming for their mommies.

We pulled into Bluelake Hospital just as these children were contemplating jumping out. I finally got my eyes to open. Doctors and nurses scurried about like live ticks on a hot griddle. They hoisted me onto a gurney and then wheeled me inside. I could see needles going into my arms, and within seconds life seemed kind of peaceful again.

What felt like years later I woke to the sound of someone crying over me. I figured I was dead and my mother was mourning the fact I had blemished her reputation by doing the stupid things I had done during my life.

"It's okay," I mumbled, too tired to open my eyes.

"Gray?" my mother said, sounding a whole lot like Rivers.

I opened my eyes. I had obviously made it to the celestial kingdom because there was Rivers. Her blue eyes were wet, and her mouth looked so concerned I thought I was going to cry. She brushed her dark hair away from her face and smiled.

No one had ever told me there was a level above the celestial kingdom.

"What's a matter?" I asked groggily.

"Some boaters found you in the middle of Blue Lake," Rivers explained softly.

"How long have I been out?" I asked.

"You've been sleeping for about two days," she answered.

"There was a tornado," I said.

"We know," Bob broke in.

Lost in the glow of Rivers I had failed to see Bob standing by the side of my bed.

"It must have picked you up and thrown you into the lake," he clarified.

"And I'm alive?" I asked.

"Alive and well," Stick said.

Now I knew I was dead. I saw images of Stick standing on the other side of the bed. He had his hat in his hands.

"You're here?" I said as excited as I could bring myself to be at the moment.

"We're all here," Bob said, sounding like a character in the closing scene of a really bad production of the *Wizard of Oz*.

"The doctor said you just had a few bad bruises and a couple scratches," Rivers reported happily, taking hold of my hand. Her touch shot energy into my tired body, filling me with strength.

"It's a miracle plain and simple," Bob said. "You are one lucky guy. I'd say Mother Nature was right nice to set you down in a pool of water. Pity Kitty wasn't so fortunate."

"Kitty?" I asked.

"They found her on the meeting house lawn," Stick said. "She was out cold. Sister Gent discovered her when she went over to run off some bulletins. That green sod saved her life."

"Is she okay?" I asked.

"She's going to be fine," Bob said. "She broke both her legs, and she's talking sort of silly, but the doctor says she'll make it. Ned's with her now. She in room 6304, up a floor and down the hall."

"Well, we'd better get back to the store," Stick said.

Stick and Bob left Rivers and me alone.

"I thought you were dead," Rivers said.

"I didn't mean to..."

Rivers wasn't crying anymore. She had locked eyes with me and she wasn't letting go.

"What?" I self-consciously asked. The drugs were wearing off, and I was beginning to see thing more clearly.

She pulled her dark hair back behind her head and stepped over to the side of my bed. Her cheeks were flushed and her blue eyes flickering. She pushed aside the tubes on the side of the bed. Like a jungle explorer she hacked her way thorough the surgical foliage and stalked her prey.

I prayed like never before.

She put her warm hands on my face and brushed back my matted hair.

"Rivers..."

She put her finger to her lips. "You've been avoiding this," she said. "Now that I've got you trapped there's nothing you can do."

"I know but..."

"How can I marry you if I don't know how you kiss?"

I started to recount a story of a couple I knew that hadn't kissed until they were married. Rivers didn't want to hear it.

I prayed for that sign I had been waiting for.

"To heck with it," I thought. Perhaps I had been like the Jews of old and missed the sign already. Maybe I had been searching for tidal waves and earthquakes, when the message had been sent via sunshine and mild weather.

Rivers put her lips on mine. I put my tube infested arms around her and kissed her back. I could feel her heart beating wildly, and I suddenly had enhanced feeling in my toes and fingers. Any and all pain I felt moments ago was now gone. My body whirled. My mind cleared. My ears rang like the bells of Notre Dame. I could feel Rivers' cheek against mine as she kissed the side of my face. There were no words to describe the joy I felt. My brain began making up new words to define the elation I felt.

Incredilentay.

Marvunderal.

The sun merged with the moon and tiny stars shot out from our beings. We sat there together like two Fourth of July sparklers, all lit up and crackling. Rivers became tangled in the tubing that was supplying my medication. One dose of her, however, was far more potent than any medicine this hospital could have administered.

"I love you, Gray," Rivers whispered as she kissed my ear.

"So will you marry me?" I asked.

"I'll think about it," she said.

Light surrounded us and the heavens laid out their finest spread. Actually, a nurse came in, flicked on the overhead, and dropped off my lunch.

This, however, was no time for splitting hairs.

Chapter Thirty-five

All Is Forgotten

I was in the hospital a week before the doctor told me I was free to go home. I was excited to leave, but not thrilled to go home. The tornado had taken my tree. It had ripped it out of the ground and dumped it about a mile down the road from Forget. Rivers had broken the news carefully to me. Depressing as that was, it didn't compare to the fact that Rivers had left to go back to California yesterday. She had some things she needed to take care of, one of which was for her to decide about marrying me. I reluctantly watched her go. I gave her the bracelet Orvil had given me. I tied it tightly around her small wrist and hoped it would constantly remind her of me.

President Gram had been by to visit me in the hospital. He was giving me a week's extension. I had only five more days to figure things out. I wasn't looking forward to finding an answer. When he came by I had tried to act really sick and hurt so he would rescind the offer. But he just kept going on about how my life had been spared for a reason.

I got together all of my things and signed out. Before I left the hospital, however, I dropped in and paid a visit to Kitty. Bob had been going on and on about how changed she was. I had to see for myself.

Kitty was sitting up in bed with her hands folded in front of her. Ned was standing by the side of Kitty's bed talking to her. I sheepishly stuck my head in the door and lightly knocked on the door frame. Kitty looked at me and smiled.

I checked the room number on the door again.

"Come in," she said.

I walked slowly to the side of her bed.

"How are you feeling?" I asked.

"Lucky to be alive," she replied.

I couldn't tell if she was patronizing me or if she was being sincere.

"Hey, Ned," I said.

"Gray," he responded.

"Could I talk to Kitty alone?" I asked him.

Ned and Kitty exchanged glances. It was obvious there was more to them than there once had been.

"I'll be back," Ned stated. He then walked slowly out of the room, closing the door behind him.

"I guess we had quite an adventure," I said to Kitty.

"I can't remember too much about it," she replied.

"Do you remember..." I began to ask.

"I saw God," Kitty interrupted.

"Really?" I said, knowing no other way to respond to such a statement.

"Well, He and I didn't exactly have a one-on-one, but I saw heaven, and He was there." Kitty leaned up further in her bed and continued. "I really can't remember much about that actual night, but I remember being sucked up. I tell you I was never so scared."

"Yeah, me too," I said butting in. "I thought I was dead.

"I was," Kitty said seriously. "That twister started pulling me apart. In fact when I finally became conscious here at the hospital I was surprised to find all my legs and arms still attached to my body."

Kitty threw down her sheets to show me her busted up, but still attached, legs.

I winced, internally.

The Miracle of Forgetness

"That tornado lifted me so high," Kitty said. "Higher, higher, higher. I finally passed out. Next thing I know, two little ladies are sitting by me in a big blue room with high ceilings and textured walls. One of the women was crocheting, and the other had a clipboard and was asking me my vitals. I told them who I was and they informed me I was deemed ready for death. The one who had been crocheting gave me this beautiful loose knit sweater to put on. Never had I felt such warmth. It was the most marvelous thing. That sweater was the nicest thing anyone had ever given me. I started to cry like a baby."

Kitty pulled her covers back up and dabbed her eyes with the corner of her blanket. I sat down on the edge of the bed and continued to listen.

"The woman with the clipboard was kind of short with me. She didn't want me sitting around crying when she had other perfectly good dead people to log in. The woman who gave me the sweater was a little more patient. She took me by the arm and walked me to the door. She opened the door and waited for me to walk through it.

"Once I had stepped in, I took off flying like a wrinkly kite. I had heard you saw a tunnel at death, but this was more like an elevator ride sideways, except without the elevator cart. I flew for so long that after a while I began to get bored with it. I felt certain I was headed to outer darkness. There could be no other place this far away.

"Finally, just as I was beginning to fall asleep, I stopped. There I was in a big field filled with ferret holes and weeds. I was surrounded by people hoeing at the ground as if there were no tomorrow. Eventually, I worked up the nerve to ask one of them where I was. He just looked at me sadly and said, 'Grab a hoe. There's lots of work.'

"I did as I was told," Kitty said. "I must have hoed for what felt like two weeks without a single meal or word from anyone else. I started to feel cheated. This was the worst death I had ever heard of. Where were the departed loved ones come to greet me? Where was the host of heavenly angels singing praises?

Where was Saint Peter and his golden gates? If this was death I wanted no part of it.

"I threw down my hoe and began screaming. The people around me became bothered and nervous. Everyone kept telling me to get back to work. Finally a tall guy with thick glasses and a limp lumbered over to me. When he couldn't get me to shut up he took me by the arm to the edge of the field."

The nurse wheeled in Kitty's lunch and placed it in front of her.

"Mind if I eat while we talk?" Kitty asked.

"Not at all," I said, looking forward to leaving the hospital and getting some real food myself.

Kitty put a big spoonful of peas and carrots into her mouth and continued. "This tall guy was mad I had stopped hoeing. He started to rant and rave about a quota or something." Pieces of peas sprayed from her mouth as she said "something." "I said to heck with your quota I want to see God. So he led me to a portable office located just off the field. He pulled me inside and sat me down in a chair to wait. Then he stormed away, leaving me completely alone. I waited for weeks."

"You were only unconscious for a day," I argued.

"In heaven, time's different," Kitty explained. "Days and weeks are longer there."

"I thought they were supposed to be shorter there," I said.

"Maybe you Mormons have a different heaven."

I sure hoped so.

"After the longest time, this nice woman with no hair came into the office and informed me that it just wouldn't be possible for me to meet with the big guy, but would I mind seeing Karen Foulten."

"Who's Karen Foulten?" I asked.

"I guess she's some woman who had lived a perfect life down here on earth at one time. She was a farmer's wife from some-place in South Dakota."

"So that made her an authority?" I asked.

"It was the best they could do," Kitty said. "Heaven's a busy place these days. Besides, Karen was wonderful. She told me all these incredible things about heaven. Things she had experienced up there because she had lived a good life down here.

"Well, I wanted the stuff she had. I didn't want to spend my days hoeing. I wanted to know that God was somewhere near about. I wanted to progress and achieve. I begged Karen to let me go back to earth for a while. She pulled a few strings for me and here I am."

Kitty was crying.

I didn't know what to make of all this. I just kept thinking that there was a trick somewhere. Kitty was probably just setting me up for something horrible.

"That's amazing," I commented.

"I'm a better person now," she replied.

I decided to test her.

"What about the UFO?" I asked.

"I heard it was picked up by the tornado and carried away."

"Yeah, but what about it?"

"No one knows where it is," she guessed.

"And?"

"And that's too bad," Kitty tried.

"Do you think it was an actual UFO?" I asked.

"I have no idea," Kitty said honestly.

"No idea?"

"None."

"Are you mad at me?" I threw out.

"Now, why would I be mad at you?" Kitty asked, confused.

Kitty appeared to have forgotten.

"Do you remember why I was out at your place when the tornado picked us up?" I asked pointedly.

"For a visit?"

"At two-thirty in the morning?"

"I can't remember," Kitty said nicely. "But I'm glad you stopped by."

Who was this person?

"My home was destroyed," Kitty added. "Not a piece left."

"I heard," I replied. "Forget took a few hits as well."

"It's still standing though, isn't it?" Kitty asked, concerned.

I nodded.

"We'll help you get back on your feet," I told her.

"You people are so kind," Kitty cried.

Kitty had forgotten.

"I'm glad you're feeling better," I said, standing up.

"I'm glad we're both feeling better," Kitty returned.

Ned came back into the room. Kitty crammed some wet potato flakes into her mouth during this break in our dialogue.

"Did she tell you about her experience?" I asked Ned.

"She did," Ned said boldly.

"What do you think?"

"I don't think Kitty would lie," he answered.

Oddly, I didn't think so either.

It seemed a miracle, but somehow Kitty had really forgotten. It was also as if she couldn't remember how to be mean. She was a completely different person. As I was leaving I turned and saw Ned spoon a healthy chunk of hospital meat loaf into Kitty's mouth. She looked almost pretty.

Amazing.

Chapter Thirty-six

Picking Up the Pieces

Forget looked so different when I got there. It had been over a week since the tornado, but things were still scattered and chaotic.

The twister had gotten hold of the parade floats. It had whipped them around, shredded them up, and then sprinkled them liberally over the barren landscape. I kind of liked the color the tiny bits of crepe paper added.

I was still bummed over my stolen tree. Forget had seemed like such a good buy with the tree included. Now with it gone I felt as if someone owed me some change. Mother Nature had selfishly plucked up my one real perk.

Bob was at the store when I returned. He was there helping Stick clean up and fix the place. Thankfully there had not been too much real damage to our compound. The store had sustained a broken front window which Bob was now repairing, and the shingles on my home had been picked over by the wind. My house sat there looking as if it had the mange. The bench at the crossing had lost one of its boards, but aside from these few things we had weathered the storm pretty well. Sure, there was a lot of trash and debris scattered about, but at least we were still whole.

I walked in and took a seat behind the counter by Stick. Everyone welcomed me back, as best as a couple of middle-aged men with insecurities and poor social skills could. It was nice to be home. I noticed a big piece of poster board behind the counter.

"What's that?" I asked Stick.

"Oh, that's for you," Stick said.

I picked it up and looked at it. There was writing on it but it didn't seem to make any sense.

"What is it?"

"It's from that rug girl," Stick informed me. "She left it here when you were in the hospital."

"But what is it?" I asked.

"Well, it did have a bunch of candy taped to it, but someone took it all off and ate it." Stick pointed his head towards Bob.

"Guilty," Bob said. "I didn't think it would be good for you to have all that sugar right after the hospital."

"Thanks," I joked.

The poster made absolutely no sense without the candy taped to it.

"So what did it say?" I asked.

"Was it supposed to say something?" Bob replied.

"I assume the candy spelled out a message," I explained.

"Huh," Bob huhed. "Clever idea."

"That rug girl's been by a couple of times to see you," Stick said. "Last time she came through she got a little mad at me because you weren't here."

"Did you tell her I was in the hospital?" I asked.

"I didn't know if you wanted me to be giving out your personal information."

"Stick," I complained.

"Don't get mad at me," he said. "Besides, you can tell her yourself, she just pulled up."

Angela was out at the pumps. I didn't know what to do. I admit, Angela was one of those things that seemed to have gotten left downstream since I had deepened my relationship with Rivers. Now here she was reminding me of a loose end that my life had not taken care of for itself. I preferred complicated things working themselves out behind my back.

I decided to get this over with. I took a deep breath and then walked out to her truck.

"Hey," I said.

She didn't reply.

"Business good?" I asked, not knowing what else to say.

Angela looked different. Her hair was dull, and her smile was completely nonexistent.

"I sent you flowers," she flared.

"I wanted to thank you, but I've been gone."

"I made you a poster."

"I just now saw it."

Angela stood there watching the numbers on the gas pump increase. She mumbled something to herself. I hoped that she was complaining about the price of gas and not the faults of me.

"I hate you," she spat.

Gas prices were unusually low right now.

"We hardly know each other," I pointed out.

"You told me to come around," she argued. "You said, 'Come around, we'll do something.'"

"We did some things," I pointed out.

Angela looked at me. I could see her temper rising beneath the surface of her face. Her eyes boiled.

"I'm really sorry," I said, not knowing what else I could do.

"I hate my job," Angela blurted out. "I hate traveling all over trying to talk people into buying rugs they don't really need."

"Couldn't you do something else?" I asked, wondering why she was even telling me this.

"Like what?"

I had no answers for her; I barely knew what to do with myself.

"So I guess you and I aren't a thing," Angela said.

"Nope."

"For sure?"

"I think so."

"It's probably best," she slurred. "You being a Mormon and all."

I tried to smile at her.

Instead of paying Stick for the gas Angela gave me one of her rugs. She also gave me one of her cards in case I ever needed another one. I had a feeling she wouldn't be buying gas here any longer. I also had a feeling one rug would be sufficient for quite some time.

"So I guess there was a pretty big tornado out here," she said, trying to sound civil as she got into her truck.

"I heard about that," I said.

I shut her door for her and she drove off, closing things up more easily than I had anticipated. She was a nice little whirlwind who was thankfully blowing away. I hoped she would be able to find someone who enjoyed angry women.

I thought of how much things had changed in the last few weeks. At one point Angela had represented hope. Now as she sped away she resembled closure. I prayed the Rivers chapter of my life had a far sweeter ending than this.

I really missed Rivers.

I went back to my house and gave her a call. Her brother Milo answered.

"Is Rivers at home?" I asked.

"She's not," he replied, sounding happier than I had ever heard him.

"Will she be home later?"

"I'm not sure. She went to see Darrell Higgins," he said proudly.

I panicked.

"Who?"

"Darrell H..."

"The missionary?" I interrupted.

"Yep," Milo said as if he were enjoying this.

Milo had never been real fond of me. He was quite close to Elder Higgins and felt he owed it to his friend to keep me away from Rivers.

"What's he doing there?" I asked.

"He came home for an emergency operation of some sort. A

punctured lung or something."

How convenient, I thought.

I begged Milo to have Rivers call me back. I hung up my hopes, my dreams, and my expensive cordless phone that now didn't seem to work so well. I needed a phone that transmitted nothing but good news.

Rivers had gone back to California to settle a few things and to make up her mind about marrying me. Me! Me, me, me. It was awful crafty of Elder Higgins to pull this lung thing. He had probably received Rivers' letter telling him it was over, at which point he just held his breath until one of his lungs burst. I knew Rivers. Heck, I'd give myself a self-inflicted case of leprosy if I felt it would keep me from losing her. I'd sooner part with my nose, ears, flesh, and face than let her get away.

I went outside and stared at the hole where my tree used to reside.

I tried not to stress out. Rivers was simply visiting a sick friend. Of course she had at one time almost been engaged to this deviant...I mean sick friend. Didn't he know it was my turn to be almost engaged to her?

I got down on my hands and knees to examine the tree hole more carefully. I hadn't noticed it before, but inside this big hole were hundreds of smaller ones. They were everywhere. They sort of looked like..."

"Snake holes," I said to myself.

I couldn't believe it. Kitty's little prank snakes had slithered and wiggled out a tiny community there beneath my tree. They had been the cause of its uprooting—loosening the soil and allowing the heavens to effortlessly pick it up and drag it away.

I thought of the Kitty who had let loose those snakes.

I then thought of the Kitty who now sat in the hospital helping the nurses fold towels and reading storybooks to the sick children.

I guess I could part with a tree to gain a cordial Kitty.

I spent the rest of the day picking up trash around Forget. At eleven o'clock that night Rivers had still not called me back. I

Robert F. Smith

reluctantly went to bed. It appeared her sick friend had later than normal visiting hours.

I called her first thing the next morning. Her mother informed me Rivers was out. She gave me no other information but promised she would have her return my call when she arrived back in.

I was getting worried. I was afraid that I had moved from in to out.

Bob had spent the night at Ned's house. He and Ned had come back bright and early to continue working on the store.

"Don't you have stuff to do in Longwinded?" I asked as soon as I saw Bob. It wasn't that I was bothered by his presence, I was just curious how he could hold down a job he seemed never to be working at.

"You've got to spread yourself around," Bob told me, waving his hands in front of himself. "The world will pass you by if you don't leave bits and pieces of yourself lying about." Bob blew into his handkerchief.

The store hadn't been opened long when our first customer came in. Stick was behind the counter organizing the film, Ned was outside sweeping the front walkway, and Bob and I were just standing around looking as needed as a mortician in the City of Enoch.

This woman customer came in and looked around nervously. She seemed so scared I thought perhaps she had come to rob us or to announce she had just received word the world would be ending today.

I was dead wrong. Things weren't ending, they were just beginning.

Bob's mouth dropped open as soon as he saw her.

"What is it?" I asked.

"Jenny?" Bob gasped.

Stick whirled around to face her. "Jenny," he whispered in unbelief.

"Francis," she said nervously. Her eyes were wet and she

262

looked as uncomfortable as a vegetarian in a slaughter house.

She took a breath of air.

I thought maybe Stick would start clapping for joy or jump out over the counter and hug her. I mean here was Jenny. Thee Jenny, the Jenny, just plain Jenny. This was the moment he had been waiting for. Here stood the reason he had spent the last twenty years locked up in this suffocating store. This was a moment of rejoicing and singing. Stick did neither of these things.

He grabbed hold of the edge of the counter to prevent himself from falling over and began crying.

I had never heard such deep and guttural wailing. His body sounded as if it were trying to digest a ten-pound brick of wet clay.

"You've come back," he cried, tears streaming down his cheeks and his chest heaving as if he were going to hyperventilate. "People didn't believe me," he managed to say. He just stood there holding onto the counter sobbing. "They didn't believe me," he blubbered. It was the most heartbreaking thing I had ever seen.

Jenny walked back behind the counter. Stick looked at her as if he didn't know what to do. He was crying so hard he kept losing his breath. Finally Jenny reached out her arms and Stick grabbed her, clinging as tightly as he could.

Stick was crying, Jenny was crying, I was crying, Ned was still sweeping, and Bob, being the master of emotions that he was, lost two pounds in tears that day. Hours later, however, he gained back three pounds in donuts.

This wasn't a day for counting calories.

Jenny had come back.

Chapter Thirty-seven

Closure and Openture

There are certain times in life when you can almost feel your eternal course shifting or yielding to allow some major occurrence to merge with your soul. My parents dying was one of those times. Their death took my spirit by the neck and shook it until there was little life left and my soul was spiritually decapitated. The Stick and Jenny reunion was another one of those times. But instead of draining me, this event had filled me with hope and left me immediately stronger.

I would never forget seeing Stick cry like that. He had wished for that moment forever. We had all doubted it would come about. But his perfect faith had been vindicated. Like the brother of Jared waiting for God to touch his rocks. Well, once Jenny had stepped from the past and shown herself it was almost too much for Stick to bear. Stick had been blown away seeing Jenny, but he was equally shocked discovering how she had come to return.

Jenny had been living in Washington state for the last ten years. She was working there as a secretary for a law firm. She had left Paul years earlier, but she was too embarrassed to ever come back to this part of the country. Well, two days ago Bishop Withers showed up at her work.

He hadn't deserted his flock, he had gone looking for that one lost sheep. The reason he had told no one about his journey was because he didn't want Stick to find out and get his hopes up. But after weeks of dead ends and bad leads he finally found her. He told Jenny about Stick and how Stick had been faithfully waiting for her. He then gave her the money to come out to Forget. Stick had been Bishop Withers' one loose end.

Stick was ashen. Only hours ago he was loathing the very man who had given up everything to find him his Jenny. Bishop Withers didn't plan to come back to Bluelake. It was time, he felt, for his ward to strike out on its own. After his initial desertion he had called Selma, his wife, and told her what he was doing. He then made her promise not to tell a soul. Well, Selma had a hard time lying so she had flown out to her sister's so as to avoid the entire situation. Neither of them would ever be back.

Now there was a dedicated bishop. I couldn't believe I was being asked to fill his shoes. I just couldn't do it. I was undedicated and unworthy. I was twenty-four and floundering in my self-confidence. How could I ever step in where Bishop Withers had stepped out? Besides, I still wasn't engaged.

Stick took off with Jenny—I guess they had a few things to discuss. Bob and I did some work around the store before we left Ned in charge and went to go see the UFO site. Neither of us had been out there since the tornado.

As we drove over Bob and I discussed what we hadn't spoken about since the night of the twister. We decided to take the secret of the UFO's real identity to our graves. There was too much at stake to step forward and tell what we knew.

"You can't even tell people who promise they won't tell anyone else," Bob said. "Because believe it or not, sometimes those people still tell."

"Just you and me," I vowed.

There was not a single piece of UFO or the fence that had once gated it off left out at the site. It was now just a big hole sitting next to Nine Month Mound. The missing "spaceship" hadn't hurt attendance, though. Hordes of people were still coming out to see the spot where the galaxy had once touched down.

"We lucked out," Bob said as we sat in his car watching people look at the hole. "One more day and they would have found out."

"Perfect timing," I commented.

"Jay's been demoted," Bob informed me. "He took his own sweet time on this one and now he's paying for it. He really embarrassed the state. He wanted to make me mad by dragging it out, and look how he's ended up helping us."

"Amazing," I said.

"I'll tell you what, there's something about this open sky down here that seems make things work," Bob observed.

"So what about you, Bob?" I asked. "Jenny's come back, Ned's been romancing Kitty. Love is in the air."

Bob laughed.

"Do you remember Tartan?" he asked, sounding as if he were leading into a story.

"The forest ranger from Longwinded?"

Bob nodded.

I nodded back.

"His wife had a baby a couple of nights ago," Bob said. "Tartan let me be in their house when she delivered it. I'm not good with blood, so I just hung out in their pantry until it was over."

"What did they have?" I asked, wondering why Bob was telling me this.

"A baby," he said. "The cutest little baby. They named her Summer."

Bob was silent for a minute.

"If I were married I'd probably have children," Bob said. "Maybe a couple of boys, and a couple of girls. I really like the name Lisa. It sounds so classy. Lissssa," he pronounced. "Don't tell anyone about me liking Lisa," he warned me. "I'd hate for someone to steal it from me."

Bob sighed.

"I wish I had had children," he finally said.

Bob had more kids than he knew. He was like the surrogate

father of us all. There wasn't a single soul in the area who didn't love him. And mixed amongst the masses of pretend prodigy were probably hundreds of Lisas.

"Did I ever tell you about the argument Stick and I once had?" Bob perked up.

"I don't think so."

"I tell you that uncle of yours can be so stubborn at times. We got into this big fight over the words to that one song, 'Skipping to the Loo.'"

"What song?" I asked.

Bob sang, "Hummm, hummm, skipping to the loo, humm hmmm skipping to the loo, humm humm skipping to the loo, skip to the loo my darling."

"Isn't it 'Skip to My Lou?'" I asked.

"I should have known you'd side with Stick," Bob sniffed. "The song makes no sense that way."

"Actually, it makes no sense either way," I pointed out.

"My way does," Bob explained. "You've had a real big soda, and now you're having to hurry up and skip to the loo."

I laughed. "Well then, what's the 'my darling' part about?"

"The singer's just being friendly, 'I'm skipping to the loo my darling,'" Bob sang.

At least his theory explained the "shoo fly, shoo" part. Bob was such an interesting person.

"So is that the story?" I asked.

"No," Bob replied. "Because of that argument, Stick and I didn't talk for over a month. Finally I swallowed my pride and went down to Forget with a friendship mending batch of cookies."

"And?" I asked, knowing there was more.

"We ate them," Bob replied.

"No," I said, frustrated. "What's the point of the story."

"Well, that was just a horrible month. I missed out on a lot of things because I had removed myself from a friend."

"Why are you telling me this?" I asked bluntly.

"I just wonder what kind of person I would be if I had gotten married. Just think what I would be if I had been hanging around with a wife the last thirty years."

Bob was everything but direct.

"It's not too late," I said. "I don't know about kids, but you could at least get married."

Bob was silent for a second. He then unbuttoned a couple buttons on his shirt and scratched his big round stomach.

"I..." I started to say something about marriage.

"Do you think carob really tastes much like chocolate?" Bob asked, coming out of left field and changing the subject we had been talking about.

I shook my head.

"Not at all," I smiled, answering his question.

"I feel the same way," Bob replied.

The sky began filling up with clouds. Light rain started to fall. Bob drove me back to Forget, then he headed on home. I sat out in the rain, thinking about Bob and wondering why Rivers hadn't called me back yet.

I was really getting worried. What if Rivers had decided that Elder Higgins was worth waiting for again? What if the California sun had filled her head with doubts and scattered her thoughts.

"Like Gray, no way."

There was a lot working against us at the moment. For one thing I was here and she was there surrounded by a family who seemed to liked Elder Higgins best.

I went to bed confused and nervous. Not even the sound of the gentle rain and blowing wind could soothe my fearful soul. I felt as if Rivers were flowing away.

Chapter Thirty-eight

Complacent No More

I had three days left to decided about this bishop deal. I was praying all the time, wanting an answer more than anything. President Gram was growing persistent, and I was growing less and less confident about Rivers and myself. For some reason she was not calling me back. I had left messages with both her mom and her brother. Where was she? Where was my "Yes"? My state of mind couldn't handle a "No" right now. My existence had been prepped to receive nothing other than a resounding "I will."

The rain of the night before had dried up under the heat of the early morning sun. Once again Forget was brown and dusty. As I walked past the tree hole on my way over to the store I noticed the bottom of it was still wet. I supposed it was just taking a little longer to dry out then the rest of Forget.

Stick had come home late last night and left early this morning. I had not even had a chance to talk to him. I was anxious to see where he and Jenny stood. When I got to the store only Ned was there.

"Where's Stick?" I asked.

"I haven't seen him," Ned replied. "Listen, Gray, if he's not here by two could you do me a favor and watch the store? I've got to pick up Kitty from the hospital."

"Sure," I said. "Where are you taking her?" I asked, knowing

269

firsthand that her house had been destroyed.

"Kitty bought a single-wide mobile home to put out on her land until she can build a new house," Ned informed me. "They were supposed to deliver it yesterday."

Nothing like a single-wide to ward off any future tornadoes, I thought, suddenly reminded of Angela and her brother Fetch's home. I had meant to tell Bob about it, to see if he knew anything more about Fetch. I made a mental note to do so soon.

A small U-Haul truck pulled up to the front of the store. I turned and headed out the back door, leaving Ned to his customers. Just as I was about to step outside I heard my name being called.

"Gray."

Every tiny hair on the back of my neck stood up. I turned around to find Rivers standing there. My heart enlarged to the size of a soccer ball which my liver, kidneys, and spleen began to kick about. She stood there like the South Pole, spinning my world around. With every rotation my heart beat harder. Her eyes were alive and her body language spoke in soft coy whispers to me.

"Rivers," I said, amazed.

She was here. I couldn't believe it. A couple of seconds ago I was thinking about flying out to California to help her make up her mind. God had obviously flicked her in the ear for me.

Rivers just stood there, fixed casually to the floor.

She was right inside the front door of the store, and I was just inside the back door. Ned was right in between standing behind the counter. There were no other customers in the store at the moment.

She smiled at me.

"Is that your U-Haul?" I asked, pointing out the store window. Rivers nodded.

"What are you doing?"

"I drove all night," she said. "I have something I need to tell you."

We both took one step closer to each other.

"What did you want to tell me?"

"Elder Higgins came home," she said.

"I heard."

We took yet another step.

"He asked me to come visit him."

"And?" I asked, having to hold myself back from physically jittering due to anticipation.

"He is so wrong for me."

My head became heavy. I was afraid I was going to topple over. Things were heating up. Electricity flashed between the two of us, making our relationship extremely current and charging my heart with more volts than it was capable of holding.

We both took another step.

We were now standing only a couple of inches apart, right in front of the counter. Ned was staring at the two of us. I felt as if he were a preacher and Rivers and I were exchanging vows.

I do.

I wanted to reach out and grab Rivers like Stick had grabbed Jenny. I wanted to kiss her like I had never kissed her before. I wanted to add my last name to her first. I wanted her.

I did.

"So what are you saying?" I managed to ask.

One word was all it took.

"Yes."

She had driven overnight to her male and delivered my "Yes."

"I've got everything I own with me," Rivers said.

She was here to stay.

"My parents suggest we get married as soon as possible."

Her parents had never seemed wiser.

Neither one of us could stand it any longer. Rivers pulled me to her and kissed me on the mouth. Her beautiful blue eyes were big and shining. She felt so right within my arms I almost passed out. She ran her hands through the back of my hair, reiterating her point while kissing me all over my face.

The store transformed itself into a beautiful garden, stuffed with bursting flowers. Nature pushed up, giving life color and making things smell sweeter than they already did. I breathed Rivers in. Her hair, her lips, her being. She was the smelling salts of my soul. My body coughed and gasped in air as she miraculously resuscitated my everything.

Ned wandered over to the cold cereal section to give us some privacy. He knew all too well the danger of staring at a full eclipse.

Chapter Thirty-nine

Full

I watched the stars burning brightly as I drove home to Forget. I was glad my meetings were over for the night, but I was sad they had gone so late. I knew there was no way Rivers would still be up.

I looked at the moon as it shined like a naked light bulb in the sky. The darkness here seemed less intense than it used to. I passed Ned's home at the edge of Bluelake. His kitchen light was on, indicating he had not yet called it a night. Ned had a lot to think about these days. Kitty had just finished her tale of near death and was looking to get it published some time soon. Yes, *Cherub for a Day* should be hitting the shelves some time in the next year. But more immediate was the fact that Ned and Kitty would be getting married in the coming month. Soon Kitty would be Mrs. Ned. They had asked me to perform the marriage ceremony.

I couldn't wait.

It would be my second marriage as bishop. Late last month I had had the privilege of performing the marriage of Brother Wendell Scatty and Cloris Plot. It took place exactly two months after Cloris was officially divorced from Todd. No one ever heard from Todd Plot again. I hoped he was well wherever he was.

Time flew here. I had been bishop now for almost six months. I had called Tom as my first counselor and Jonathan Call as my second. The bishop position had been harder than I ever imagined it would be. But I was finally beginning to feel as if our ward were coming together. Don't get me wrong, I was still messing up at almost every turn, but the heavens were pushing me back on course with great regularity.

The first thing I had done as bishop was to order curtains for our tardy window. This had turned out to be a smart move. People were so relieved about not being stared at if they came late. It changed the entire spirit of the meeting. I had overheard Sister Buswidth telling Brother Scatty that my decision to put up curtains had been divine and inspired. I don't know about inspired, but I sure felt much better about speaking from the pulpit knowing someone wasn't behind me looking in. I had heard another member explaining to Sister Lark that the window had been fine when Bishop Withers was around, but the current bishop always supersedes old policy. I guess that made sense. Enis McCaffy was so proud of me for being bishop. She sat with me up on the stand almost every week.

Yes, the Forget First Ward was really coming together. I took great comfort in the fact that the members were gaining testimonies in other things besides me. The numbers were rising back up to where Bishop Withers had them before he left. The stake was already planning to make an official split. I would do everything in my power to help make that happen.

An added bonus to all of this was that Stick had been coming out to church. With the store closed on Sundays he found he had little to do. He worked in the nursery, where he scared the kids into being quiet. Stick wanted to get his life in order so he could go through the temple if Jenny ever did say yes to him. Jenny had gone back and forth from Washington about five times in the last few months visiting Stick. I felt confident the two of them would come to pass.

I thought often of Bishop Withers and what he had done for my uncle. I hoped someday I would see him again and be able to thank him. He had done more for me than he would ever know. I couldn't believe someone could be so concerned about

The Miracle of Forgetness

another to go through the things that he had.

Forget was dark and lonely looking when I finally got home. Only the two streetlights at the crossing and the small light above my front door were lit. I walked inside and set my things down.

There was a message on the answering machine from Bob. He was inviting me to go fishing with him and Orvil this next Saturday. I would have to decline due to my school schedule. I was actively working on getting every aspect of my life together.

I sat down on our new couch and smiled. I had never been so happy. I couldn't believe how my life had become so complete. There were no voids any longer. Rivers supplied me with all the substance I could ever desire. I looked at my wedding ring. The gold band allowed me more freedom than I thought possible.

Our wedding had taken place in the Oakland Temple, and the reception had been at her parents' house. Bob and Stick had both been there as my best men. It was weird to see the two of them in tuxes. The wedding had been perfect, and the reception went off without any real hitches. Sure, Bob had helped himself to half the wedding cake before Rivers and I had a chance to cut it. But that was Bob. With him and Stick, I finally had the family I had lost a few years back. I knew my parents were as happy as I was.

My sister, Maria, had come to the wedding and officially given me away. I was reminded how much I missed my big sister. I was currently trying to convince her and her husband to move to Forget.

You see, the miracle of the UFO, the twister, and Kitty forgetting were all part of a chain. They were just links in the great work of God. And those miracles had since been overshadowed by the next link, which was the fact that Forget now had water. It was discovered months ago after the hole in my backyard refused to dry. Stick had some friends come out and just for fun drill a well. Well, one hundred feet down they hit an aquifer so large we couldn't stop the water from pushing up out of the ground. No one could explain it.

Bob thought perhaps Kitty had known there was water for some time and that this was why she had never allowed people into her house. She was afraid they would find out about the water and then insist on moving in around her. Bob did some checking and discovered that Kitty had not had any water delivered to her house in years. He concluded that she must have been pumping water out of the ground for quite some time. Thanks to the tornado, however, there was no trace of Kitty's home or well.

When Bob questioned Kitty about all of this she said she simply couldn't remember. It didn't matter. Forget was now blossoming like a rose as Kitty joyfully sold off chunks of her land to people wanting to move in.

I got up from the couch and went out back to look at the new tree I had planted days before. It was dark but I could tell that it was growing all right. Of course I would be dead before its branches were big enough to climb up into. It didn't matter. I would try to enjoy the now.

A shooting star streaked through the sky, bidding the eye to follow. I watched it burn bright and then fizzle out. The sky here had brought many of the miracles we had witnessed in the last year. I loved knowing God was loose amongst the vast stretches of blue. I often imagined him taking a break from it all and resting on the small red bench out by the road—simply waiting for the rest of the world to catch up.

The wind tumbled softly through Forget. I looked again at the sky. What was it with this place? How could everything I need be right here in the space of thirty acres? I loved the land and the people who had come with it. I couldn't remember anything before them. I searched for my parents in the stars. I hoped they were happy with their son.

I felt the real miracle of Forget was the power God had extended to let me change. He had helped me find my way. There were no unidentified objects in his universe. He knew me, and like a jagged rock I had been worn smooth under His hand. My entire existence had been peppered with things I had handled badly or could have done better. But God in his mercy saw fit to help me Forget. There was only forward now. My investment had paid in huge dividends, and it was now time to reinvest. I could only imagine the gain.

I was so wrapped up in the stars and the moon that I didn't notice the sun slip up from behind and put her arms around me.

Rivers kissed the back of my shoulders. She took my hand and pulled me in.

Words I had once heard, or read, or sang blew through the cold sky and entered my mind.

> Beneath his watchful eye,
> His saints securely dwell;
> That hand which bears all nature up
> Shall guard his children well.

How gentle God's command.
I was finally connected.

About the Author

Robert Smith lives in Albuquerque, New Mexico, with his wife, Krista, and his daughters, Kindred and Phoebe. He is the owner of Sunrise Bookstore in Albuquerque. Inspired by the saying, "Given enough time, a thousand monkeys banging on a thousand typewriters could eventually write a book," Robert picked up a pen and began writing early in life. As a result, Robert is the author of BAPTISTS AT OUR BARBECUE, the book you are now holding, and the forthcoming FOR TIME AND ALL ABSURDITY.

If for any reason you wish to talk to, scold, criticize, compliment, or bother Robert, please do so by writing to:

Sunrise Bookstore
7200 Menaul Blvd. N.E.
Albuquerque, New Mexico 87110